Wolf Runaway: Escape

Wolf Wars, Volume 4

Alex Ankarr

Published by Alex Ankarr, 2016.

WOLF RUNAWAY: ESCAPE

First edition. February 24, 2016.

Written by Alex Ankarr.

Chapter 1

He's panting, with his back up against raw rough-finished stonework and the frame of a window digging into his shoulder-blades. Panic gives the look of dark shapes in the darkness a wild unreality. Almost, he expects to be pounced on, for Parrin to refuse to listen to Penn's objections. He could impose his will – his excellent idea, as he no doubt sees it – as imperiously as any wolf, as completely without regard for a stupid weak human's wishes as any gentleman-wolf of the old school, who regards humans as not just lesser beings, but as little more than tools and capital, to be pointed in a particular direction and set about their task, without volition or thought.

But Parrin doesn't leap on him. In fact he pauses and quiets, at Penn's words. If it's making him think then it's some kind of miracle. Perhaps Penn isn't going to have to fight off a different kind of rampant and eager wolf, this night. Good, because there's precious little he could do, if Parrin were truly set on such a mad idea. But by the devil, his voice is sulky when he replies, "You're sure? Damn Chac and Zamn both together, Pennorth, but you're a stubborn little piece, aren't you? I offer to wipe out your problems and captivity at a stroke, and how do you respond? By tossing your pretty head, with your pretty hair flowing, and putting your nose up in the air like a thoroughbred filly, too full of its own consequence to condescend to give a moment's attention to a fellow's ridiculous suggestion. What's so bad about becoming a wolf, after all? Speaking as one myself, I'll give you that they're an impossibly arrogant bunch, and responsible for about eighty percent of the problems of the world – well, the half of the world that belongs to us, at any rate. But actually being one – that's not so bad. And you'd be free."

He utters the last four words as if he's dangling them before Penn's nose, tempting him into insurrection and bad decisions. Penn's not such an addle-pate, nor so weak-willed. "I have no desire to be a wolf," is all the response he allows, firmly and with decision. He's pushed himself to stand up straight, and he forces himself to look direct at Parrin, against every inculcated reflex. (And against his personal preference. Benedict Parrin is trouble, that's the final conclusion he's come to: nothing else, nothing but. And limned in moonlight against the starry sky, smirking and gazing at Penn, the expression on his face confirms Penn's opinion. That smirk, as far as Penn's concerned, suggests not an iota of seriousness, gives no indication that Parrin is taking his statement right to heart. He mistrusts it: and as he moves forward, to circle around Parrin and take his leave, he watches him warily, for any sudden lunge or grab, any hungry leer. "I hope you can accept that, sir. I'll bid you goodnight."

And it's creepy as hell, the way that Parrin rotates slowly to watch and follow Penn's journey, eyeing him up with a pleasant composure. But he at least doesn't grab, and doesn't argue, doesn't threaten in any way. Indeed all he has to say is, "Well, I regret your decision very much, Pennorth." The look in those hazel eyes is quite severe, but there's a twinkle in there too. It doesn't make them one jot less creepy. (He wonders if Parrin is genuinely a little mad.) "But I would never try to argue someone out of an honest conviction. Or turn someone against their will. It would go against every principle and belief that I possess." His tone is quite sincere, believably so. And as he takes the last step to make his way to the other side of Parrin, and finally – carefully and thoughtfully – turns his back on him, to head towards the door... Penn draws a long breath, finally relaxing a little.

Relaxing, just as Parrin says casually, sounding more amused that he was a moment ago even, "I'll just have to find some other way to get the job done. Have at him, boys."

And this, this is the reason *never* to turn your back on a wolf. Or wolves, perhaps: and Penn can only deduce, later, that this is the moment that two burly and swift young wolves sweep out of the shrubbery, and seize him from behind. It's a damn sight too quick for him to really be aware or to make sense of what's happening, as it actually takes place. His body is just taken out of his control, and then everything's dark and uncomfortably stuffy and his shouting is muffled, with something fabric stuffed in his mouth. He realises after that he'd had a bag shoved over his head as well as being gagged, and they must have carried him off at some considerable speed. Very advisable for them, what with Renally Hotstaat and Lettice Parrin sleeping only a few flimsy walls away. Well, rough-hewn stone and brick, in fact, but to a wolf it's very little more than plasterboard.

He doesn't know any more than that at the time, and he doesn't remember much more than that later. There's Benedict's voice here and there, indistinctly directing and ordering – he thinks that's what's going on. He does fight, of course. It's not even a sensible thing to do – he's caught and doomed, and whatever Parrin wants to happen, is what's going to happen. And it might invite retaliation and forcible control, where a floppy obedience and passivity would be least likely to result in injury or highly constrictive binding. But he can't help it, because that's just his nature. He flails with an utter lack of co-ordination or awareness of his position in space. Perhaps he manages to hit a target here and there – there are a couple of muffled snarls from the two who are manhandling him as if they're removals men and he's an unusually recalcitrant wardrobe – but mostly it seems he's more hitting walls or trees or inanimate objects. He's hurting himself, more than anyone else, and doing not the least good in terms of getting himself free and making an audacious escape.

And then – he remembers this bit with a certain vividness, compared to most of the rest of it – a hand is shoved up inside the darkness and cloth covering his head. The stink and reek of something halfway between raw gut-rot alcohol and bleach feels like it leaves the insides of his nostrils bleeding and his lungs shrivelled. Then he can't remember a damn thing for a while, because he isn't consciously there for any of it.

WHAT HE KNOWS NEXT is discomfort, quite a lot of it. He's bloody cold, that's the first thing that impresses itself upon him. And it's dark – darkish, at any rate – but he hasn't got a bag on his head any more. Or the cloth that was stuffed into his mouth to keep him quiet, and less trouble than he might be. (Thank heavens. At least someone had some concern about his possibly choking while unconscious.) Still it's an infinitesimally minimal improvement, considering the other circumstances he encounters on opening his eyes.

He's moving, that's the second thing that's obvious. Or, rather, not he himself – no. The floor's moving underneath him, carrying him with it, and it's made of pressed steel, corrugated and with regular stamped out holes at certain points. It's shabbily painted, paint flaking off and showing the dull scratched gleam of steel. And the holes make clear the movement beneath: new tarmac road, flashing by, at a cracking rate. He's been thrown in the back of a van – perhaps a post or police van, judging by the dimensions and the dull formal green, the wooden slatted benches built into the sides – and his hands are tied at his back. Tied nice and tight, and they would be an absolute bugger to get free. And he's still wearing nothing but the light bed-chemise he came out in. (Which was fairly ill-advised, he sees now, what with summer being largely over, and even the days lately not as balmy as an English autumn day is capable of.) His sandals are slung into the far corner. And the light blanket from the daybed in the sitting room back at the lodge, the one he'd come out with, with it around his shoulders – it's thrown over him. It offers the only source of warmth in this bitterly cold box of a prison, draughts and gusts of cold air blowing over him from every corner.

If he wasn't as liable to be killed by a psychotic slave-running wolf, as soon as the vehicle stops and he finds out where they're at and what's going on, then he might be at risk of catching his death and dying of pneumonia.

And he takes a minute to curse his life, and to wonder why, when things seem as if they couldn't honestly get worse, they do. And when things seem to be going unusually well, that's the moment just before utter and gutting disaster strikes. That's how it usually goes for Penn, at any rate. He can't speak for anyone else, of course.

Up ahead, in the metallic housing of the cab that constitutes the fourth wall of his little gaol, there's a sliding door, instead of a window. It has a handle on one of the sides, not that that does him a powerful amount of good in this situation, with his hands bound. But at least he knows where his captors reside, and from where he needs to seek attention and demand succour and release.

He doesn't have a great deal of hope regarding that last point. But damned if there's any point just lying here meekly and waiting to arrive at some pre-set destination point, then to be collared and hauled out of this chamber by the ear, and dragged off much like a sheep to the slaughter. If nothing else, drawing attention to himself and demanding explanation and assistance might cut short the long and agonising wait and build-up, to an unfortunate end to his personal history. And, to look on the bright side, alternatively disrupting the course of events might spark off incidents such that he finds an opportunity to disable one or more of his captors, and make a run for it or otherwise evade a grisly and disagreeable ending. (Damn Benedict Parrin, damn him. So much for his offers of freedom and sponsorship, of support and a new life in one of the wild and desolate regions so drab, forlorn and unattractive as residence that no wolf would find it worth its while to conquer or inhabit it. Is this where all of his hints, seductions, persuasions and strong-arming have led? Yes. And Penn can only wonder what he's really been after all this time, and what he's up to now. But it seems doubtful that it can possibly be any good thing, considering that it's an endeavour that starts out with a kidnapping. And even that, after a rejected offer of giving Penn the bite, which Penn does not look kindly upon.)

It's no easy matter, however, to drag himself up from an unsteady and rapidly moving base, and an uneven one too, to get himself up on two legs. And especially not with his hands bound, and all of the twinges and sudden burns he's feeling. They suggest that the ways and means employed by his current chauffeurs, in transporting and depositing him in his current abode, while he was out for the count, were rather less than gentle and compassionate.

But Penn has always been amazingly persistent in pursuing his goals. (Perhaps not everyone he has encountered has described it in such a neutral and even complimentary fashion. In fact the phrases 'persistent little bugger' and 'bloody-minded swine' have been thrown in his direction a time or two. Penn takes it as a compliment, actually. It's still a tribute, in its way, to his tenacity and endurance, his dogged ambition. His bloody-minded obsession, you might alternatively put it.) One way or another, with only a casual couple of knocks to the head, and the slightest graze to his knees – followed by a rather nastier gash when the van goes hard left around a corner at some speed, and he's tumbled almost off his feet again with only his joints and his skull to support himself as he hits the wall to one side – he gets himself up, and standing, and shuffles over to lean against t'other side of the vehicle. He gets his breath, panting, feeling the vehicle's motion and vibration all through his shins and thighs.

But he can't hang about this way, however absorbing an occupation grimacing and cursing his life might be, while wondering if the pain in his knee is likely to turn into any permanent injury, or have the chance to. Instead he takes a great deep breath, and shuffles forward – hands flexing and testing at the rope at his wrists. He thinks that perhaps he ought to try to get his hands free, before alerting his captors to his wakeful state.

And he seeks out the sharpest edge and the most easily available that he can find – the hinges on the outer doors, a little lower than waist level so that he's obliged to bend his knees, as he begins to attempt to scrape and tear at the rope enough to loosen it and free himself.

But the slight edge that the hinges present isn't quite sharp enough. Or he can't direct the knots accurately enough, or some other issue or combination of issues that prevent it from being the least damn good, or anything other than a failed and futile attempt. Which leaves him with two options, or rather three. To alert Benedict Parrin and his two lupine goons to his presence, his being awake, and his extreme dissatisfaction with the current state of affairs. Or to begin to kick as fast, as hard and as effectively as he can possibly manage, at the doors of the van, in an attempt to bust them open and bust himself out. He'd have to roll out on the open road, and then just run like hell and hope for the best, hope for readily available shelter, helpful strangers willing to give aid and succour to a bruised, shocked, semi-dressed and apparently runaway slave, hope for a lack of injury in the fall. And hope to be able to outrun three wolves who've already tacitly expressed hostile intent to his freedom and his person.

Of course there's also the third option open to him. But Penn has never had a talent for sitting on his hands and quietly hoping for the best. Not when there's an alternative of action and enterprise and possible more favourable outcomes available. Even if there's also a possibility of distinctly less favourable outcomes as a result of said action, too.

It has to be better than doing nothing, Penn thinks. Or, even if it isn't, then at least he won't spend an indeterminate amount of time waiting and wondering, with no control over how long he waits or over his eventual fate. Penn would sooner invite disaster, than put up with that prospect. You might call it his greatest failing. But on the other hand, it's got him this far, which might be said to be a case of *quod erat demonstrandum*. Of course, also it's led to his preferment in a great household, and a lot of highly valuable gifts that he might be able to – or might have been able to – sell and add to his slave price at some future point. And marked, vowed, promised, hand-fasted favour, from not one but two powerful wolves.

Anyway, his restraint is always buffeted most severely when he is cold, or tired, or mistreated, or hungry. Or tied up. Or in spring, summer, autumn or winter.

The choice is made, then. And Penn sighs, and closes his eyes a moment, at the prospect of how many further bruises he's going to acquire in this endeavour. But the price must be paid. That's all the repining he allows himself, and then he puts his shoulders forward and runs at the doors, hammering into them with all the grace of a small bull, if not the brute muscle power. Unfortunately.

Damn, and it hurts so much! And it does nothing at all, no hint of give in the stolidly unresponsive chunks of metal and paint, and the glass in them boarded up even if his hands were free, offering neither purchase nor a view. He staggers back, with nothing achieved and the doors still stubbornly fixed in place, unmoved. He resolves that this is clearly going to get him nowhere – his shoulders are going to give before that door ever does. And although it's a riskier approach regarding his stability and centre of gravity, that most probably the only way he even has a chance of exiting the vehicle under his own steam, rather than at the hands of others, is if he uses his feet.

He's going to be so bruised. He's going to fall so many times. But he could be dead in an hour or less, so he doesn't even give himself a moment to think or plan. He just straightens up and careers towards the door, kicks one-legged, falls over. Gets up, drags himself up, and goes at it sideways on this time, and jumps two-footed and forward. He actually puts a dent in one of the doors that way. But still, the lock holds, and nothing shifts. Another try, then one-legged again, then two, then one last single-footed kick, reckless and abandoned and hurting all over... He should be in bed, right now. He should be curled up against Ree's side, pulled in a little tighter than is comfortable. Ree never likes him to be too far away, likes to have him close as skin on skin whenever possible. (Likes him under the thumb and well-trained as a dog or a performing seal, Penn frankly thinks. But no, he wouldn't like it expressed that way. Not half enough hearts and flowers about it, not a poem or a love-song in sight. Renally Hotstaat, who thinks he's a romantic. Penn thinks there are other words for it.)

He should be there, though, still back at the lodge, with Lettice Parrin tucked in to the other side of Ree. Sister to this hound, this robber, kidnapper, and if only she knew, she'd have his beta hide! The three of them, snoring and safe and cosy, and if his heart hadn't been stoked up into a fire of rebellion, if he hadn't resented being tucked like an adjunct, a sidekick, an afterthought into Ree's side – if he hadn't been damned uncomfortable – if he hadn't been gasping for a smoke – then that's where he'd be, with them. But no, he'd had to go out, and invite trouble. Not as if he shouldn't have expected it, by Perseus. Not as if Benedict Parrin hadn't explicitly invited him to an assignation, hadn't given him the fullest warning of what it was about, hadn't expressed his intention of being there, in the moonlight, hanging around at the back of the lodge and waiting for Penn to show.

There's scarcely any excuse for Penn having allowed himself to walk directly into the hunter's trap. How much sympathy would he have himself for any prey, given that prey first had fair warning, and second, forgot all about said warning, and wandered into the mouth of the beast just the same? He can hardly believe it himself, and yet it's the facts of the matter. You might as well say he's a runaway. He's practically a volunteer, at least.

Being handed over to his lover wrapped in a bow as a gift... And held in something approaching solitary confinement, for an hour or two, even holding the key himself, while said lover chased after a new flame... And being taunted, teased, kept in the dark, seduced into a threesome by terrifying supernatural aggravating creatures... Hand-fasted and promised and mated. Apparently, all of these things taken together, within the same twenty-four hours, is enough to quite turn Penn's wits. Or at least to scramble them sufficiently that he forgets extremely pertinent facts he's been presented with, and goes toddling off in the very depths of the night to satisfy his hunger for nicotine and tar, and the desire to smoke-blacken his lungs.

(To be fair, it's a hell of a bill to add up. If it was paid for with a reduction in mental acuity and short-term memory loss, it's really not all that surprising.)

And so, due to his own absence of mind, he's gone from the arms of wolves, to... Well, to the arms of wolves, in a certain manner of speaking. But from being caught up in those arms in a fairly agree-able manner, to being thrown into a van and kidnapped, driven off into the night, there's a vast gulf in terms of the satisfaction arising from the experience. If only, now, he could turn the clock back a couple of hours... He'd be happy enough to forgo Ree's expensive French cigarettes, or any stimulation or satisfaction at all. He'd be happy to stay put and endure insomnia, right where he was.

He was dissatisfied enough at the time, but now it seems like a vastly preferable option.

Here's where he is, as a result of the decisions he's made, though. And the last kick – which may have damaged his big toe, may take his nail off at the bed – is the last one for a reason. He's made too many attempts, and made too much noise doing it. The van veers off to the side, and slows. And stops.

Penn knows a good many useful curses and oaths, mixing with slaves and servants and wolf gentry. He hears the choicest epithets that all of them have to offer. None of them seem adequate now. He hunkers down quietly, braces himself, his legs, tugs again at the rope around his wrists. And he tries to ready himself for whatever greets him when the doors open, because he's lost, and bruised, and anything could happen.

Everything's oddly quiet, with the engine cut off. He hasn't wolf hearing, and after all of the banging around he can't hear birds outside, or voices, or the distant hum of civilization and activity and people. They might be there anyway, but he'd bet odds against it.

They're not going to open up those doors, not anywhere with an audience, witnesses, anyone who's liable to aid and comfort Penn. He has a damn shrewd idea that that's inflexibly the case. Not even anyone who might report seeing an unusual tableau to the local sheriff or magistrates or the nearest most powerful pack. (Local jurisdiction and authority, under the wolves, being a complex web alternating in levels of seniority and influence and power, final authority, that's very near-incomprehensible to any non-wolf.)

There are few surprises, then. But he still jumps, at the clanking noise of the doors opening up, and sticking as they're dragged open – that dent he put in the one of them evidently rendering it a trickier job to open up than it must have been to lock him in, in the first place.

This is where he ought to leap through any available chink between his captors, perhaps. Or fight his way out with brute force, or talk his way out with Machiavellian cunning much like another Scheherezade, or some other option that results in a free – or relatively free – Penn, evading a pursuing Benedict Parrin and his assistant wolf thugs.

And if there weren't three of them, carefully and thoughtfully arranged at the door of the van and covering all angles, watchful for any break for freedom, then perhaps he might have. Or if they weren't damned wolves, after all. Any one of them has twice his physical strength and endurance, at a very bare-bones minimum.

Or if he didn't, very rapidly, have a fairly clean rag stuffed in his mouth. He does struggle, a bit, because he might get lucky, who knows? He doesn't get lucky, though, spots no opening, doesn't duck under a wide-angled arm or get in a very lucky punch. It was an unrealistic hope, after all, but he was fool enough to try anyhow. In fact he's pretty rapidly dealt with, and there he is, slung over one of the goon's shoulders, tied, muffled, gagged and re-located to the cab of the van, with the other goon taking his prior place in the back, settling down with a news-sheet and a flask of coffee. Penn is squashed and arranged into the middle seat of the second row of seats, behind the anonymous faintly grinning young wolf he doesn't know, and Parrin, at the wheel. There's liberal use of rope and bonds and Penn's pinned there in majesty, on the narrow seats levered in behind the driver's row. Pinned, and helpless.

Benedict Parrin is quite calm, and a little reproving, when he turns around in his seat, squeezing against the wheel, and addresses Penn. "Really, Pennorth, do you need to kick up that kind of a fuss?" He smiles, and Penn glares for a second. Then thinks better of it, and drops his eyes. To say he's one down in this situation doesn't cover it, worse than even his usual position being chided by a wolf. Chided by a wolf while bound and gagged. If he was more helpless then he'd be a wooden dolly, lifeless, spiritless. "You act as if you think I'm out to do you harm," Parrin continues. The hurt look in his eyes is no doubt mocking, designed to provoke Penn into impotent fury.

Isn't it? He reaches over the seat-back and pats Penn's knee, and if he's not sincere, he does an excellent imitation of a wounded friend, at least. "Aren't I the one who wanted to make you free in the first place?" he asks, and the gleaming half-silver hazel of his eyes is only grey in the dimness of the night, that hasn't begun to fade into dawn yet. But Penn can still make out the soft gleam in them, even by moonlight. "Didn't I tell you you were too good to be a slave, to brutes? And," he says, with a considering expression, magnanimous and pleasant, "I can understand that it's difficult for you to break through the years of conditioning, when you've lived your whole life in conditions of subjection, when you've been brainwashed from the ground up and you've never known anything else."

Across from him, on the other side of Penn, the other young wolf – dressed in casual black as if he's considering a spot of cat-burglary – nods solemnly. "Some you can't win over, sir," he agrees. "They get 'em too young and it's hard, when they've known nothing else. It's like they breed servility into flesh and bone, they know nothing else bar tugging the forelock and serving the young master. If you can't educate 'em into an enlightened state of consciousness and political awareness, sometimes it's inevitable. You just have to take 'em by the hand and then take 'em by force, and hope for the best. That they'll understand and be grateful once the choke collar's off, and they have a life that belongs to 'em."

His voice is more cut-glass, carelessly refined and full of upper-class arrogance than Ree's, even, despite the careful slanginess and contractions, and that takes it to some impressive extent. And if Penn wasn't already half-choking on a bit of crumpled linen, then he'd choke, quite probably, on his indignation. The almighty patronage of it! As if it wasn't enough, for the great general mass of wolves, to treat men as property and exploit their labour, confine and chastise them as if they could be truly owned. But hell, no, the small percentage left over, the ones endowed with any scrap of conscience and misgiving, they can't just work for universal suffrage and take the consequences in a repressive society? Will they accept the upheaval done to their own lives, and win a few converts amongst timid and hesitant slaves via earnest persuasion and example?

No, it blooming well seems. These ones, at least, have to make converts by force, presume to do a slave's thinking for him, and rope and tow him off to, well, to *mysterious gods know where*, to be plucked out of his accustomed life and presented with a new one of suspect, nasty and inferior quality, however he likes it, good or ill. And they expect that the magical word of 'freedom' will excuse all methods.

Bloody hell. Penn could honestly spit with rage, if he was free to do it. He does glare at Parrin's assistant, nonetheless. He doesn't even feel the normal, well-inculcated apprehension at the thought of giving offence to a wolf that he'd normally be flooded with. All for slaves, this bunch are, isn't that right? Slapping themselves on the back about their ideals, and their holy bleeding mission, saving any consideration of whether the recipients of their noble generosity like it or not.

Maybe he's being unfair. There is some nobility in it, or there would be, if he wasn't in the process of having freedom inflicted upon him. Even a wolf – even a high-born and moneyed wolf from a powerful pack – takes a significant risk, when he allies himself to the cause of abolitionism, and signs up for practice rather than words. He just resents the very notion – and now the experience –of having it decided that he isn't capable of choosing for himself what he wants, and needs to have it hashed out and decided for him by his betters, inflicted on him as a done deal that he has no choice in accepting. How is that so very much different from being a slave, born into a life of being a chess-piece manipulated about and used as if a pawn? If he'd gone seeking them out and asked for assistance in escape and running for the few free lands, that would have been one thing, and a very different thing too. But this, this isn't what he wanted, and he didn't sign up for this deal. He's a conscript, and a bloody angry one.

He's capable of making up his own mind, that's the thing. It's the thing that even the best of wolves don't seem to understand. And maybe he's capable of choosing his own life, and conniving and plotting and striving in order to damn well create it, too. He'd been bloody close – closer than he'd ever really expected to come, no matter his bloody-minded refusal to accept anything less than a free autonomous creative experience. Refusal to accept reality, it's not the same thing as honest optimistic expectation. It's just been all that's kept him going, half the time. Blind faith and pig-headed insistence, in fact. And now here he is.

Well, in fact, now here he *is*.

It's not as if Parrin's *aide-de-campe* – or whatever kind of status and title he cares to give himself, in their disreputable little organisation – appears to take any offence at being regarded with a glare that could take the hide off a leather armchair. In fact he snickers, and Penn's hands twitch, where they're hidden behind his back, with the urge to rip and tear as if he was wolf-born himself. "Don't worry, little man," the unspeakable bastard says, "we'll take good care of you. You'll be glad of it in the end, you'll see."

And he reaches back himself, to Penn's seat, and ruffles Penn's hair. If only he was a wolf, if only, Penn thinks beseechingly, yearningly, for once in his life. At least he'd have fangs three-quarters of an inch long, to take out this bastard's throat, or remove the offending fingers that have the temerity to fondle Penn as if he were a pug.

It makes Benedict Parrin laugh. And, it seems, allows him to divine something of the true thoughts running through Penn's mind. "I'd be careful," he says, casting a very meaningful look at the fellow, and nodding in Penn's direction. "Looks to me as if he'd have your hand off in a couple of snaps if he once got the muzzle off." And the other fellow laughs too: but he doesn't pat Penn's head again. Instead Parrin puts the key to the ignition, starts the engine, and pulls out into the road again. And there's not a single damn thing that Penn can do about that fact.

But that doesn't mean that he's given in. That's the surest route to ignominy and misery, after all. Once you"ve given up, even the chances that do come your way you'll never recognise nor capitalise on. He can still listen, and he can still keep his eyes open, since they've not thought to blindfold him into the bargain.

He can still count his blessings, such as they are. From what he can deduce, from what's escaped Parrin's lips, and those of his companions, or the one here in front at least, then Parrin isn't cherishing any homicidal intentions towards him. It's a relief, although given his current circumstances, it's a relatively small one. Penn has to admit it's an improvement upon that suspicion – although not one that gives him huge amounts of satisfaction – that Benedict Parrin seems to have been sincere about his objective, in his discussions with Penn. He wants Penn to be free, the bolshy little adventurer. He seems to view it as a matter of his honour as a Parrin, given old Jay Parrin's alleged wishes on the matter. And since he conveniently has access to, or runs, or is the head man of – how should Penn know exactly how this organisation is structured – an underground slave-smuggling abolitionist network, then he has the means to put that desire into action, and see fruit come of his labour.

Whether Penn likes or approves his scheme, or not.

Penn growls, behind the gag, and he hears Parrin sigh, as he negotiates a level crossing by the small town railway tracks they're approaching. Penn knows this town, he does, if he can think of it: and the red boiling fury that's he's been stewing in since he awoke in the back of the van dies down a little bit – as his calculating, cold-blooded, computer of a brain regains ascendancy and cools all his emotional responses right down to absolute zero. He knows where they are, and yes, he's watching, and he's listening, for all he's worth. Not too obviously, though – he obtains a measure of subtlety, and recreates the grumpy and enraged look of a thoroughly disgruntled and furious captive, as best he can. If they're suspicious that he's listening in too closely, they're only going to initiate more discreet procedures. Or still worse, throw him back in the back of the van, where he'll have no chance of using his eyes and ears.

Now, he casts his eyes down, and observes as covertly as he's capable. Yes, he knows this town all right: they'd been making good time through the county while they'd had him in the back of the van, and now they're right up against the border to the next. And going a roundabout route as they do it, because of course Parrin may be slightly unhinged, but he's not *stupid*. He's kidnapped Penn – stolen a valuable highly skilled upper slave from the most powerful and prestigious wolf-clan in the county, it amounts to – and he knows better than to advertise the fact. Parrin's taking quiet back-roads, avoiding the bustling middle of market towns, roads past farms with a multitude of homesteads and outbuildings, dignified wolf-pack residences and gated communities and freed human slums alike.

Only the most desolate roads, only the most lonely areas. It may be not quite the dead of the night – with dawn an hour, two hours off perhaps. But even so, it's all relative: and Parrin is going to want as few witnesses as possible to his journey to wherever it is that he's going.

Wherever it is, that he's taking Penn.

Of course, it's as he resolves this, that he'll squirrel away every word and look, will figure out what the hell Parrin's plans for him are – or the specifics, rather than an unasked and unwanted ersatz version of freedom – and he'll bodge together some means of foiling his plans and returning to his own chosen life, choosing his own destiny – that they decide to go quiet. Just staring out ahead, into the still oncoming night, as Parrin passes county lines, and *Welcome To So-And-So* signs and *Garden City Of Suchlike* signs blip past in the darkness.

First off, Penn's waiting for other traffic on the road. Even if it wasn't still dark, still night, there'd be precious little of it. Out here on these backwater stretches that Parrin's deliberately sticking to, there's probably little traffic normally even in the daytime, barring farm carts and delivery trucks and the occasional motorised van. Judging by how the van tackles half the roads, they're not even tarmacked tracks half the time, just gravel or beaten earth tracks. A horse and buggy every so often, a horse and rider here and there. Personally owned motor cars almost invariably belong to a wolf: and even then, here in 1930, although ownership is on the rise it's still uncommon. Seeing a motor car on the road is still an occasion for comment and excitement. In human slums, even amongst the small freedmen communities, a real actual motor car rumbling over cobbled streets is occasion for notice and hallooing, kids gathering in doorways and on stone steps to watch its passage by.

Thus Penn knows he'll have very few opportunities, even once day sparks into being, and he needs to keep an eye out. He strikes lucky, though, not quarter of an hour into a silence that's mutinous on his part, and seemingly absent-minded on the wolves'. Parrin's humming a gay tune – the cheerful *bastard* – and the other wolf is simply staring out the window with what looks to Penn like vacant self-congratulation on his heroic uprightness. Also, the *bastard*. Probably admiring his reflection too: he's as handsome as the rest of them, not that it makes him anything so remarkable.

That's what Penn is thinking – mutinous in his silence, and he'd probably be fuming and fulminating silently even without the gag – as the light and flash half blinds him in the near-dark of pre-dawn, and he almost misses his opportunity. It's another vehicle on the other side of the road, and he flinches in the first instant. And then he lunges. He lunges at the window, sideways, and bashes his head against it, and uselessly gives a wild muffled shout through gagging folds of fabric – as if the driver is going to hear.

That's as much as he manages, before the car's gone past. And he has no idea if the driver noticed or was watching or cared, but at least he tried. He'll have to satisfy himself with that, because now he has an incipient headache, not only from his own efforts. But because as soon as he's done it, Parrin's young assistant reaches back into the back seat himself, plants his large hand over Penn's skull and shoves his head back into the seat, hard. Not hard enough to qualify as punishment, perhaps: it's certainly nothing in comparison to a dozen, or a hundred chastisements he's received from wolf owners and their friends, pack members and passing wolves who've taken offence to his demeanour, or expression. Or existence, for that matter. It's just a reminder and a bit of advice, that's all, administered with the accompaniment of a verbal warning too.

"You can pack that in right now, lad. Try it again and I'll hog-tie you and throw you in the back again, so you can't stand up or try any little tricks like that. You want that? What good do you think it'd do you even if that driver did a U-turn and came around and stopped us, wanted to know what was going on, called the local pack or sheriff in? All we've got to do is say 'runaway slave' and nobody cares. There's the brand, right on your shoulder, we'd have to have extraordinary bad luck to get so much as a quibble out of anybody. So I strongly advise you to settle down and shut up. Stop getting het up and making such a fuss, and accept that you're getting rescued and freed. Whether you like it or not, boy."

And he reaches back far enough to give Penn another light tap, almost affectionately. Patronisingly affectionate, of course. "A bit of gratitude wouldn't go amiss!" he booms, in that depth and richness of voice that seems to be as much a genetic issue for wolves as pelt and fur, under the influence of rage or excitement or their lunar mistress. Parrin's an odd exception, his voice light and smooth, and oddly feminine as his maroon-purple tinted hair and the platinum-hazel gleam of his eyes. Perhaps that's what growing up with an alpha sister does to a young beta wolf. Or perhaps he's just an odd fish to begin with. The Parrins are an uncanny crew, after all, by reputation and by Penn's own experience. Whether that's good or bad, it's hard to say, given that he can't fault their ideals, half the time. He only mislikes how those ideals play out in practice, and their effects on him when he's the target and recipient. Or the timing and expression of them, given the assumption that Lettice's bit of unintended revelation that she let slip, about old Jay Parrin having intended to free him but carelessly dying before putting intentions into practice, was true. And Penn thinks it was probably true. That would be pretty accurately representative of the luck Penn's experienced.

Anyway, a threat like that is enough to shut his mouth. The advice is good, and he takes it. But Benedict Parrin, who has kept his eyes on the road, has his mouth twisted up into a viciously thin line, from what Penn can see in the wing-mirror. And he turns and gives his dissatisfied companion one look, before looking back at the road, that has the young thug crumpling into a softer pose and looking uncertain, chastised without a word being said. He meets Penn's eye in that mirror, a brief flash of communication, too. "Sorry, Pennorth," he says – and after all this, with Penn tied up and bound in rope, and any input from him into the situation barred by a mouthful of handkerchief, how can Parrin sound so exquisitely polite and genuinely lashed by regret? "Some of our happy band – a very few – get a little bit carried away by the excitement of liberating the captive and downtrodden, and being the saviour and hero of the hour. Eh, Harry? Isn't that right?"

His tone is severe enough to demand a reply. And the other fellow – this Harry – says in a low voice – that is fairly admirably not sulky, but definitely a little chastened, "Um, yes. I suppose so. Sorry, Pennorth."

It's odd, that that actually helps a little, tamps down on Penn's feeling of raging insult and the will to smash something. Preferably

– inadvisably – a lupine jawbone. It's certainly something he's never had a chance to get used to. It's hard to remember the last time a wolf apologised to him over anything, not a punishment or a slap or a harsh word. In fact, he can't remember it ever happening – except then he remembers, and actually he's wrong. Old Jay Parrin would apologise to him quite often, in fact. Not about anything important – but then, Old Parrin never did anything so heinous and memorable to Penn that he would have needed to apologise about something important. Instead it was about having sent him to the wrong room in search of an item for his perpetual experiments in rose-grafting and hybridizing, or regarding having corrected Penn on his translation of obscure French poetry, and then finding himself in error and Penn correct, after all. Things of that nature, obscure and courteous and scholarly.

Stupidly Penn feels his eyes suddenly a little moist, and he's briefly glad of the night and the distracted attention of both his captors. He isn't going to dignify what he's feeling with the name of affection. But Old Parrin was not a bad sort, as wolves go. Penn would allow that he misses him, here and there, would have liked to be present for his last moments and exchanged a few last words of respect and service.

And, while he's so busy being wrong, he may as well allow that Ree also has been known to say he's sorry for things. Idiotic things, like buying the wrong present. And also meaningful things, that graze over sore wounds that Penn doesn't even want to think about, like persisting too long in trying to discuss the bite, or Penn's mother. For not finding him sooner, and sparing him a few vicious masters, for another thing. Once, for their first night together, which came so close to being a violent and violating disaster that would have warped anything they could have or be. (And any chance of Penn's at freedom and self-determination, along with it.)

He never apologises for Penn's captivity, or for not freeing him thus far, though. To do so might, Penn supposes, be to admit that he needs to keep a hold of that card, to keep something to hold over Penn. How else would he keep him amenable and outwardly affectionate, after all? But he does apologise, about selected things. He's capable of it. And Lettice too, he thinks. She has been sorry about a number of things, and said so freely, in her friendly and incautious way. But she's a Parrin of course, and with Parrins it seems the normal wolf rules do not apply under most circumstances.

It's a lot of thinking to be doing, but he only works and worries at it intermittently. In between times, he's listening to these damned wolves chat together intermittently, and keeping his eyes open for signs, following where they're heading. They're not totally alone on the road, and the odd other vehicle goes past in the dim dark-grey dark, now. But he minds what – Harry? - had to say to him, and doesn't try to attract anyone's attention again. Parrin may have reproved the abolitionist young fool, after a fashion. But Penn notices also that he didn't contradict him, or suggest any alternative outcome, for further breaks for freedom. Penn doesn't want to be locked in the back of the van again, and most certainly not with his arms and legs both bound and really no chance of taking advantage of any chance at freedom. It's not worth it, not when Harry was very probably right, and the mere sight of the brand on his shoulder would be enough to discount his word in any account of the past few hours, even assuming the situation got as far as him being asked for it.

Even if a passing motorist gets as far as thinking that perhaps the county sheriff's office ought to be notified of suspicious activity relating to a motorised van passing by on the county road by the next county's reservoir, he doesn't doubt that there's false number-plates on this vehicle, or that Parrin intends to discard it and swap for another vehicle or means of transport at some point on the journey. He doesn't strike Penn as a careless type, when it comes to nefarious schemes and plotting to bring down the current system. Reckless, yes, but that's another character trait altogether. His choice of objective might be insane, but the means he uses to achieve it would be perfectly plotted and comprehensively researched.

So Penn just listens and watches, carefully, as Aylesbury and Northampton go by, with his head aching from the chloroform and his muscles and bones from the carelessly rough handling. He listens as they bicker pleasantly about whether it's a good idea that they've arranged to pick up *the Holmford boy* in Nottingham, or rather on the furthest reaches of it. Penn speculates about whether the Holmford boy is a running slave or colleague, but he's in little uncertainty really. That level of patronage certainly indicates to him that it's a slave. So he's to have a companion in captivity, he muses, tucking it away as potentially useful knowledge at some point. Well, or a companion in escape from captivity, depending on how you look at it.

When the van stops at Nottingham – or in fact, on a green sward at the side of a farm-road that isn't even tarmacked, is nothing but dried out mud and gravel – then of course Penn's left in the cab, while both Parrin and Harry jump out, and lock the doors on him. Really, as if he was liable to be going anywhere in any case. He doesn't get a glimpse of the boy, even, who must be lurking in the shadows and waiting to meet his contacts, if he's unaccompanied in his flight. How frightening for him, Penn thinks, and he feels a real pang of sharp sympathy as he thinks it. It seems almost worse than his own plight, 'rescued' unwillingly and carted off from everything familiar. Instead, to have the familiar be so dreadful that this kid is willing to risk the liberation network, with all its horrific potential consequences, for the sake of the possibility of the starkest most disagreeable chance at liberty. His life must be all but a hell right on this planet, for him to jump this direction.

He barely hears even murmurs of conversation, not that whatever discussion and negotiation is going on lasts for long. Then there's a bang that has to be the back doors of the van, and the shuffle of boots on gravel. Penn can hear clunking and movement in back: now they have an extra soul aboard. And the front doors of the cab open, and the two wolves are back. "One more for the liberation trail!" Parrin exclaims as he climbs in, with a fiercely feral grin in Penn's direction. And he fires up the engine, and they're back on their way.

To be fair, he does ask Penn if he needs a call of nature first, which Penn was beginning to wonder if they'd ever think of. But in truth – without the advantage of getting a look at the new kid, of scoping out chances and information and having the wolves distracted by another body on board, he doesn't. Which is disturbing in itself, and if they let him dehydrate much longer – well, what does it matter. He could be dead in hours. And gagged, it's a fair way too complex a message to put across.

"You're taking the Pennine route?" Harry asks, unmeasured minutes later, when it comes to the county line out of Derbyshire, and they head for the hills instead of to the east. "Wouldn't it be quicker to stay to the east?" It's true: Penn has been passed from owner hand to owner hand geographically about the British Isles enough to know it, has ridden a fair bit of the country guarding herds from rogue pack rustlers and securing the boundaries of an owner's land. It would be a lot quicker, to take the main travel routes and skip the scenic areas.

"Maybe," Parrin concedes, looking out at the horizon as he takes a turn signposted for Ashbourne from Nottingham, and his eyes scan the roads. "But it's getting on for six and it'll be light soon enough. There'll be a damn sight less traffic, and less chance of getting collared up on the moors, and anyway it's the scenic route. Do you want to look at back streets and factories and smoking chimneys for half the way there, or would you rather have wild spiritual moors and beautiful bodies of water, moor-hens and geese? We could even get out and have ourselves a little run about at some point, maybe."

He looks charmed and exhilarated at the idea, in the wing-mirror, as far as Penn can judge. And it's exactly the sort of feckless exuberance and risk-taking that Penn would expect of him at this point. If he's caught running slaves to freedom through the abolitionist network, then it isn't only Penn who'll pay a heavy price. To escape with his life, Parrin might be doing well. It's not an offence that's looked upon lightly, even for an eccentric well-born wolf.

Harry hasn't finished arguing, however. There's clearly little respect for the chain of command in this ramshackle *sub rosa* organisation. It's not run along military or pack lines at all. A damn sight too much pally disrespect and argy-bargy between the ranks, Penn wouldn't stand for it in Parrin's shoes. Not that he's liable to be, of course. "All right, yes, it'll be less populated, over the moors. Those roads are quieter, but anyone we do meet is a lot more liable to be trouble. Half the rustlers and rogue packs in the country use those routes, since the private parks were opened up, and the last thing we need is to run across one of those and have any trouble. Wouldn't it be better–."

"Don't worry about it," Parrin interrupts him, casual as a cat swats and teaches a younger kitten. And he reaches to flip open the glove-box, and takes out something that clanks and scrapes across the surface veneer inside. That's before he holds it up to shine, eerie in the flashing gleam of the moon, that's the only light barring cats-eyes on this lonely road flashing past.

The gods would attest that there's barely the light to see his own nose on his own face, Penn thinks. But he's pretty damn sure about what it is that he sees now, and that thing is a gun. He knows a little about guns – because he knows a little about everything, with the variety of owners and clans and training that he's had. He thinks it's a German-made revolver, usually used by armed wolf-sheriff's deputies when a slave runs or goes rogue or kills its master, to hunt it and bring it down, to kill it in the field if necessary. "Pretty little thing, isn't it?"

Parrin enquires, proud. "Rifles for long-range, back there under the back-seat. But I like something a little more flexible close to hand."

"What use is that going to be?" Harry asks, and the incredulous note in his voice might earn him a smack across the face, if Penn was his superior officer in however clandestine an organisation. Perhaps something in the stone immobility of Parrin's face gives the intimation that his thoughts are following much the same lines as Penn's, because Harry's next words are delivered in a more respectful tone, even if they're still packed full of dissatisfaction. "Sir," he says, with a little emphasis, and a half-joking tip of his hand to his brow in a mimicry of salute. "But if we're confronted by rustlers, or an unfriendly pack, say, then we surely don't want it to come to pelt and claws, do we? But a gun won't do us a damn bit of good against wolves, it'll only make them angry if you have to use it, and hardly slow them down."

And that, there, is the reason Penn's somewhat familiar with guns, and none of the masters who allowed for that familiarity and learning were troubled or spooked by the idea of a slave with experience with firearms. Because while you can injure, wing, slow down a wolf with human firearms and human bullets, you'd be doing damn well to kill it. Not that it's impossible: sufficient explosive bullets to the head, the liver or the heart might do enough tissue damage for mortal injury. Just as long as the person shooting is quick enough to do that damage before the wolf injured is on him and savaging him to death, because with human bullets it takes an awful lot of damage to even slow a wolf down. Without multiple assailants and a nice long run-up to the target, it's damn hard to do, by reputation. Just the same as it's hard to intoxicate or drug them to any effective degree, not with human drugs and drink, and they throw it off quicker than any human could.

But Parrin doesn't seem all that bothered by his young acolyte still putting up an argument against his stated decision. In the driving mirror, Penn sees that he smiles faintly, and nods quickly again at the glove-box where he pulled out the gun in the first place. He's driving one-handed, still waggling the gun up in the air a little, and Penn can only hope that he's got the safety catch on, and that they don't meet any ruddy great articulated lorries, coming the other way around a blind bend without warning.

He didn't ask to be illegally freed tonight, and he doesn't want to die tonight. But most especially, he feels, he doesn't want to die *by accident*. Getting killed, he would not like that, he would rage against it most especially before having achieved any of the things he wants to drag out of his life by the very unwilling roots. He'll fight and fight and fight against the circumstances of his life, and everything he can't tolerate to his very last hissing breath. But if he's actively deliberately killed while fighting, and he still fights as he goes down, that's one thing. So much another, to be taken out by fate as a matter of mischance, a slip on a stepladder, a wet plug socket or a banana peel. The former he can accept, reluctantly. But the latter is unacceptable. Silently, he wills Parrin to keep his eyes on the road and his damn hands unoccupied. Put the bloody gun down, you idiot, he thinks. If I'm going to wind up shot tonight, then I'd at least like for it to be intentional.

But with grubby flannel in his mouth, he hasn't a current chance to make that interjection into their cosy little argument between aristocrat abolitionist wolves, unfortunately. It's Benedict Parrin who makes response, adding to his nod with the words, "You have a look in the glove-box, where I got this. Take a look inside that cardboard box, see what you can see." And he's grinning to himself, fully pleased.

Harry – the pack-nameless and packless wolf, as far as Penn is concerned, and no doubt careful to remain so – does as he's told. Good to see he's not totally insubordinate, Penn thinks critically. And he wonders why he cares, except that shoddy organisation and inefficiency never fails to annoy him, even when he's at its mercy and a little slipshodness can only benefit him. Harry pulls out a small cardboard box, which looks suitable and designed for storing bullets. Unsurprisingly, it proves to be so. And he draws one of them out, scrutinizes it in what limited light's available, and puts it to his teeth, bites down.

"Oh," he says, quietly. "That's handy. *Potentiated*. Where did you even get those?"

Well, Penn can understand that response. And soon as he hears it, he drops his head, scrunches up back against the back of the car-seat, and looks as little alert and paying attention as he can manage.

Parrin laughs happily, and guns the engine a little as they hit a long straight stretch on the road. "Better not to enquire, young 'un," he says easily, looking out into the misty air, brown fields and grizzling cheeping sleepy birds. "Some things you're better off not knowing."

Potentiated silver, Penn thinks. Damn it, Parrin has done well getting hold of that. Old folk stories tell variants upon the tale that once upon a time, a century or three back and for a few decades after the invasion, silver bullets alone were enough to kill a wolf. There must be some truth in it, because for a few decades after the European occupation, records suggest that the human population held out and held off the wolves, in most settlements in any case. (And Penn is a librarian, an archivist. He's read the records in the original, and he knows what they document.)

But eventually – from what the records hold, the little hard data that's available going that far back, during times of such raging upheaval and disaster for humanity – it seemed as if the wolves developed a degree of immunity. Silver bullets worked no better than steel or iron in the end, even where cities under siege didn't simply run out. And the human race was overrun, vanquished and made a vassal race in a state of subjugation. They were enslaved, barring a few favoured examples who were allowed to live free on account of influential positions, or their unusual skill, ability and charm. Or because they were favoured pretty pets, even in those times. (Not all humans know this much of their own history, either before or after invasion, or whether they're slave or free, Penn has found over the years. Not many slaves have as much education as he's had, nor the scholarly tastes that Ree teases him over.)

But before the final complete defeat, there'd been a couple of strongholds where humans not only held their ground, withstanding assaults and attempts to starve them out of walled cities in England and what Germany was at the time, but also made ground in assaults against the wolves. Silver, the records show, that was what made the difference: but not regular plain mined and smelted silver. What was used, was treated with secret ingredients and alchemical preparations, wizards and viziers making undocumented pronouncements over the smelting mix. A special and potentiated active silver, smelted and cast into bullets, a silver that could still kill a wolf with a single bullet, to the heart or the head.

But it was too late, the discovery, and they were too few holding out, and those cities had fallen too. And with them the secret was also lost, all records destroyed and all possibility of any real resistance against the invader disappeared.

Well, that's the story that does the rounds and made it onto paper records, at any rate. But judging by subsequent incidents, rare and notorious, but hard to explain otherwise, there's still an effective explosive and deterrent against wolves out there. Every so often in Penn's experience, also, he's come across someone – a slave or servant or freedman with an inexplicable experience, or a wolf who lets slip a little something he'd do better not to have – and they also suggest that the knowledge of how to activate silver to maximise and restore its lethal capacity against wolves was never destroyed, after all. Only hidden, and very carefully retained, and kept by the wolves themselves. For use on their own kind, against the rogues and the criminals and the outlaws they throw off here and there, even by wolf standards. Just to make sure that in terms of wolf against wolf, the established packs and the wolf-recognised authorities always have the upper hand.

But even in the circles where it's known of, Penn has heard whispers that it's semi-legal and quietly proscribed, except for those very highly placed and authorised.

And Penn doubts very much that Benedict Parrin and his couple of daring, idealistic young wolf-accomplices here, are high in wolf-council and sheriff's office circles, high enough to justify possession of wolf-bullets that can and will disable or kill one of their brethren. Which means they're illicitly in possession of them, and Penn can't say he's surprised. Parrin has struck him as a resourceful type, before now. He feels no dismay or disapproval at the knowledge. It's potentially useful, that's all.

In fact, it could be very useful, to know that Parrin has weapons stashed here that are lethal to wolves. Really, how very careless of him to discuss it with his young friend, in Penn's hearing. Of course Penn might not get the chance to put that knowledge to use: but it's an option tucked away out of sight, and suddenly Penn feels a lot less hopeless than he was five minutes ago.

But not any less constricted. There's a dim hint of dawn that's flushing up the eastern corner of the sky into a tawny rose-pink, and it reminds him that time's passing, and he should be utilising it to the fullest, while he can. He's pitted against two – no, three – wolves, who are armed against human and wolf alike. And he's a poor soft human, with his hands bound, unarmed, weaponless.

Well, mostly. Penn has always found that his best weapon is his mouth, in more ways than one. Ree's often found it so, although weapon probably isn't the word that he'd choose. But if Penn isn't using it to advance his ambitions, in the most direct manner possible, then he can always use tongue, teeth and lips another way, i.e. by talk-ing. He's used it to talk himself right into and then again out of a tight spot before now: and if nothing else, he's willing to bet that his ability to provoke a response out of almost anyone, when he chooses to, will at least alter the situation. For good, or for ill, or in unpre-dictable ways that might neither advantage nor disadvantage him.

But Penn feels willing to risk an uncertain outcome, given that he has so little to his arsenal at present, nothing to plan around or use. And all he needs is a measure of freedom. Not his hands, because it's not as if he hasn't been trying all this time – as subtly and discreet-ly as he can manage it. But they'd expected that, of course, and taken it into account. He doesn't consider Benedict Parrin a fool, or only a very particular and specialised kind of fool. He wouldn't do any-thing as slackly incompetent as tie knots so amateur that they leave Penn with the slightest chance of escape and getting his hands free. Not without assistance, a penknife or a wickedly sharp edge some-where to rub up against, and none of those things are immediately available to Penn. Because Parrin isn't such an idiot as not to check the immediate environment for that, too. And nor, probably, are his colleagues, even if they seem a bit dimmer than one might expect, from wolves willing to trust to their wits running a covert and pro-scribed slave-freeing organisation, only their mental agility and acu-men to keep their furry hides off the chopping block for doing so.

His mouth, though. Not that he hasn't already been trying, this past, what, hour, hour and a half? But only half-heartedly, absent-mindedly, while surveying the land and looking out the window to watch their route, while observing every little thing that these two get up to and listening to every word out of their mouths. And back in the back of the van, a still smaller fraction of his attention paid to getting back the capacity to speak his bloody mind. (A capacity that's always been dear to his heart, and not one he gives up with the least willingness if he can damn well help it.)

But now, he's sucked in all the information and tips that it seems the environment and his companions are prepared to yield up, at least without a little further encouragement and prodding, of the Machiavellian and sneaky kind. (Ah Machiavelli: now there was a human in a wolf world whom Penn could wish to emulate, whose starry, shocking career from slave to freedman to landowning bitten and made wolf is... Well, it's impressive, even if Penn would vastly prefer to leave off the latter part of that sly devil's ascent to power and status within the seventeenth century wolf community, and the wider culture and society both wolf and human. Not that Penn is ever going to advertise having read his seditious and still applicable writings, since in some jurisdictions it's a punishable offence and a dangerous pastime: unwise enough that old Jay Parrin provided and approved him reading them, the revolutionary old codger. Jay Parrin, a scholar to the bone, who loved words more than he feared the threat of censure over keeping blacklisted writings in his library.)

There's nothing more that Penn can find out, without having a more active role in events. So he focuses every last bit of his attention on the rag of grubby linen rammed between his teeth and to the gagging point of his throat, and he really puts himself to work on it. After all, he's always been talented with his tongue, and throat, cheeks, lips, all the rest of it. With the uses he's put them to, and the workouts that they've had – not pleasantly, always, but with the efficient resolve of a job to be done – then they've had the opportunity to reach peak condition and match fitness, to be capable of much more than a less-trained and honed set of muscles and bone.

In short, if anyone can tongue and tease and ease a gag several inches out of a mouth and throat, then Penn's the lad to do it. And with the light brightening and gathering in the east, and the van trundling through lighter and lighter back roads, he puts all of his skill and ingenuity into achieving the object. The signs read Ilkeston, Ripley, Alfreton, as he works steadily, with careful unobtrusiveness, his head down as if he's dozing. Baldur damn it, it takes so long. He's only half-aware, concentrating hard upon both the task and its concealment, as Parrin takes the van up onto the moors and they're travelling through the Peak District, speeding along narrow roads between fields of dozy sheep, massed and huddled together in fast sleep in the very early morning mist.

As he begins to make some real progress, and is working and doing his best at not actually choking as he does so – the bastards, in their eagerness to free him did they have no concern over whether or not he survived the experience? - the increased light and brightness seems to loosen the wolves' tongues, wake them up beyond a mere intermittent mumble, into alertness and communicativeness. Enough that Parrin is minded to include Penn in the conversation, which is damn good of him, if pointless at present. They're talking about the Holmford boy, the one that Penn still hasn't laid eyes on, but is close enough anyhow, stuck in the back of this vehicle that Ree wouldn't condescend to acknowledge, let alone drive. And Penn listens to them talk, about why the boy's run and what he's gone through before lucking into a connection with the network, who's been sheltering him until they could come pick him up and why he's alone. (Indiscreet, Penn thinks disapprovingly. He's been loaned out for labour to a sheriff's deputy before now, he's run a small household and kept order and discipline, and if he had the running of this little cadre then it would be a different story, very different indeed. This is no way to run a surreptitious organisation dedicated to the overthrow of the current social order. Not that it matters, of course, and he shakes himself out of the thought, gets back to pressing himself back into the shadows of the back seat, and dispensing himself quietly of the obstacle to his use of his favourite weapon. Yes, it sounds like the unseen lad's had a rough time of it, and Penn can understand why he made the choice he did. If it's a free choice, he has no quibble with it. It's only himself, brought along as ballast, and no more asked for his opinion on the matter than a parcel packaged up and thrown in the mail van for delivery, that he takes issue over. Bloody wolves, always deciding a man's fate from on high, thinking they must know best whether it's for his good or his doom. And half of them without the education to read and parse a contract or an essay, even regarding their own history.

Up in the driver's seat, Parrin shakes his head, and from the glimpses that Penn gets of the side of his face, he looks solemnly concerned. "Poor lad, eh, Penn? Do you not think so? There must be many an experience you have in common with him. And see the choice he's made as a result of it, all the brutality and suffering that he's endured at the hands of my brother wolves. Perhaps if you'd had less of a mixed experience, and mixed feelings about the race of wolves of late, it would have been easier for you to come to the same conclusions that he has. That it's worth the risk, and the privations of the life you're bound for, to have freedom and security from such abuse and such maltreatment. Eh, what do you think? What would you say?"

It's the Platonic ideal of a rhetorical question, of course, and Parrin's just enjoying hearing his words evaporate in the cold rushing early-morning air. That's all, he expects no answer unless young Harry chooses to butt in. But he doesn't know everything. Because Penn has been working, working all this time, working without cease at all, and now he's almost there. The scent and camphor on the linen is extremely unpleasantly bitter against the wet inner flesh of his cheeks, and it almost squeaks, setting his teeth viciously on edge, against his molars as he finally forces it forward enough to be spat out. If he chokes a bit before he speaks, it's understandable.

Chapter 2

"I'd say, that if I'd been asked for my opinion, then I'd have given it," he says. "But no, wait, I was asked, wasn't I? And I said no, no, I didn't want to be freed, I didn't want to be rescued, I had my own plans. So you had my opinion, and you ignored it. Sir." And he'd congratulate himself on just how cool he manages to make the words themselves, no screaming or imprecations. Except that his voice is unsurprisingly hoarse, and there's a little crack midway through where it gives out completely. It's still a reasonably creditable effort, though.

It's effective, too. It makes Parrin jolt in his seat, risk a quick glance in the driving mirror before returning his attention to the road where it's floating with early morning mist and rolling waves of rain. Sheep are eyeing them sceptically in the distant fields, disapproving of their morning slumbers being disturbed. And so is co-conspirator Harry, who's turned a little in his seat, arm along the length of it to trail behind Parrin's back. And he's watching Penn with an interested gaze.

To which Pen casts him a chill look, and looks instead at the back of Parrin's head. That glance is apparently all the visual attention that he's getting, but Parrin does respond. "Well done, Pennorth," he says coolly. And you'd never be able to tell whether he's annoyed or pleased or merely neutral, to have Penn unexpectedly half-free himself and leaping into the conversation unasked – or, well, not asked with the expectation of any answer. "I appreciate your input: we merely expected you to be a little, ah, noticeably vocal initially, on finding that the decision was made for you, and I'd decided to gift you with a better life since you're currently too brain-washed to make the decision yourself. Hence the gag, you see, but you've done a nice job dispensing with it. Very impressive."

"Thank you," Penn says blankly. Because what else can he say, to that level of self-possession? Parrin isn't going to care, not about his opinion, not about the life behind him that he'd almost, almost... Was on the point of dragging into a semblance of a shape that was pleasing to him, that might have satisfied him. Perhaps.

He doesn't even trouble to make it sarcastic. It seems a waste of effort, and it's not as if Harry hasn't cuffed him once already tonight. He isn't looking to invite more casually violent reproofs. But there are none forthcoming in any case from that direction, although Harry is still taking an observant and alert interest in him, and shows no sign of turning back around. He smiles, now, and says, "The boss-man's right, you know. We understand that it's difficult to come to a decision to make the break, when you've lived in captivity all your life, been used to abuse and had mixed experiences with different packs. Sometimes you form bonds with an owner-pack, sometimes the odd wolf here or there seems to have an affection for you and you get caught up with it. If it's the only emotional warmth that's on offer, if it seems as if it's all the love you're ever going to get. But once you get away from that, you'll see how much better it is to be free. Even if the life in free territories can be a little harsh, compared to the civilized lands."

Which says a lot, as far as Penn is concerned. The civilized lands, where he's stored and built all of his hopes and ambitions, where the living is soft and relatively easy – unless you get caught as a runaway slave, unless you're a slave at all, as long as you're a wolf or a freedman – aren't open to him, as a 'liberated' slave. Not now that they intend to free him, against his will and his better judgement. No, he's stuck with the dregs, with the most remote and desolate scrag-ends of homeland available on earth, the remnants that no wolf would deign to set paw in.

Presumably, he's supposed to be grateful for his liberation, as well. Perhaps the stony echo of his response shows in his face without need for words. Because this Harry, this bright young wolf with a nice face and an unfortunate manner, laughs, and reaches out to pat at his shoulder. A bit much, a bit rich, considering that, what, an hour or so back he was shoving Penn halfway through the seat-back? He doesn't open his mouth: Parrin comments before he can. "Harry's right there, Pennorth, and you might want to consider his words. A wolf might be fond of you, there's plenty that have a soft spot for a weak pretty creature. Something they can fondle and fancy themselves a protector to. Harry here's a case in point, eh, Harry?"

The tone is extremely dry: and perhaps it's referencing something previously discussed. Because Harry abruptly removes his hand from Penn's shoulder, and retreats back into his own seat, giving a swift hot mutinous glance in Benedict Parrin's direction. Parrin laughs, shoots up a tight hairpin bend and rounds an impressive great boulder at the corner, a monument in the mist set in wet grey grass. "Yes, I think Harry has a hankering for a pretty human boyfriend. I've noticed it before. But we have strict rules and prohibitions about that kind of thing, you don't need to worry, Pennorth. He knows it's more than his hide's worth to fondle the goods or make an approach, to a human we're restoring into the wild. With us, you're safe from that kind of exploitation. Which is more than I can say for the Hotstaats, with their esteemed and noble Alpha being a prime example. That bastard was never going to free you, Pennorth," he says, and there's an undue warmth in his voice, a coaxing come-on in the undertone that's more personal than he's allowed, up until now, with his sensible withdrawal into a businesslike detachment. "Not even through the bite. Did he not even offer you the bite? Still, you'd still have half-belonged to him then, as one of his betas or worse – you're better off without that, too. No, I could see it perfectly well, watching the two of you, his eyes on you all the time he was supposed to be courting my dear sis. He was going to dangle you on a string until the end of time, keep you waiting and waiting with hints and half-promises. Till you were old and tired and too defeated to even hang onto any resentment over it. He'd have turned you into the model of a perfect old retainer contented in his duties, praising the master and the family up and down and doting on every new litter of cubs like half the human fools who spend enough decades in service of a pack. And then, perhaps, once he was absolutely sure you weren't going to disappear over the far horizon the minute he did it – once he knew that all the fight had gone out of you – he might have freed you, yes."

He accelerates violently, and glares at Penn via the driving mirror. "That isn't what old Jay wanted for you, Pennorth. He respected your mind, and he was amused by your spirit. You served him because you liked him, and I'd like to see you deny it. Remember we visited a time or two – me and dear Lettice – and we saw the pair of you together. You deserve more than that. You should be free while you're young still, with all the spittle and fire and bile still in you. While it can still do you some good."

Penn would sorely indeed like to deny it, all of it. He's not a hundred percent sure that he can, especially regarding Ree's intentions vis-a-vis himself and manumission, whether those intentions are conscious or otherwise.

But he feels his heels dig in, mentally, and the urge to contradict is strong. And less easy to quell than it normally would be, in the presence of wolves. These circumstances are special and unusual, after all. Perhaps that's the explanation. Anyway, it's the only one he can think of, when he snaps, "I'm sure you know your future brother-in-law better than I could. Sir. But perhaps in some ways I know him better than you." He's being sarcastic, of course. Benedict Parrin doesn't know Ree well: apart from anything else, Ree doesn't care for him at all, and has kept him at a good long distance as much as possible. Not that it seems to be other than mutual, what with Parrin seeming to bear a combination of wariness and hostility towards Renally. Who is of course a perfect example of the arrogance and entitlement of the slave-owning wolf class, which he both despises and belongs to. Perhaps there's some projection in his attitude, but it seems sincere too.

And Parrin lets it go for a moment, gazing out the window. They're winding around small towns and narrow roads towards the moors, heading towards the Snake Pass that winds through the Peak District in the North of England, and if there wasn't still so much mist obscuring the view then it would probably be beautiful, if still grey and dimly lit. Harry's brooding quietly to Parrin's left, and he murmurs, barely audible over the slightly straining engine, "Do you think I'm unfair to Renally, Pennorth? I wouldn't have thought it possible you could bear him much affection, rationally speaking. He owns you, he hasn't freed you, he's bound you to him while taking my sister to mate, and for all you were children together, he still has the upper hand in every interaction you have with him. What loyalty do you imagine you owe him?" He sounds sincerely curious, not as if he's seeking to provoke.

Well. Penn's hands are sore, well beyond chafing, and he has been half-choked with a gag for hours, and he has not rested well for obvious reasons. Chloroform lends itself to unconsciousness, and in unfortunate circumstances and incompetence death, rather than restful sleep. His chemise is unsuitably thin, and the autumn morning's cold, and the back-seat blankets half-pulled over him do almost nothing to ameliorate it. Perhaps his temper's a little sharp: perhaps it takes the edge off fear and blunts wisdom. "Does it have to be about my feelings for him?" he asks, and that is definitely a little sharp. "Perhaps he serves a purpose for the plan of what I want my life to be: isn't it still my plan to make? Or I had a chance at that, at least, until you threw me over your damn shoulder and carried me off."

"You'll come around," Harry states in a monotone, blank-faced and with his eyes on the horizon. "They all do. Now you're free of that animal."

Ree, Penn supposes he means, and he feels it as the last tossed splint that ignites a great fire in his chest. Even the irony of the epithet – from such a source – matters less than his rage. His face is hot, he can feel it, and he says, "What do you know about it? Or him? Actually – sir," – and the respectful *sir* has never been more irony-laden – "Alpha Hotstaat *has* offered me the bite. As it happens." Which is a slight stretch of the facts: since Ree has in fact hinted around the subject, at first teasingly, and then much more cautiously after gauging Penn's reactions to the idea. Which are not warm and excited, it would be true to say.

"Really?" Parrin asks. His eyes are still on the road, by necessity: the tracks in these hilly formerly-private parks are winding ribbons of road that require careful attention. But Penn can feel that he has commanded a good deal more of Parrin's attention, with this. "So, you wouldn't take it from me. I thought maybe you'd just got something against me, Pennorth: you seem strangely resistant to my irresistible charm. But it turns out it's the bite itself that you object to. So why is that? Care to explain?"

No. No, Penn never cares to explain. He's never fully explained to Ree, although perhaps Ree's researches on Penn's ownership history have turned up enough clues that he's worked it out by now. He's never touched on the subject nor gone anywhere near it with Lettice Parrin, nor any other, even those few old slave compadres who knew the little of his history he confided after a little ale. Anyone who knows, knows a lot better than to bring it up.

But now it spills burning and bitter out of him, because–. Because. "Maybe you wouldn't want the bite either. Not if your mother was bought by a rich merchant wolf when you were six, and you were bundled along as bags and baggage. And then he decided that she had pretty eyes, and then that he'd take her to his bed, and then–." Oh, his voice is not doing good things. It's all over the place, and if Penn was operating according to his usual standards and precepts, then he would certainly have the dignity to shut up. He doesn't, though. Both of these damned wolves are ramrod straight, upright in their seats, eyes forward in this little tin can of a vehicle, but totally aware of him. He knows it: his fury must be scentable easily, and just how close he is to humiliating tears. He will control his voice, though. He wills it, forces it steady.

"Then he was in love with her, took her with him everywhere. I was along for the ride half the time, for outings and treats, only dumped in a nurse's hands at the door of the bedchamber. Another household where I was quite coddled and indulged. You'd have thought I was a wolf-kid, the way they spoilt me. Brat of the master's favourite, of course: it pays to keep on the good side of someone who's on his good side." He gargles down a breath that's long and not steady at all, but it's air and he sucks at it like a lolly.

"It's not that uncommon," Parrin says remotely. It's chilly, antiseptic, but somehow Penn can tell that it's carefully free of any outgushing of sympathy. That much feeling at this point might put the final crack in the dam of Penn's control, and Parrin is wily enough to see that. He does have mercy, if not wisdom. "You should know, if anyone."

Penn swallows the rush of bile – literal, metaphorical – that he could spurt forth in response. "Maybe not," he allows, and shivers in the dank and sweat of his chemise. "And it's less common for a smitten wolf to offer the bite to a pretty slave, I suppose. But also, not unknown. And yes, I should know. Some refuse it, of course, like me. It's known to be dangerous, or more slaves would be looking to court the master and seduce him into it, I suppose."

It seems that young Harry can't keep his composure and his careful detachment, face forward, any further. He shifts a bit in his seat, then twists around, to look at Penn out of wary, but potentially kind eyes. "It's not that dangerous," he says, hesitantly.

And Penn snorts. It's not becoming, or the kind of doe-eyed seduction he'd practise on Ree, but it's expressive, all right. "Statistically, maybe," he allows. It's strange to look a wolf full in the eyes, and have that wolf flinch away a little, not to insist on dominance. Perhaps this Harry is intuitive enough to have a suspicion of what's coming. "But if you're the one bitten, then statistics don't count for much. They didn't for my mother, anyway. She was one of the small percentage of the bitten who don't survive. Would you have told her how it wasn't that dangerous?"

Well, the air in the van goes very still, very quiet. "I'm sorry," Benedict Parrin says after a moment's pause, hands on the wheel to steer around a long slow bend in the road. There's a mumble from Harry that suggests assent, and he straightens back up in his seat. Penn doesn't elaborate on his own personal tragedy in more detail than that. But he can't stop it all from unspooling without restraint or decent, merciful blotting out, not in his head. A new home, if you could call it a home at all – new owners and new lodgings, that was all it amounted to really. And this, coming after the loss of Ree – Ree as was, the Ree he still holds dear in memory and does his best to disassociate from the troubling, demanding, confusing stranger encountered so many years after. He'd been still mourning the loss, not that his six-year-old self would have described it that way. There was just a horrible empty absence in his heart, and he filled it up with anger and misbehaviour, that did little to impress their first owner after the Hotstaats, and was probably half the reason they were sold on again so quickly.

Sold to a wolf who looked at his mother with thoughtful eyes, that were still all wolf in his human face. And regarded Penn with a mildly amused indulgence, searched candy out of his pockets to silence his wailing as he was loaded, a new purchase, onto the wagon for their destination, their new pack-owners. "Good healthy lungs at least," had been his only comment, but Penn can remember now the way his eyes lingered on Penn's mother's form, still young and supple.

Two weeks later and she was being teased by the new batch of house-slaves about the master's clearly favouring her. A month, and it was different from that, although a six-year-old Penn hadn't been able to define exactly how, beyond a few bare facts. The facts, that the unwed, unmated master took his mother out and about with him everywhere, and bought her gifts, and Penn too sometimes. That his mother didn't always sleep with him in their little room any more, but instead he was foisted off to one of the wet-nurses working in the pack nursery, who smelled of baby-sick and gin, and was gentle enough but still not his mother and therefore quite unsatisfactory. As well as being unwilling to answer questions such as *where is my mother* and *why can't I sleep with her?*

His memories of mama are more vivid around this time, not less. She'd been excited, a little bit on edge, extremely easy to provoke to either laughter or tears. At this distance of years, he can see it. She was in love. Damn it, but she'd been in love, with that wolf.

And if that had been the worst of it, it would have been quite bad enough, Penn thinks, feeling the distance and the loneliness, far far away from that other self. If only it had been, he could have lived with it. Quite well, because he hadn't learned different, then, and maybe he never would have. Not in a household where his mother was prized above all others, treated as almost free, almost a lady. Almost a *wolf,* by the time three, four months were up. Not that the wolf was a substitute father to him, and didn't pretend or try to be. But he was indulgent and amused. Penn can only speculate that he might have been freed himself, perhaps on reaching his majority, if things had gone differently. They would have had to go a lot differently, though.

He might never have hated wolves, might have lived free eventually, might have seen his mother grow old. If things had been different, and the wolf hadn't decided that it wasn't enough to have a pretty human darling on his arm and in his bed. That he wanted her turned, wanted her wolf, and he was prepared to bite her for it. That was the worst.

No, no, the worst was that she agreed. This bit he was in on, if not explicitly, this part he knows for sure. Even so little, even as a kid, he knew when a pack-run was coming up. When the moon was fattening and getting greedy and full and every wolf in the pack houses and habitations was getting restless, wild in the eye and smirking with teeth that little bit too long. He knew it wasn't usual, when his mother took him aside specially, to tell him that she was required to help at the run – which was normal, for any slave of the household. But that she wouldn't be back in the morning, but might be gone for as long as five days, perhaps even a week. (That wasn't.)

He hadn't known she was preparing him for, protecting him against, the long recovery from the bite, usually and ceremonially practised at the end of a run. When it was consensual, at least. He hadn't realised at the time, of course. He'd only known it was wrong and strange, that it wasn't what normally happened after a run, even in these few short months they'd been with this master. Afterwards he hadn't understood either, but then he'd been too busy howling and crying and raging against her loss. Once they'd explained that she'd died, after the run, after – well, after, and it was very sad. Everyone was very sad, and sorry.

Even the wolf, the master, had said how sorry he was. Probably he felt it was an absolute moral requirement, to apologise after a fashion to the brat he'd bereaved, the child of the pretty human girl he'd loved. Not that he'd done a good job of it, but then he was grieving himself, probably too much so to give himself to the job and pay all of his attention to a small child who couldn't possibly understand sad and serious adult matters. Penn will give him that, will pay him that due. He was grieving and more than grieving, it was plain as day at the time. His hair was wild and his eyes red and he was unable to stand still a moment, barely able to speak at all. It was more of a low rolling grunt, half growl, as he forced out the words about *your mother* and *very dear* and *the sweetest* and *we will sorrow forever, you and I.*

Penn will concede him that, and will never, never forgive him.

And then he'd turned away, with his duty completed, and said to someone else in the room that adult, twenty-seven year old Penn can't at all remember now, not with the fuzzy memories of remembered childhood once you're grown, "Send him away. It's not good for him to be here, now."

Sent away: a nice little euphemism for sold, on to the next household that wasn't a home, still less of one than any had been up until that point, for obvious reasons. And then still another, since he'd been little use as any kind of apprentice, wild and emotional and raging, still and shell-shocked and almost mute, alternating between the two and barely aware of his surroundings. The first master hadn't bothered to beat him much for it: just assessed the value of his purchase, marked it down as money thrown away, and sold him on to the next pack.

And that household was the one he'd burned down.

Chapter 3

O ops, no, better, oh much better, never to phrase it that way, even in thought. Just lest it ever slip out before some other ears. That was the wolf house that burned down. That's it. Much better, yes. It wasn't that it was so bad, either, that pack, that bunch of new owners. They were no worse than any other pack he'd encountered at that point, at any rate. It was the old house he wanted to burn, the old owner, the wolf who'd taken his mother away. And changed her. Changed her wrong, carelessly, messing it up somehow, so that she died, leaving a grieving lover, and one child.

The new house had been only a substitute for that desire, once the thought had entered his head. But once he'd thought of it, he was only looking for an excuse. And a beating after failing to spot a pair of shoes left out for cleaning had been sufficient. He'd put his fantasies into practice: only careful to be noisy and careless enough, returning to his own quarters, to disturb and awaken most of the slaves, so that they at least had fair chance to escape. To escape the fire, and to escape altogether, most of them: very few survivors were reported. But Penn remembers damn well one quick restless body after another slipping out of those quarters, consulting together about the likely results for slaves outliving masters burnt to death. A quick plotted plan put together, and half of them were away up over the hills, seeking out what freedom a branded slave might be able to find.

Leaving himself behind, forgotten, a recent addition to the household and not yet even branded. He was a small child, who could only be a hindrance in flight and no aid. All of his memories of the episode are vague. The next thing that blips up in his mind is wandering through narrow slum streets, shaking and freezing cold. And then being picked up by a county sheriff's deputy – numerous counties distant, somehow, in a space of hours or days that will be a mystery perpetually – and then the narrow path back to captivity, as a slave in possession of the county. He'd kept his mouth shut under questioning, and feigned vagueness even about what little he could remember. He was young, but not stupid, and was no keener than was wise to be associated with a fire and dead owners.

It's not something he calls to mind often, and when he does it's disturbing as the rest of his life. He was a bereaved and broken and frightened child: and the people he hurt weren't *people*, he self-justifies in harder moments. They were wolves. And they'd hurt him, besides. In more honest moments, he doesn't buy it, but probably it's good that it makes him uneasy. Even his life, even all these years, have failed to make a psychopath out of him. Even at the time, as far as he can drag it to the forefront of his mind, he hadn't had actively homicidal intent. He'd wanted to hurt, and to destroy something: but he'd been aiming for the house, not the inhabitants. Aren't wolves expected to be able to leap any height, with little hurt taken, if any? It must have been well-laid, and the wind lucky, and the sleep of the wolves deep. And except under the strictest duress and with strong incentive, he doesn't think he's liable to go on a murdering spree, even with wolves under discussion. Even if he was physically capable.

(Except that this isn't how it actually happened. He knows that, that it's the fantasy he cherishes, the edited re-written story he tells himself, to soothe (or aggravate) his fury and resentment, in times of punishment or humiliation. Perhaps that doesn't say anything good about his mental state, either. The truth: his child self had woken in the night and stumbled out from his bed and into the corridor, out to the dirt closet for bladder relief. He hadn't expected to encounter another slave while doing it, but he hadn't thought much of it at the time. It was an old fellow, and sometimes the cook brushed him gently away from this man. There were whispers that too much brutality and too many beatings had addled his wits. And on that night small Penn had faced him, and wondered what the petrol can was doing in his hand. And felt somehow uneasy at the wild grin on his face, as old Rictall stood and stared at him, a bit white about the eyes.

"Off for a slash, son?" he'd asked. And not waited for an answer, before adding, "Yes, you get along and do that. You do that."

He had: out in the cool of the night and the darkness, he'd relieved himself. And heard a great quiet rumble from a distance, and a shattering of glass. The walls about him had shaken, a little. When he came out the masters' side of the house was ablaze. He thinks, now – the memories are dim, re-written over, vague – that he stood a minute, slack around the jaws, uncomprehending. And then, the rest of it, as in the story he prefers, the one he tells himself like a bedtime fairytale. That's the truth. That's the truth. Not that he did anything about it, not that he raised the alarm. Perhaps that was helping to kill them, after all. Old Rictall wasn't one of the ones who slipped away in the night, either. Perhaps he was content to die in his own conflagration, an old man with a lost life and lost wits. As long as he took a few wolves with him.)

But even so. None of this seems advisable to let slip. He's done enough confiding in wolves for this day, or this year or decade, for that matter. He calms himself, takes a few deep breaths and braces and relaxes his legs, his arms. His face feels stiff, with the effort of abstention from tears, and everything aches. His heart, yes, but damn his heart. He's more concerned with retaining function and feeling in his arms, at the moment. He's about to open his mouth, and cautiously suggest that they hardly have much to fear from him, and freedom won't do him much good without the use of his arms, and how about stopping a moment and at least re-positioning and re-tieing them... When Parrin clears his throat, and speaks. He looks hard-faced, considering the sad sad sob story he's just been told. But then, he's a wolf, whatever his sympathies.

"Well, now that I know, Pennorth, I can understand." His voice is a little softer than his face, though. "It's natural that you'd object even to the suggestion of taking the bite. I'm sorry that I brought the subject up, and persisted with it when you clearly weren't interested. How would it not be a sensitive subject? I'm only surprised–." Parrin pauses there, chewing at his lip, stuck. Penn hopes, vindictively, that he slips into wolf mode by accident, and chews a hole through, but he knows that it isn't going to happen.

Young Harry slides his face around, and takes a contemplative look at his technical senior officer's face. His slightly sceptical expression confirms what Penn's thinking anyhow. That Parrin is fishing and angling, is waiting for the enquiry. And Penn doesn't mind providing it, taking the bait off the hook, getting hooked at the same time. Isn't that what he's playing at, seeing what he can do with his mouth, luring them, collecting information, surveying the field and building on his strategy? "What surprises you, sir?" he asks softly.

Parrin sighs. "That you're still calling me sir, to begin with. I'm not one of *those* wolves, Pennorth. You know I'm not. None of us, risking our lives to do this, are."

But you *are*, Penn thinks, meanly, coldly. You like to think that you're not, but you're ordering my life from the lofty height of your superior wisdom, and taking no account of my opinions on the matter. In lots of ways, you're exactly like any other wolf. The pack you were born into exhibits the traits differently, that's all. This he keeps his mouth shut about, though. It's Parrin who keeps on talking. "But yes. I'm surprised, Penn. Surprised that you took up with Hotstaat at all, now that I've heard your mother's story. How did you ever think it was going to go well? That's what wolves *do*, when they become infatuated with an alluring slave: they pick up a pretty thing, and they play with it for a while. Then they break it, and they throw it away.

I don't even know how many times I've seen it." He sounds sad, and patient, and utterly patronising, as if he's in the middle of explaining something to a child. "You've seen it before, haven't you, Harry?" he throws out, flinging a hand out Harry's way and negotiating a hair-pin bend single-handed. It's a good thing he has wolf reflexes when a hay-stacked farm vehicle comes around the other way, laxly steered. In the grey-green fields down below, a human tenant farmer looks up at the passing van, and sees them passing by, but Penn doesn't even think of throwing himself at the window, of yelling for help. Too far away, and too human, besides the consequences he's already been threatened with. (Human, yes, but how does he know? He just does. Often enough you can tell. There' something in the line of the haunches and the shoulder-blades, that's subtly different be-tween most wolves and most humans. Though occasionally you can be fooled. Some humans are a little closer to wolf than others, in in-definable ways. He has been accused of it himself, and offended by it.)

Harry grunts, but it sounds pretty much like an affirmative. He probably just thinks that Parrin is having a dig at him, about his own weakness for pretty humans.

"Would you say so, sir?" Penn asks. He lets the tone of his voice lash out with a cold, cold civility. "And yet you're letting your sister marry him."

He doesn't expect the laugh he gets for that, the harsh burst of amusement that has the faintest echo of a growl down deep in it. "I am that, Penn! Yes, I'm letting dear Lettice do as she pleases, just as I always do! As if anyone could prevent her." His face in the driving mirror is sly, now, amused. Then it turns serious. "She's a wolf, and she can take care of herself. None have more talent for that than dear Lettice, believe me. She'll keep him on his toes and keep him hop-ping like a frog, not half. It's a different thing for a human, Penn. If he's let you think that he cares for you, then he's – well, maybe he's not lying. You're a delightful creature, and that's a face no-one could forget, and you were boys together. No doubt the fool has something of a *tendresse* for you. But that's not at all the same thing as being able to give you the life you want, or having the slightest intention of ever making you free. Or condescending to acknowledge you publicly, without a bite you don't want. Or allowing you to take another lover or choose your occupation or live apart from him – until and unless he decides he's dispensed with you, and then you'll have no choice about any of those things, again. He'll sell you on, and you'll be up on the auction block once again and wondering what the hell happened and how you displeased him enough to wind up here. While he's living the life of Riley with my dear sister, once she's given him a packful of ratty little half-Parrin cubs. They'll provide him with hellacious torture and amusement, enough to take his mind off you permanently."

It's incredibly harsh – and probably true – and it hurts his chest, like it's punctured a lung. He just gasps, with the pain, for a moment. He hadn't known it would hurt so much, for someone else to see these things clearly. It's much different to lecturing himself to the same effect. And he never argues with himself on it, but he can't bear to hear it from someone else and not fight back. "Do you think so?" he spits out, a deal sharper than is wise. "I don't. And I've been close enough to know – to know he's marrying because he must, and he's marrying your sister because I picked her out for him. If I'd blacklisted her then she'd never have got near a Hotstaat for mating or marriage or a quick fuck in a dark wood at full moon. For that matter I could still edge her out now, if I felt like it, if I put my foot down, if you hadn't carted me off and safely off the premises and out of the way–." He stops, breathing fast. He isn't sure that last is true, isn't sure he can. And putting the wind up Parrin like that, giving him only an extra incentive to want Penn out of the picture and unable to do harm to his charming sister's marriage prospects, probably isn't the wisest thing that Penn has ever done.

"I wouldn't, though," he says, hastily repairing the damage as far as can be done. "She was the best of the bunch and has been good to me, I suppose by her lights. I like her. You, on the other hand..." He's pulled back from the indiscretion of mentioning the hand-fasting, the threesome and the three of them, sharing a bed and sharing vows. Vows, that ought to mean something, surely? Whatever snide aspersions Benedict Parrin might cast. He's only huffed out a soft laugh, at Penn's defence and battle for his own dignity, his own claim on Renally Hotstaat. But it would be risky to allow him to know that Penn's position is sufficiently privileged that he's actually been accepted into the mating ceremony, however covertly and discreetly, not to be publicly acknowledged. At present he's headed for freedom at Parrin's hands, however unwelcome and unwanted, unasked. If he gives Parrin reason to consider Penn a true rival for Renally Hotstaat's affections, favours and fortune, a powerful one and to be taken seriously, then his attitude might alter to something a good deal less benign. Provocation's one thing, but still Penn thinks he'd better be careful what he lets slip.

Yet he can't resist adding, "I think you're a dreamer, if you think Hotstaat's going to just let it go when he wakes in the morning and finds me gone." The morning that's already with them, brightening a little as the sun pushes its way up out of the east, and it gives Penn a disagreeable pang to think that that might already be happening. Ree, stirring and rising, waking Lettice and looking about, then searching about, for a Penn who isn't there, nowhere to be found.

It's Harry who shrugs, looking out into the morning where fields and farms and animals are waking. "What do you imagine he's going to do about it? You'll just be one more runaway slave, a statistic. He'll notify the local sheriff and hunt about a bit, but when you don't immediately turn up, he'll shrug and chalk it up to being too damned soft with the livestock. Then he'll keep a closer eye and be a damned sight less relaxed with the next nice bit of flesh he buys to warm up his bed where you've left it cold." It's rather brutal, perhaps because of his rebuke at the hands of Parrin.

And Penn could honestly spit acid, could throw an impressive fit. "Do you think so?" he asks again. His voice is very soft, and could still pass for respectful. "This is the wolf who spent twenty years, two decades searching for me after I was sold away from the estate when we were kids together. And he didn't give up, even though I was lost early on and there was no way of tracking me down from the records. He just kept going – like any hunter – and in the end he found me. Just the same way he's going to do this time," Penn snaps, and he feels a pang in his chest, burning with the truth of it. It had better be true, he feels. He can't tolerate a world where it isn't. "He's going to come and get me, just the same as he did last year, and what do you honestly imagine that he's going to do to you when he finds us? It's not as if he likes you much in the first place: and he thinks already that you're hot for my pretty face. He'll rip you apart like a deer in the hunt, and roast you for a pack feast into the bargain." Penn's breathing fast, and he wants it to be true. He's shocked by just how much he wants it. This isn't keeping a wise level of detachment and rationality, this isn't strategic. This is Penn tangled up in Ree's life just like when they were kids, following him around with dumb – well, knowing him and by all accounts, extremely chatty – adoration, persisting in a one-sided hero-worship until he'd harassed and poked and coaxed Ree into a returned affection.

He'd laughed, and felt incredulity, when the Dam had given that account of him. It doesn't seem like such a stretch of any possible world's history, now, in fact.

And Parrin is only smiling, at his account. Smiling, there in the mirror, quite blithe and cheerful, as if he has perfect confidence that Ree, now he's had a taste of the adult joys that an adult Penn can offer him, and has moved on to one of his own, to a proper little wolf bitch who can give him cubs and respectability, will be an official mate… That Penn is dispensable, and Ree can't help but have found that out, whatever his declarations and promises. Penn would like to break him apart for it. And an addendum to his little tirade just spits itself out. "Your sister, too," Penn adds, and he can see the minute stiffening of Parrin's spine in the driver's seat, that he pays just that fraction more attention, with Lettice thrown into the equation. "She knows what she owes me, and she's a good girl, for a wolf." Why trouble to hide his contempt, at this juncture, with this pair? They know what he really thinks, and how he really feels about wolves, no matter how he dissembles. "Ree and her both, they'll come for me. And then you're going to see how it goes, when you cross Ree."

Oh, it's embarrassing how childish, how fiercely petulant those last words sound, in the grey air inside the cab, the scenery whizzing past on the narrow breadth of the Pass. But Penn can't bring himself to regret it that much. He means it, and Ree and Lettice will, they're bound and hand-fasted with him, are they not? They volunteered that, no-one coaxed or cajoled or forced it out of them. He's given good enough service in return, well past any reasonable debt due. He's given his pound of flesh and then some, and they owe him. They *owe him*, he thinks, and it makes his jaw go rigid, his teeth clench, how very much they owe him that. They owe him a rescue – a rescue from unwanted freedom, by his owners, oh it's the very pitch of irony – and they owe him plenty more besides. That's the rock-bottom minimum. Aren't they technically his mates, for Pete's sake, after all? Why do it, why bodge up an off-the-cuff spontaneous ad-lib of a ceremony, if it's to mean nothing when push comes to shove?

But Parrin doesn't seem to be disturbed, not in the least. His eyes never leave the road, and his response is cool, bordering on chilly. "Do you think so, Pennorth?" He even smiles at the idea, his lips twitching like there are words waiting behind them. "Perhaps we

should have a bet on it. But I'm betting that you're just believing all
the lies that Renally Hotstaat's filled up your head with, and you're
over-estimating your worth to him. Even if he could find you at this
point, do you think he's going to bother? Even wolves have limits,
Pennorth, when it comes to the internal combustion engine. Even
if we hadn't carefully crossed water at a couple of points along the
way, and we've come a long, long way since two a.m., believe me. You
over-estimate wolf endurance and powers of perception in the hunt.
Do you think he's going to revert to wolf and go galloping across
country, trying to follow a trail that doesn't exist, and would have
been split by water even if it did, through hundreds of miles of county after county, other pack's territory? No, Pennorth."

His voice is kind, as if he isn't doing his best to eviscerate Penn
with a careful precision, with a surgeon's hands. "All he's going to do,
is to write you off as another runaway slave, over-indulged and ungrateful. And notify his sheriff's office of your brand-number, and
distinguishing characteristics, and let them hunt you down. With
dogs," he adds, cheerfully, and Penn knows enough to know that it's
the crowning insult. A slave not considered important enough for a
master to hunt down personally, with his own pack, should he run,
is negligible indeed. But Penn doesn't believe it. Ree will come after
him, would always come after him. Is bound to him, hand-fasted, by
his own free choice.

Isn't he?

"Although they'll never find you, not at this point," Harry points
out. "Not the Hotstaats, and not the sheriff's office. We've gone too
far, we're way ahead. Not even an alpha could catch up, now. You're
free now, Pennorth," he says, quite jovial and cheerful. "They'll never
be able to drag you back into captivity, not now."

"He will find me," Penn says, but even he can hear the shaken
dullness of his tone. "He promised me. That he'd always look for me,
and always find me." And he can't believe that he's defending a *wolf*,

this particular wolf, standing and speaking for his honour and his trueness and believing it too. But he is. He will. Many things, he's called Ree, in the peace and silence of his own mind, and few of them complimentary most of the time. But he remembers them, two tousle-headed little chaps falling into streams and with licence to run over the whole estate, sometimes two boys running wild and creating havoc, sometimes a boy and his wolf-pal. Thinking of the yells and tantrums and tears shed, when they were separated. Thinking of that, how can he believe Ree insincere in his protestations, now they're grown?

"Well, don't worry about it," Benedict Parrin says comfortably, "Certainly, one of us must be right, and it'll work out one way or another. Now, I need a piss, and we should check on Gus and the Holmford boy in the back, make sure they haven't expired of starvation or boredom." And he pulls over to the side of the road, and Penn gets the first dose of fresh air he's had in a long while, when they let him out of the van.

Penn stumbles out of the van with his arms tied still, only his legs free. He does it slowly, and taking care not to tumble down off the step, because he's damned if he'll accept the eagerly welcoming offer of support from the wolf Harry's arm extended, hovering at his side. He isn't sure if Harry is worried that he might abscond, even bound and exhausted and clad in a thin chemise, as he is. Or if his intentions are more amorous, more inclined to hover and offer protection in the way of one of those wolves with a fancy for tender vulnerable humans. Parrin's accused him of it, after all, and he must surely have some prior knowledge of the other wolf's character.

At any rate Penn makes sure he gets down from the van under his own steam, and keeps a careful distance between himself and young Harry, who still hovers with a solicitous interest. At this point, he's had quite enough trouble and *sturm und drang* resulting from amorous interested wolves, Penn thinks. One extra would be absolutely the outside of enough – unless he was useful. That's the only circumstance under which he'd consider a little discreet flirtation, encouraging any advances from the young wolf. And this wolf, considering what appear to be his fixed beliefs about manumission and slave liberations and whatnot – and his disinclination to listen to the opinions and objections of individuals out of that group he proposes to assist – isn't liable to be the least damn use to him, in getting free, and returning to his slavery. (Penn is fully aware of the irony of his plans and restless musings, but even so. His choices are his own, wise or foolish, rational or biased. It's not a matter for someone *else* to decide for him, high-handed, no matter how well-intentioned.)

It's briefly wonderful, to stretch his lanky frame to its fullest height, to flex his arms as far as he's able and move from one foot to another, easing aches and soreness. To draw a full breath, not the stuffy stale soup of the cab, and to let his eyes rest on the rolling curling grey mist in the valley below them, down below where the road winds and coils, a thin gravelled track that can barely take two vehicles abreast.

He's not the only one let loose, of course. Once Parrin's relieved himself up against the stone crags on the upper side of the road, he takes the gun from Harry, that he's been discreetly bearing – the same dull silver loaded revolver that he'd fondled and played with while driving, the careless swine. The one so potentially useful against wolves, and Penn notes its presence thoughtfully and carefully. Because you never know when opportunity might strike. But he's not discreet enough about his scrutiny, since Parrin notices and laughs, waving it around a little in a way that seems idiotically careless. "Yes, better behave yourself, young Pennorth," he advises – the little squirt, as wolves go, barely having attained his own majority. Yes, Penn remembers him, a couple of times here and there visiting at Jay Parrin's residence. He remembers a moody fierce-eyed young lad watching Penn curiously, disturbingly observant and pensive.

Well, it's not surprising, now, given what his preoccupations and avocation have turned out to be. Not considering he's a Parrin pack sprig, too. "It works just as well on humans, if not better," Parrin advises him, giving the gun an ostentatious jab. And he gives a jerk of the head in Harry's direction, where he's still hovering, still watching and pretending not to watch Penn. "Oi, make yourself useful, then, young 'un." And he extricates a key-ring out of his trouser pocket, and throws it, jingling, in Harry's direction. Who catches it as perfectly as any other wolf would, of course, predictably.

And he lets one stretching, wide-eyed figure out of the back of the van. This must be the aforementioned Gus, Parrin's other assistant in subterfuge and larceny of human property. He's a meaty, broad fellow, muscular and chunky about the chest, built like a bull, like a rugby player. The dark-gold glint of his eyes and the developing shadow at his chin suggest the wolf, even if he didn't absent-mindedly sharpen his teeth with a metal nail-file, instead of poking his cuticles. He looks every inch the overly-muscled and stolidly loyal pack beta, not especially gifted intellectually, ready to steamroller over any enemy to the pack. What he doesn't, at all, look like, is an idealistic soldier in the battle for liberation and enfranchisement for slaves. But what does Penn know about it, after all? He's always stayed strictly out of that kind of trouble.

There's no second person following on from Gus, though. A moment, two moments, and no-one appears out the wide-open van back-doors.

"Thank Wotan," Gus says sourly, stamping around to loosen stiffened legs. He ambles up to Parrin and Harry, without taking a blind bit of notice of the slave he's supposedly selflessly releasing at the risk of his own life. "I thought I was going to die in there. Either him talking me to death, or asphyxiation. Damn, it's nice to get a fresh breath out here. I thought you were never stopping."

Penn isn't the only one who's noticed a certain absence, though. Parrin waves his gun in the direction of the back of the van – and, Penn thinks sourly, he really wishes Parrin wouldn't *do* that. An accidental death during an unscheduled unwanted escape attempt is not how he wants to go. "Where's the lad?" he demands. "Did he aggravate you enough that you opened up the doors and shoved him out the back, while we were on the move?" And then they all laugh together, as if it's just a jolly hoot and a bit of foolery, instead of life and death to the slave concerned. The one that they're joking about.

"He's asleep," this bull-shouldered brute explains casually. "Must have talked himself into exhaustion, because I swear he's never stopped since we picked him up in Nottingham. All his plans, what he's going to do once he gets to the Canadian territories, the contacts he already has there, undying thanks and promises to name half his grand-kids after me. By the devil, it never stopped. Ten minutes ago he conks out cold, and it's the first bit of peace I've had in hours." And he sighs, and turns about, and gives Penn the first look he's honoured him with, a hard scrutiny that only seems to intensify. "Well, so that's the Hotstaat bit?" he asks. But he's talking to Parrin and Harry, not to Penn. "Fetching bit of flesh, I'll allow. You can understand how Hotstaat went nutty and head over heels for him. Ciggie, Ben?"

Penn is busy grinding his teeth, biting his lip to keep himself from an untoward interjection. And that's not all that this hearty public-school-type young wolf has to offer to the conversation. After jabbing his jet-and-silver chased cigarette case at Harry, too, he leaps a step forward and proffers it in Penn's direction. Which is a novelty. He's had elaborate displays of egalitarianism in private, amongst Ree's closest friends. But not with wolves he doesn't know, when they're having a private conversation with himself as a dumb ignored witness. "How about you, old son?" he enquires jovially. "Smoke?"

And Penn's still sharp enough not to rebuff the advance. Because whether it's guns or wolves or a little bit of intel, you never know what's going to come in useful. But he quarter-turns and indicates his well-bound hands to the wolf, wriggling them a little bit, chafed as they are, in their hempen bonds. "Oh, we should have re-tied and re-positioned you by now, Pennorth," Harry cries. And what Penn will concede is that there's real remorse in his voice. Not that it does Penn a blind bit of good.

But it's the new boy who actually makes himself useful, stuffing his cigs in his pocket as he turns Penn around and has him free in a moment of utter relief. Prods him in the direction of the inner wall, first, which has Penn bamboozled. Until he gets the idea, and takes a leak while he can, and hadn't realised how much he needed it. And then he's bound up again in an instant, too, but at least with his arms forward, this time, and the position of his shoulder eased. Which both accentuates the fiery burning discomfort in them for several moments, and then eases it considerably. Of course the new boy – Gus – is as proficient at knots as the other two. It's not as if Penn's a Houdini, to be flexing and playing tricks and ensuring he can get out of such intricate webs five minutes later. Unfortunately.

But it's a sudden access of comparatively blissful comfort. Harry – a little tight-faced, jealous perhaps – offers him water from a bottle. It's not really enough, but then they won't be wanting to stop every hour or so, he supposes. And feeds him a ham sandwich in torn-off bites, which he'd object to on grounds of dignity. (And because he thinks Harry gets a kick out of it.) Except he's damnably hungry. And what's more, Gus doesn't forget his initial offer, but pulls out his cigarette case once again with the job done, shoves a narrow elegant cylinder between Penn's lips and lights it up for him. "Better, eh?" he asks, with casual off-hand kindness that doesn't completely make Penn want to kick him. He still looks like a cross between a bull and a brick wall, though, and his wolf-eyes are narrow and very dark against his fair complexion, sliding around observantly and taking in everything there is to see.

And Penn's noting Gus, is noted by Parrin, which is no surprise. Parrin waves his own ciggie around freely. He has cig in one hand, gun in the other. It's brilliantly clear that he's a wolf on a mission, to free the slaves and infuriate every other wolf in the land, bringing down storms and violence on his own head. Penn thinks he'd as soon pal up with a hand grenade, or a landmine. He is a little struck by the image, though. "I think our Pennorth is trying to size you up and take your measure, Augustus," Parrin says, smiling and soft-voiced. "You're probably not exactly what he expects from an abolitionist, an idealist out to save the world. Being... *you*," he says, with another expressive gesture.

This seems to amuse Gus a lot. He turns back to Penn, thickly handsome, arrogant features creasing in a toothy grin. "That right, Penn? Do I not look the part? Well, you know, you can't always tell only by looking. My old da's a magistrate, a pillar of the community, a loyal beta in his pack – they think – and couldn't be more the template of the perfect wolf. A social animal, serving the pack. Except my old grandmama was a suffragette and a Quaker – a bit of a one-off, the old lass, a human sect you'd call it really. Never has caught on with most wolves, a damn sight too much emphasis on personal responsibility and conscience, dangerously close to pacifism. None of this *follow the pack, rrr-uurrr haroo, live with the pack, tantivy! die for the pack* stuff. And she got a hold of me early, got me properly indoctrinated, and I know my duty. Not that you'd ever suspect it," he adds, leaning in to Penn and grinning more hugely. "From the outside I look like a jolly good chap, don't I? A howling beast to take a piece of calf-muscle out of you at the full of the moon, and a rugby-playing jazz-loving lawyer, in with the right families and packs, the rest. My cover, you see, Penn? Think on, my lad. You *can't* always tell who it's going to be."

And Parrin cackles with laughter. He seems a sight more relaxed in company with his fellow wolves, less the melodramatic villain or show-off showman. Although still sly, and full of pointed digs and sub-text. "Don't destroy all of his illusions there, Gus, lad," he admonishes. "I've just been trying to disabuse him of the notion that his love is going to don pelt and claws and run to the rescue, to save him from terrible freedom and autonomy. I don't think I've quite got through to him yet, though."

"Really?" Gus asks. "Well, I wouldn't peg Renally Hotstaat for the sentimentalist type. But I suppose we've been proven wrong on that one, what with him taking a human concubine. And not just any concubine, but his childhood sweetheart, eh?" He twinkles at Penn, and Penn re-thinks the whole issue about not kicking him. "Still, I wouldn't get your hopes up," he adds cheerfully in Penn's direction. "He's still a wolf, after all. And to him, you're just a human pretty, done with and on to the next."

"Hsssssh," Parrin says suddenly. It's the first time that Penn's seen any evidence of real authority and leadership from him. But the other two wolves, both bigger and wider than him, more obviously dominant, quieten and turn, alert, at his hissed instruction. They all perk their ears up to the wind, something Penn's seen wolves in pelt do a million times. It looks odder in human form, but it's more important that they're listening at all. And what are they listening *for*?

Whatever it is, it galvanizes Parrin, who pulls the car key out of his pocket. He snaps, "Let's get out of here," and then, "Put him in the back," nodding at Penn. "I need to talk to the two of you. Penn, ruddy behave yourself this time, or I'll let Harry throw you out the back when we reach Haworth, if you're so damn keen to return to captivity. You can wander across the moors until you either find the road home, or expire of exposure out with the gorse and the heather and the ghost of your pelted Heathcliff."

It's Harry who lays hands on him and swiftly manhandles him, down the length of the van and into the back – again. And Penn cooperates, if minimally. Mostly because he's more likely to get an answer when he asks, "What is it? What the hell's going on?" in civil enough tones that it's not liable to aggravate.

Harry rolls his eyes, as he boosts Penn up into the waiting maw of the van doors, hands still bound, without consulting him first about if he's steady on his feet and ready to be tumbled into the interior. He's speaking as he's heaving, directing and pushing. "How d'you cope with human ears, lad? It must be like being half-deaf most of the time. That we were just hearkening out for, it was a wolf cry. Wolves out and on the hunt, not even as close as the horizon, but still heading this way. And so we're up and off, boy! To Scotland, ahoy, away we go!"

Chapter 4

Penn's mouth is jammed with a dozen different questions in response to this, including *how many*, and *from what direction*, and *how fast are they coming on*. And, he supposes, most importantly – *is it Ree?* He barely gets three or four words out of his throat, though, before a negligently inattentive, distracted Harry shuts the big green doors of the van on his face. He's left in the near-dark of the interior.

In what light's admitted by the high, narrow windows at the top to each side, he can view his new companion in the journey, too. Judging by the supine form slumped in the far corner of the van, the Holmford boy is asleep. Penn still hasn't heard an actual name in use for him by the wolves, a detail that's telling. No doubt he's exhausted from his adventures, his travails, the danger he's faced in his escape and the stress of his experience. It's not that Penn doesn't sympathise with him, the poor kid. He knows something of what a really brutal position in a hostile environment and aggressive pack is like, and in fact his heart goes out to the poor bastard. The choice he's made is natural, and even admirable, if extremely risky, Penn feels. It's simply not the choice that Penn wants, given his druthers and the actual freedom to choose.

But although it might seem to be a pressing matter, Penn doesn't give it over-much attention, no more than those few thoughts. He has a more urgent matter to attend to, much more so. As soon as he hears the lock and bolts rattle and bang behind him, he's dropped onto his knees on the corrugated and pressed steel floor of the van, disturbing flakes of paint that haven't been treated or cleaned in a good few years. And he casts another thoughtful look his companion's way. But this one's not for reasons of concern and compassion.

It's because he'd rather not burn his hand, and possibly set his chemise on fire. But on the other hand, he wants to be damn careful about what he does in this bijou little box, with an audience. But no, the boy's out cold. Even without being able to see his face, underneath a carrot-top mop of ginger hair, the slumped line of his back and the absolute relaxation of his lithe young frame tells Penn that he's out for the count. Which is good news, and leaves Penn free to get on with the business immediately at hand, and rapidly becoming something of an emergency. To wit, the cigarette given him, and lit, by the third of the trio of wolves hauling him off to an unasked and unwanted liberty.

They'd all, especially Parrin, been in too much of a frenzy to get on and out of the way of the wolves hot on their trail and in pursuit of them. Too busy to remember, and think of the casual kindness bestowed upon someone who's never failed to take advantage of an opportunity, to take the high-stakes risk and the unscrupulous venture. Penn isn't one bit ashamed. If the miser gives a shilling to charity at the winter solstice, how much should he be applauded? Plus, Penn's burning his damned fingertips off. Worth it, though. Well worth it.

He'd half-fallen into the van, and huddled into a corner, without making any attempt to extinguish his light. Only a very concerted, discreet and successful effort to conceal the fact that he had it still, and it was still lit. Penn's not a bad actor, if he makes the boast himself. Perhaps not up to the standard of the classical thespians in the performances of Shakespeare and Webster that Ree's taken him to see, up in a box discreetly away from *hoi polloi*, where he can do as he pleases and fondle where he pleases. But quite a good enough actor to convince, when he adopts an utterly casual manner, enough to suggest merely a sulky slave bidden where he doesn't wish to go, and obeying with some reluctance.

Not one carrying a weapon, and concealing it with every bit of craft of which he's capable.

Now, he has peace and is – up to a point – in solitude, however. And that means that he gets to work at once, preferring that to scorched wrists and a chemise aflame. His attachment to Ree may be admitted, at this point, undeniable, and regrettable. But that doesn't mean that he's willing to undergo *suttee*, like the Indian brides engulfed in mourning fire, for his sake.

But he would be willing to undergo quite a bit of discomfort, and even a few blisters, for the prospect of freedom. Even so limited a freedom as the ability to release, flex and examine his two hands, right now. He promptly gets to work. Carefully, he adjusts the thin stalk of tobacco between tense, manipulating fingers. And he burns a little of the rope – then presses back against the wall of the van, to put it out. He doesn't want to go up in flames.

Better slow and steady, than a little hasty. Better than for three wolves to open up the doors however many hours from now, and find nothing more than a sleeping adolescent, and a small pile of ashes. But he repeats the process – maintaining the same stealthy manner and continuous surveillance over his companion – until finally, one sharp unrelenting tug to the tattered, burnt bindings at his wrists finishes off the job. His arms are loose, he pushes them up and flexes them, and kicks the remains into the darkest corner. Much better for his companion not to suspect Penn was ever bound, when he wakes. Penn has his own concerns, and no time for someone else's awkward questions.

The lad doesn't wake for a good long time, though. It gives Penn plenty of time to think. More than is useful or cheering, in fact. He does try to stick to facts, rather than any maudlin considerations about what Ree is going to feel about all this. What his true position might be in Ree's life. Whether Lettice will, at this moment, be providing comfort and support, or alternatively soothing Ree's rages and pointing out to him that a runaway slave, while possibly an embarrassment and an inconvenience, is still in fact only a runaway slave. No matter how indulged, how petted, no matter any amount of spurious hand-fastings and pleasurable deceptive consummations.

They might, at bottom, have been doing no more than humouring him, or even purely amusing themselves at his expense. (And they'd got enough amusement out of it, if so, he thinks with a sudden flow of bitterness. They've had his co-operation in it, with how he let Ree make him a third, a substitute and a place-holder in consummating the hand-fasting, a human link between the two of them in an act that offends against Miss Lettice's tastes and tendencies. He wonders if that's all he was, a means to solemnize the bond between two packs, without offending the delicate sensibilities of a wolf-lady. The thought is like finely brewed, rendered and concentrated gall.)

But the facts and the essentials, the things he can use and can do something about, that's what matters, he reminds himself. His delicate wounded feelings are not the essential point. What he needs to consider are the following things. One, that Scotland is the final destination, as far as these three maverick wolves are concerned. It's useful intel, that he needs to ponder over. Not surprising, in some ways. Other ports and jump-off points to freedom might be more accessible, and better equipped, with shorter journey times to free territories. (And quicker to get to in the first place.) But they also tend to have a greater concentration of wolves. This is a major drawback. Scotland, on the other hand – or the more remote regions of it – has a lot in common with the unoccupied territories, the ones that the wolves never wanted in the first place, without actually technically being one of them. It's bloody cold – and, for pelted creatures, the wolves have a distinct aversion to extremes of temperature – and it doesn't support a lot of game. Barring oatmeal and whiskey and heather, it doesn't produce many things that wolves are actually interested in. Not enough deer for more than the odd visiting hunt, and thin stringy gamey rabbits. Hence, very few wolves, and a much quieter route and venue for a bit of slave-running, and the abolitionist network in general. Much more scope for seditious plans to take shape.

Two, Ree is coming for him. Who else can it be, that Parrin and his associates heard when no human ears could detect howling or wolves in the breeze? To have attracted the attention of some other pack, with sufficient keenness that they've followed and hunted Parrin and crew down, along with his human... companions, seems unlikely, unlikely in the extreme. Why else would Parrin take such carefully roundabout long-ways-round routes? Ree, though, has considerably less incentive to evade notice. Running and hunting over another pack's territories may be a matter for care and caution, but Parrin is awfully confident, about the triumph of modern automotive engineering over mere wolf speed and limitations.

Perhaps Ree and any companion he might have can't quite go as the crow flies. But he thinks on, to his first weeks back on Hotstaat territory. Ree had been missing then because he was busy brokering business for other Northern packs, who would surely owe him favour and indulgence as a result. They're not the only ones. There's a reason the Hotstaats are a powerful and courted pack. If anyone might get away with taking liberties over the land of another pack, while on an emergency mission, it's Ree. He could cut miles and miles off a long long journey. Ree could make good time, could make a damn sight better time coming for him than that damn fool over-confident Benedict Parrin takes account of. And of course he *is* coming.

Penn feels a small measure of triumph over it. He knew it, he *knew* it, he thinks. Parrin scoffed, and his two companions too, and see, see how much they know?

He knows that it's Ree pursuing him, who will come for him, and as he sees it, by his lights, will rescue him. This he knows, and holds to it despite all the mockery and dismissal of such an idea by Parrin. What he knows, he knows. He won't be budged from it by mockery or by logic. You know what you know, and this he knows in his bones. Why it's so important, no-one can make him consider. Lettice may be with Ree too. It's quite probable, since she belongs to Ree by some lights, now, at least technically.

Third point, he has his hands free, and the wolves up front don't know it yet. Better to be ready, surely, when Ree catches up? He might prove to be of some assistance in the struggle, if there is one. It's not as if he'd back a humble and barely competent trio of betas like these ones, against even Ree alone. Let alone if he's brought Lettice with him. But still, it's a good principle.

Ree won't have brought more than Lettice with him. To bring more witnesses than that to fetch Penn home would be compromising and dangerous, and risk some fools with pretensions to minds of their own deciding that Penn could not have been taken by abolitionists without his consent, or at least that it's a mite unlikely. (It is a mite unlikely, Penn will concede. Most slaves have considered the idea of running at some point, whether they'll admit it or not. And a slave not in dire circumstance, conversely, would think carefully before assenting to such a proposition, and going through all of the danger and difficulty of contacting the runaway underground. Not to mention that it's unheard of for the underground – as opposed to rogue slaver thieves – to take an unwilling slave. He's never heard of it himself, even. But then, he's probably never met such a reckless fool, combined with ruthless idealist, as Benedict Parrin, not until this past year. For a wolf, he'd make a pretty good human, given that he seems to have little pack sense, little willingness to respect the chain of command and follow the given party line. Perhaps the Parrin pack is a sufficient explanation in itself, and to be a maverick is to conform, as far as the Parrins are concerned.

Fourth, there is weaponry and ammo, lethal or at least highly dangerous to wolves, present in their little caravan. And, access or no, currently, that might be useful knowledge if he just holds on to it and keeps a weather eye out for events. He might get the chance to use it – or to prevent these three loose cannons from using it. Or get it to Ree, somehow. Whatever the outcome, it's better to have the information than to be flying blind.

Fifth, he has company, here in the rear of the van. And that bears keeping an eye on, because any unknown quantity is potentially an unknown danger.

Thus he moves over to take a look at the boy, who's slumped limp and immobile in the draughty corner. A voluntary runaway, he thinks, who didn't have to be drugged and kidnapped and slung over a wolf's shoulder in order to end up here. It must be a vastly different experience, in comparison to Penn's. The lad doesn't stir an inch under Penn's regard, which considering how lightly most slaves sleep, sensitized to any sudden demand from a master or imminent danger, suggests ill-treatment, or extreme fatigue and long hours, or emotional wear and tear. Or a combination of those three, likely enough, given his circumstances.

Under the rough brown tunic the kid is wearing, and on what skin it leaves exposed and available to view, Penn can discern the odd bruise here and there. Not enough to definitively suggest repetitive beatings under circumstances of abuse and oppression. But nothing that would conclusively rule it out, either. Although it might still be a combination of carelessness, accident, and the rough and tumble of a rapid and urgent journey under stressful conditions. It might.

But considering that the boy's desperate enough to seek out help from abolitionists, and risk re-capture and brutal punishment in so doing, Penn doesn't lend a lot of credence to that possibility. Penn feels his heart tweak and leap in sympathy, in pity. He wouldn't do what this kid is doing, not in his present circumstances, and not even in more desperate circumstances and with worse owners and packs that he's known. But he has fellow feeling, as a slave, and can well imagine such circumstances that he'd be willing to do what the boy's assented to. And in fact he finds it admirable, the risk, the nerve, the willingness to disregard the respect and fear of wolf authority he's been schooled into for all of his life. It makes him a lad after Penn's own heart, in fact, in a lot of ways. Just also a lot more direct and open and straight from A to B in achieving his desires. Less sneaky, less stubborn, and perhaps less simply set on having his way and having his life ordered up *à la carte*, exactly the way he wants it.

Penn won't accept or brook a fate that's less than what he thinks he merits and is owed. It may be entitled and it may be unrealistic, but so what? It makes him a little like a wolf, perhaps: and considering his early youth, and how he was spoiled and pampered, perhaps that shouldn't surprise in the least. He broods on it, and he watches the kid carefully, in case he's taken a blow to the head or is sick in some way, to be out cold so deep. But he's breathing even, and has a bit of colour to his skin, which is freckled and has a healthy sheen too. He's just out cold, despite the cold and the draughts and the uneven floor of the van. Penn wonders if it's true, what Gus said – that the kid's talked himself to an absolute standstill and exhausted himself with it, fallen into sleep from it.

All the better if he sleeps all the way through, if so. Penn isn't any more fond of an inveterate talker than wolfy Gus appeared to be. A little gossip over servants' hall weak ale is one thing, but the kind of fellow who can talk for hours non-stop all night, is quite another. Penn's had too frequent experience of fellow slaves who live for gossip and chat, since they've little else to entertain 'em. If he wakes up and won't shut up, then Penn just might have to give him a bop over the head with a lat of the bench, and send him back to dreamland.

But the kid snores heavily, as if he's responding to Penn's thoughts, and it's a reassurance both in terms of his health and his mute peacefulness. Penn leaves him to his slumbers, and goes to leap on the latted wooden bench to the side of the van. Because from that vantage point, he can peer out the narrow strip of window at the very top of the wall before the ceiling, and hear the wind rumbling past up above. More to the point, he can get a look out of the window and see the moors rushing past, squint out at the pale grey early morning and search for signs going past, for habitation, signs of where they are and how fast they're going, for indication that they've hit the border and are moving on into Scotland.

Can they outrun wolves in a van, he wonders? It's not even a high-performance little one-person race-car, after all, not one of Ree's Italian models that he likes to take out at dawn on a little private race-track in Essex. He's taken Penn a couple of times, and even set him off on solo circuits of the track. (Oh, the excitement, the heady thrill, the danger. It shames Penn to think that he could be bought with such gifts and treats, could have his head turned by the toys and experiences that his rich wolf lover uses to buy his affections. And not even unconsciously. It's not as if he's not fully aware that Ree dangles these pretty things and special outings as bait to distract him from the plain and brutal fact that he belongs to Ree as much as any automotive gewgaw or toy. Oh, but the excitements of those days at the track, mechanics tinkering with high-speed high-voltage beautiful creations of petrol and steel and inspired demonic speed, before they go whizzing around the track, waterboatmen insects on a high-sheen pond surface. The mechanics mostly freedmen, an honest trade being a damn sight too honest for most wolves, who even if they deign to soil their hands with labour at all, tend to favour the white-collar professions, the administering of the complex *lacunae* of pack law, the strange and difficult practice of wolf medicine, architecture, scientific research. Engineers, except at the highest levels, are mostly freedmen, and oh, how Penn would love it, building and creating and testing prototypes. When he's free, when Ree has been finally seduced and pinned down and bound by his word into signing off manumission–.

Well. Before that can ever happen, Penn needs to get out of this pickle. It's not going to happen while he's standing on tip-toe, peering out of a draughty, too-slow box on wheels, trying to make something out of the grey and green landscape whizzing by.

He can't really see a damn thing, and it's not like he could change or affect anything locked away here, whatever goes on outside, in the chase and pursuit. He jumps down, and sits on the bench, puts his head in his hands. And wonders: how far away Ree is, how many borders and counties a wolf can hear howling and thundering paws across. (It must be Ree. It must be Ree.)

The boy stirs, after all, perhaps alerted a little by Penn's descent onto the bench not being as stealthy and considerate as it might have been. Penn eyes him very narrowly. "What do you say, lad?" he asks. "Do you think that a mid-powered motor vehicle, with a two-human sized load in the back, can outrun a wolf? Perhaps a wolf taking a little care not to use and abuse the territory of packs he has no treaties and understandings with, mind you. It's not as if he can make free and go quite as the crow flies, not unless he wants inter-pack trouble to follow. Or not unless he's very reckless about his objective, and attaining it. Do you think he's running with a rational mind, eh, and keeping to the rules, observing due respect and caution? Or is he running roughshod and trampling over everything in the way, to get to me?"

He gets no response, barring a mournful grunt that seems to issue up from the depths of someone's bowels. And the boy rolls over, clutching at the rough blanket over him while still sound asleep. It's well enough, because he wasn't really expecting an answer anyway. A magnificent snoring starts up – the boy, not Penn – and Penn shrugs.

Snoring means breathing, and saves him having to check the boy's health and mortality status every five minutes. It may, of course, also mean having to kill him at some point, if he doesn't wake up soon.

It's hard to calculate and track time, though, without a timepiece, without someone to talk to and gauge its passage with. How long now since he was bundled into the back of the van? They must be past Haworth in terms of how far north they've got, by now, he thinks. Parrin can't have meant seriously that they'd be passing it, since they're going quite the wrong way – over to the west and then hugging the coast along north-ways, he estimates. He was only mocking Penn, and his supposed romantic fancies about Ree – Heathcliff, and Rochester, and a lot of Gothic romantic nonsense he imagines Penn is taken up with, to cherish a mistaken loyalty.

The very thought triggers off memory so deep and intense that Penn has to close his eyes. It's not that it hurts, exactly. Not exactly. Just thinking – vivid, heard and felt and smelt and seen – of his first day on the Hotstaat estate, a piece of property reclaimed and the paperwork filed. (The paperwork that he himself had responsibility to archive copes of, stored alongside purchases of rare-breed pigs and farm equipment.) Well, to say it was his first day is to mis-state a verified fact of his history. He has been Hotstaat property almost since his first breath, in fact: just with a prolonged intermission in between, a chance to get his breath before being sucked back into a binary star constellation with Ree. Orbiting each other, once again, just as they did as kids: himself the small dried-out white star, circling around and around Ree's giant hissing furnace of a sun.

That's how it felt, back then, Penn is pretty certain. If only mostly from other peoples' accounts, and his own memories of an aggressive loyalty and possessive affection. Of his Ree, his *wolluf*, his furry yelping friend and exasperated thin dark quiet protector, short pants and short back'n'sides and not physically much different from his nephew, from young Gerald now. And now, now it's not so different. Not most of the time, and not if he's honest.

That first day of Ree's return to the estate, after Penn's purchase, though. Penn hadn't understood that he'd returned home, or that the estate had ever been a home to him, not with his spotty ownership records and spottier memories. Even when Renally Hotstaat had arrived, had turned up in the family library where Penn was working, no bell had rung, no spark of real deep recognition and knowing in the gut had flamed up between them. Or not for Penn, at least. There'd been nothing to connect this sleek wolf-stranger, this alpha who owned Penn's arse and every other particular about him and had the deeds to prove it, with a small dark taciturn wolf-boy, who used to tolerantly put up with it, when Penn trailed after him every waking hour of the day.

Not until he'd quizzed Penn upon his duties, and his experience thus far of the Hotstaat estate and his fellow slaves, had set him back upon his tasks and then required of him to read aloud, from a novel upon the great extensive library shelves, and of his own choosing. Penn had put no meaning into his choice: *Jane Eyre* had come to his hands as a matter of chance and convenience, and he'd set about reading it with a mindless care and precise diction, merely obedient to the whims of a new master.

And when he was done, Ree had commented on what an annoying whimsical bit of French fluff Adèle was, and how they themselves, as children together, had surely never been so pert and demanding. And that was that, and Renally Hotstaat was Ree, and that was when he knew. So it is that he associates the Bröntes, and Haworth, and perhaps the characters of Brönte novels, with his own Heathcliff.

(He deletes that thought immediately from the forefront of his mind. What a bit of foolishness.) But the important thing, the thing that Parrin scoffed at, is that Ree is coming for him, is on his way.

Penn couldn't honestly claim to be calm of mind, right now, as he settles up against the van wall on his haunches, watching over the sleeping, bruised boy. But he's not unhappy or despairing, either. Isn't his mate coming to fetch him? Aren't they, both of them? Yes. So all he needs to do is to watch out carefully, and to seize his opportunity when he sees it. That's the life he's been living all along, these many years. It's what he's trained for.

He settles, and watches, and thinks a lot of conflicting thoughts. The van rumbles over what seem like poor back roads, and rough tracks, and rougher tracks, and time passes. He hears no wolf howl, only the rain that starts up and hammers against the windows, against the roof, almost hard enough for hail. The moors, the desolate northern territories, are made for wolves and a wolf run, though. They can't possibly be that far behind.

OF COURSE IT'S EASY to think deep thoughts, and wait for events you have no control over to unfold, when you have relative peace and silence to do it in. It's a bit different when you have company, depending on the company involved.

Maybe half an hour, or maybe an hour passes. It's hard to judge, very hard, and Penn has little in the way of light or natural acuity of vision to judge by. If only he'd taken his spectacles outside, as well as Ree's cigs. Then Penn has a companion in this solitary section of the journey who is no longer unconscious, snoring or muttering and snuffling in his sleep. It takes five minutes to explain who he is, where they're going and apparently why, and to swap a basic outline of their stories. (Very basic, on Penn's part. He's not eager to disclose to this kid that he's not a willing volunteer on this escape bid, that he's waiting to be captured and returned to the life that had him in the chains of formal slavery. For his own ends, yes, but still it would be hard to explain to someone with urgent, damn good reason to want out, to want out enough to take the risky and potentially lethal underground short-cut to freedom. That's strictly for the desperate: Penn knows enough about the potential consequences, if caught, to know it. A couple of acquaintances, along his long route as an object and a possession, have opted for it, and one of them didn't make it. He has the occasional nightmare about that. So all that Penn discloses is that hello, he is Pennorth, his mother was Margaret and lately before her early and unfortunate death belonged to the Gateley pack. That, yes, he's *en route* for Scotland and the Canadian territories and freedom, along with Sam. (For Sam is the Holmford boy's name, or Samuel, late of the Holmford pack. He's surrendering safety for freedom, after one vicious and unearned beating too many, after injury and mortal threats.) Penn fails to add that he's here unwillingly, and that they are pursued by wolves as well as 'rescued' by them.

(No point panicking the boy, when Ree is coming for Penn, not for other creatures packaged up and delivered to a life of liberty by Parrin and his associates. Also no point in preparing him, if he's the kind who'd be willing to fight and perhaps fall alongside wolves for the sake of freedom. And merely by being here at all, the suggestion is implicit that he's willing to take a risk and put flesh on the desire and skin in the game. Well done to the boy for that, but Penn's not arming him with knowledge, if it makes his own safe return less likely.)

The boy has no kith and kin left, Penn finds out, and nor friends in a pack run so harshly that fraternisation between slaves is monitored, outlawed and punished. He made contact with Parrin by observation of his conduct at a pack dinner, and is suffering a dreadful degree of hero-worship. And that should be enough: it's a basic outline of his situation and his reasons, and Penn would be well content with it. They could, for his opinion on this matter, settle back into a silence that was companionable enough. (When the lad was sleeping.)

But the lad won't settle back, and he won't rest, and he won't stop talking, either. Isn't Penn excited about the new life and the new home that they're promised, he wants to know, hugging his knees squatted up against the wall, and shivering with the cold so that Penn feels compelled to donate his own blanket to take the chill off the boy's thin underfed bones. Aren't Parrin and his friends heroes, risking their own lives for the sake of giving liberty to the trapped and the suffering amongst enslaved humanity? Has Penn suffered much, what is his own tale of woe, what about his reasons for running and his story on how he made contact with the network?

None of these are things that Penn is eager to discuss, most especially not with a wet-behind-the-ears young man, however maltreated and however admirable regarding pluck and spirit. And certainly, however talkative. It's worse when the boy becomes a little embarrassed, and shuffles that bit closer to where Penn is crouched against the wall near him, glaring into the dim corners and listening with increasing urgency, trying to make out any clue or hint about their headlong flight. But no, the rain pelts, and the engine rumbles, and the road gets steadily worse and more potholed, judging by their ever slower and more impeded progress.

Not that that's not all to the good, considering that the slower they go, the sooner they'll get caught. Probably it won't be a popular sentiment with his present company: and he feels bad enough about it anyhow, as he hears in more and more detail, more and more of what he didn't wish to know anyhow about how much the poor lad's suffered. It's not that he wants the poor boy to get caught and copped and returned to captivity. He only wants to be able to make the same free choice – with a different outcome – that Sam's been allowed to make. But he gets more uncomfortable as the boy talks – because whatever the outcome, one of them is likely to be unhappy with it, and more than unhappy, desperate and bitter.

It's only worse with his face up closer, thin and sharply defined around the jaw and cheekbones, his russetty hair and green eyes making him not pretty, no, but noticeable. (He's probably had trouble with wolves of the kind that most slaves fight a bit shy of discussing in more detail, other than with their closest intimates. But he doesn't bring it up, or only with the vaguest allusions to the beatings and casual blows that he's more comfortable referring to. Penn doesn't blame him – who wants to trawl through all of that with a stranger – but it only makes him feel worse.) Sam's eyes flick around all over the place before he can actually bring the next subject up. You'd think that Penn was a wolf, the way he has such trouble meeting his eyes. But it's the subject that's making him uncomfortable, not Penn.

"You know, there's more than one way of getting free?" he says, in a tone that's a definite question, that's aware of its own daring. He knows it's a potentially controversial subject, and gets a violently disapproving response from some slaves. As well as a furtive interest, a prurience and excitement, from others. Because Penn knows perfectly well what's coming next, as the boy leans into his ear and hisses – terrified at his own daring - "You know, if they bite you, they have to free you?"

Perishing hell, but this kid must have been kept in a cultish seclusion and the equivalent of purdah with that pack's other slaves, in a way that makes Penn's own experiences look even halfway benevolent, Penn thinks, slightly appalled. It's common knowledge amongst owned humanity, after all, even if not much publicly discussed, frowned upon unsurprisingly by the owner class. But Sam talks as if he's dredging up a deep dark secret from the bucket of a well with no ending.

He also talks as if it's some joyous and thrilling gift, to be mangled by a wolf's jaws and left possibly in one piece, possibly with the odd fragment hanging off by a shred of flesh. And the boy may be young, but he's not *that* young: quite old enough to be making his own decisions, acting the part of a man, and throwing his weight behind the decision to risk everything and run for liberty. Therefore, in Penn's opinion, he's also well old enough to know the bare unvarnished unromanticised version of what getting bitten by a werewolf involves.

"True," he says, and he knows it's harsh, but the kid's asking for it, or asking for something anyhow. "As long as you actually survive it in the first place. And as long as it actually turns you wolf, which is pretty chancy and by no means guaranteed. You could just have a nasty bite, if it's not deep enough and near any major blood vessels – a very nasty bite, and quite often infected. The wolves can withstand and co-exist with bugs that our immune systems can't fight off, so that their bodies don't trouble to dispose of them at the first sign of trouble. They just pass them on to us if there's any unsafe contact, and they *wipe us out*. Or alternatively, your body might try to change, but be too weak or tending to violent allergic reaction to invasion to fully accept it, and it just leaves you sickly or wounded, or changed in the wrong way, in unpredictable ways. They say some stay human, and don't pelt up or bow to the pack, but gain unnatural strength, and the wolves can't have that. Wolves generally take care of those end results amongst themselves, with no fuss made. But mostly, it's the survival issue that you need to keep an eye on."

And the kid's eyes are very wide, round and unbelieving, as he turns them to Penn. "Most people survive the bite..." he says, a bit tremulous and uncertain, not half such an excitable brash proponent as he was a moment ago. Good. If Penn's brought him down to Earth a bit, then he's done him a favour.

Penn nods, and if the bitterness comes through, then he doesn't have it in him to care right at this moment. "Statistically. How would you feel about being one of the ones who don't?" He doesn't mention his mother at this point: bad enough that he spilled his guts to Parrin and his cronies, just now, without compounding the offence with some random runaway he'll never see again. Let his poor mother have a little privacy in her tragedy.

What he expects is for that to shut Sam up, though. Why wouldn't he expect it? It should be the trump card, the untoppable common sense that stops up his mouth with a cork. But probably, even after forty minutes' acquaintance, he should have known this Sam better than that. "Worth the risk, though, eh?" he whispers. And it's aggravating enough that Penn begins to understand the wolf Gus's point of view on the boy.

He's still cold, and though Ree's surely in hot pursuit he has no certainty of the events of the next few hours. And he has a guilt towards this boy that he can't even touch upon. Even so, this is the most irritating thing that he's currently putting up with, the one that chafes and aggravates him most, and he simply can't let it go. "Really?" he snaps. It's sharp enough to cut through the whine of the wind as it buffets at the sides of the van, and over the rattle of what might actually be hail on the roof. "Why? Why would you want to be a wolf, even if none of those possible bad things happened? Even if it took, and changed you right?"

The boy's been respectful up until now, even if he clearly doesn't know how to shut his mouth and keep it that way. Penn may be a slave like him, a runaway slave too for all he knows – but he's older, senior, more experienced and wise in the harsh ways of the world. And those things are evident, even to a dumb kid like this one. (Not too evident, he hopes quickly to himself. He's found more than one grey strand amongst his fair locks lately, which is ridiculous when he's not even thirty. Although he's already older than his lovely daft mother when she died, and bless her, she had a little grey among the fair too, quite early even for a human. Not that it marred her beauty, but only gave it a distinguished, slightly eccentric emphasis. Not that it put off the wolf, either. His poor pretty foolish mother, and he has to swallow quickly, just thinking of her. It's not just the fact of her death that hurts, and how unnecessary it was, the reckless gift of an infatuated wolf. It's that she went to it eagerly, excited. And even to Penn's six-year-old eyes, visibly in love, although he probably didn't have the words to express it at the time, nor the adult willingness to recognise it and not flinch squeamishly nor giggle. She'd gone with joy, and almost forgetting him: the last things of her that still retain dim shadows in his memory, are the kiss to his cheek as she handed him over to the wet-nurse, and the ruffle of his hair, telling him to be good, and she'd be back in due time. She'd been utterly willing, excited: no doubt at the prospect of freedom and power, and even more at a more equal alliance with the wolf-owner who'd seduced her, and meant to take her for a true wolf-mate.

He'd said goodnight and then panicked as she disappeared out the door, her bright hair swirling down her shoulders, over the pretty dress the wolf had bought her. Had shouted after her, shrieked for her to come back, to stay another minute, begged for another kiss and a little reassurance that he was remembered, loved. (Hadn't he already lost one beloved person already? His little heart had known that that was quite enough. But he doesn't know, from this distance, if instinct had told him to hold on tight to his remaining precious person, for fear she might be taken. Perhaps it had only been another tantrum, little fighter and brawler that he'd been.)

And that was the last of her he'd had. The wolf bit her, and she did not fare well, and she died. The story's simple, and the pain never ends.

The irony isn't remotely lost on Penn. It hasn't been, not from the first moment that he registered that Ree had retained a softness for him, a warmth that Penn could use to worm his way into his good graces and gain a strategic advantage. His mother was loved by a wolf – and loved one, too, even though it's mouth-puckering gall to Penn to admit it. And if she'd been a little more crafty, had even a tenth of

Penn's own wiliness, then she might have got her freedom out of it, and Penn's too. A slave's children are freed the moment she's freed, which is sometimes why it's reckoned such a great step by the wolves to free a slave at all. It might have been done, without having to take the reckless shortcut she'd been seduced into, thinking it such a great honour, such a mark of favour. His mother: she'd been lovely, and fond, and pretty. But she'd never been canny.

So Penn's had it on his mind, since the first night and the first time with Ree and even before that. Back when he was carefully judging and guiding Ree's old affection, and marking its progression into infatuation and desire. It would be a lie to say it hasn't disturbed him, the parallels between his mother's situation and his own. But he's been resolved – since long before Ree, since long before meeting him once again, being his property once more – that he'll never take the bite. Never. He has his mother's example not to follow, after all.

And even if he wasn't content to take the long road around to liberty, why would he want to be a wolf, in any case? After all. He hates wolves.

He (still) hates wolves. With a few specific exceptions, that aren't really exceptions at all, but only weaknesses.

But this boy, this damn fool Sam, with more than enough reason to hate wolves himself, and probably a damn sight more reason than Penn, even, judging by bruises and things he hasn't said and his sheltered, cultish innocence – he doesn't seem to hate wolves. Or not enough. Not judging by his response, which becomes a little irritable. "Why wouldn't I want it?" Sam asks, and his tone has definitely lost the tinge of deference and respect that it had – is peevish, resentful, mardy. "A wolf's free, after all, right? And – and strong, and does what it likes, and has somewhere it belongs with all the food and drink and nice things a slave never gets near. And marries who it likes when it likes, and never. Never has to be afraid. Things are afraid of wolves, wolves aren't afraid of anything."

His face, staring in the dimness of the back of the van at Penn, is defiant, anger hidden under a fearful gauze of politeness strainingly maintained. Underneath that, Penn is pretty sure, is fear. Well-grounded fear. He wouldn't have run if he hadn't been given just cause, and Penn feels worse and worse about the part he intends to play. It would be good if there was a way to ensure the boy getting free, without endangering his own rescue and safe return to captivity. Perhaps Ree... No, he can't imagine Ree ever countenancing turning a blind eye to a runaway slave. Not even for Penn's sake, at his request, combined with all his most persuasive cajolings and the considerable inducements his body can offer. Well, perhaps not.

It's a hard argument to counter, at any rate. At least for someone as set in opposition to it as Penn, with such personal reasons for his grudges and his bias against taking the bite of a wolf. If they truly tried to argue it they'd only end at loggerheads with nothing gained, and any friendliness and good understanding between them that's possible set aside. He could tell the boy that a beta wolf is as much property to the alpha of the pack – in a way, and admittedly in a very different way – as any human slave. But it isn't as if he'll listen or believe it. People don't observe much, even when it's in their best interests to pay close attention. That's what Penn's observed, over his twenty-odd years, because he's one of the few exceptions. Sam's seeing what he wants to in the life of a wolf low down the pack dominance diagram – which is what bitten-not-born wolves tend to be. Anything that doesn't suit him he isn't going to register at all. He needs the dream, the promise of a perfect solution and a free, satisfied, powerful life, even as he gives up on ever getting it, and runs.

Which forces Penn to ask himself a question, and not only himself. He's been offered the bite, himself. Not only the once or by one wolf, either. Not by a long chalk: by Benedict Parrin. And by Lettice Parrin. And, rarely putting it into explicit words, but hinting around and leaning heavily into the subject, by Ree. And even before him:

a couple of his wolf owners have taken enough of a fancy to him – or thought it might make a useful tool, a carrot instead of a stick to manipulate him with – to drop a few hints and try out Penn's reaction to the idea, too. Altogether, when he thinks about it down the years, he's had a queue of wolves, practically, all eager to get their jaws clamped around his neck and to give him the full lupine experience, running beneath a mother of pearl moon and with thin faint high howls disappearing over far green hills.

But it seems as if Sam hasn't. Because if he's so very enthused about the idea, then if he'd been offered, he'd have been a wolf long since. Perhaps it's not tactful, how Penn phrases it, when he says back to Sam, "So he hasn't offered it you? Parrin, I mean. He hasn't offered to make you a wolf?"

The implication isn't absolutely logically necessary, isn't a necessary follow-on – but Sam seems like a bright boy, and he jumps to it anyway. From a little lippy, jumpy and increasingly assertive, a touch of resentment enters into his expression. "What?" he says, a little incredulous. (It's not exactly flattering.) "You mean that he offered it to you?" He takes a moment to let the thought digest itself in silence, and that moment of silence is quite blessed, a brief gap in the non-stop little-bird open maw that he's presented since he woke up. (Yes. Penn does begin to see Gus's point.)

Actually Penn had rather assumed that his case wasn't anything special: that Parrin perhaps has often offered to make wolves out of slaves, as an alternative to smuggling them away to freedom. But on second thoughts, he hadn't thought it through clearly at all, obviously. Making a wolf is a serious matter, and there would be trouble between packs and fights between wolves, for any to go about casually depriving a pack of a perfectly good slave by giving him an effective bite. (A mere savaging in a fit of temper would be treated much less seriously, provided the victim survived and the pack was not left without his person and service.) The presence of a great many more made wolves, and the gradual disappearance of a great many slaves at the same time, would hardly go unnoticed. And all of that leaves aside the point that to be bitten and made wolf is far from a risk-free endeavour.)

In fact, seeing it in a clearer light, it's less surprising that Parrin hasn't offered a bite-based change to this Sam, and more surprising that he did offer it to Penn. And the more he considers, the more unlikely it seems that he goes about randomly offering the bite to discontented slaves as a matter of course. It would be unwise. Penn had thought he'd taken his measure of Parrin, that he was reckless and foolhardy enough that any bit of folly couldn't be put past him. But there's folly and then there's suicidal disaster, and such a course, making new wolves *en masse*, would lean a great deal more towards the latter. A course of action like that would result in detection and punishment, inevitably, eventually: too many witnesses, bodies here and there, made wolves taking territory and game and without pack history or a nameable sire. Parrin would have to be not just an idiot, but certifiably crazy. Penn doesn't think that he's actually all that crazy.

Which means that Penn is actually a special case, and has received special treatment. (He ought to have known already, perhaps. He doubts that abolitionists and slave-liberators often have to kidnap the subjects of their benevolence, and still less that they routinely expose themselves to the danger of making or offering to make wolves out of them. Of course, thinking of Cousin Jay, he's been a Parrin special pet project for quite some time at this point. And what with his patron mating and marrying and hand-fasting with Benedict Parrin's sister, that makes him a special case twice over, no doubt.)

It's still quite extreme, the kidnap, though. Penn is *annoyed*, at that. Perhaps his response to Sam is a little bit curt, when he says, "It doesn't matter. It's nothing you'd ever want, anyway. Not if you had the least idea." He's older, after all. He's seen more of the wolves, and he knows better.

The patronage at least manages to shut Sam up for a minute or two, and he wraps himself in the two blankets he's got. (Without the least thank you to Penn, for the donation of the second one, either.) He lets his face do the talking for him. By the looks of it, he's young enough to think it most unfair that pretty indulged older slaves with wiles and seductive graces get to entrap a master into infatuation, get all the favours and all the gifts, including the chance to be wolf themselves. It's almost enough to make Penn glad to be nearly thirty – nearly thirty, in hell's name – and a little less of a sulking truculent fool than he probably once was, just like this near-child.

He's glad that the kid's shut his trap, too, when he thinks he hears something that he doesn't hear. Then he hears it again. Then he shushes the kid when he stirs and asks questions and cocks his head to listen too. There's a moment's pause, of silence barring wind and rain on the roof and the buffeted sides of the van. And then Penn's sure. He hears it, and when the boy flinches and huddles back, fast and scuttling, into the very corner of the van, it's only confirmation.

It's a wolf's howl, carried on the breeze as it buffets past them. It's made Sam panicky and wild-white faced, and he flings out an arm wildly and makes contact with Penn. His grip is impressive, or perhaps just impressively crazy. Penn may be bruised tomorrow. "Are they after us?" he asks. "Is that, is that my pack? Am I hearing things? Do you hear it?" His voice is a little high, and almost breaks on the last question. But really it's impressively steady, for a runaway who hears the sound of a wolf baying for his blood. Penn remembers that even if the kid is annoying, there are things about him that are admirable. And moreover he's suffered at the hands of wolves, just the same as Penn.

"If I don't, then we're both suffering from severe auditory delusions," Penn says, a little brusquely. Because sympathy won't get the kid anywhere: what he needs to do is to learn to deal with the facts as they are, the way Penn has had to. And then to discard them, use them, play them like a hand of cards and turn and twist them to the shape he wants them to take. Because only a fool or a serf accepts irrevocable facts as irrevocable, and fate as something out of his hands. You have to keep fighting until the game's reached the very end, and steal another hand of cards if you've lost decisively, at that point.

This is maybe possibly the fundamental thing, the bedrock, that Penn has learnt.

Is it really wolves? He cranes again to hear, and it seems unlikely, even with the moderate progress they've been making in a moderately powered van that's hardly the latest model. He doesn't want to delude himself, to get excited over nothing. After all, when he was put into the van, half an hour or an hour ago or more, the howls that were clearly audible to the wolves in whose care they reside, were a whole breath of nothing on the air to him. Ree must have made considerable gains in that intervening time. Unless it's Sam's pack who've made still better time, as he's clearly fearing, with the efforts he's making to cut off Penn's circulation at the wrist with his grip.

The poor kid's white, terrified, and Penn reaches out to give him an absent hug that can't be any adequate kind of comfort.

Himself, he's excited, but he does his utmost not to show it. It would hardly be tactful, or discreet for that matter, after all.

Of course, if a couple of under-sensed humans can hear it – a little louder, now – then the wolves up in the driving cab can certainly hear it too. Penn expects the van to speed up, perhaps: to swerve a little around the next bend, to accelerate wildly. He's surprised that any of their pursuers have caught up to them, so relatively quickly. They must have been far, far behind originally: and even half-unconsciously, he's been taking note of the van slowing up at what must be small conurbations and tiny hamlets, with the more frequent junctions and right-angle turns, shorter straight stretches involved. There's been a couple of brief stops before picking up Sam, re-fuelling and calls of nature, Penn thinks. And judging by the sounds of running water, he's pretty sure also that the wolves have been careful to cross water at fords at least a couple of times, a standard precautionary measure.

But it hasn't been enough, clearly. These wolves are on the trail, and catching up. And now the question is whether there's enough power and acceleration in this underwhelming example of automotive engineering, to outrun them to wherever it is in the northernmost part of the great islands of Britain that Parrin has contacts, transport and a route to the liberated territories. It seems hardly likely, but what can they do but try? So he's waiting for the leap forward, the burst of acceleration, almost without being consciously aware of it.

It never comes. Instead, whoever's driving hits the brakes so hard that Penn almost slides up the wall his back's against with the force of it, his teeth vibrating in their roots. Sam goes flying too, of course. It's an emergency stop the likes of which Penn has never experienced before. And he's ridden in the passenger seat at the hands of some truly appalling amateur drivers, what with the driving test only lately having been introduced at all. Wonderful reflexes, nerve, judgement, wolves have it all. But that doesn't always compensate for a total disregard of the rules of the road, a casual attitude to motor vehicle maintenance what with always having slave and servant mechanics and chauffeurs on hand, and a natural arrogance that means the driver is always right. Or, in the case of a head-on collision, that both drivers are always right. It makes for some interesting – well, terrifying – post-accident conversations. (Conflagrations. If everyone manages to end one of those in human skin and with no chunks ripped out, then that's a win all round for all involved.)

The whole van, cab and cage both, is shaking with it, and doors slam on the cab up ahead. There are feet running and clicks and shouts. And there's nothing Penn can do about it, not a damn thing to find out what the hell's going on, let alone Sam.

Well, he can heave himself up from a crouching position, actually, and go hammer on the doors of the van, yelling to be let out. It may be the least acute thing he's ever done, but although he has a sharp intellect and a whole bag of wiles... Penn knows well, by now, that he's not always wise, just the same. He's doing it before he's thought to talk himself out of it. He just wants to know what the heck is going on, that's all. There are wolves howling, wolves following, wolves who might be *Ree*. And they've come to a dead halt, probably somewhere in Scotland, or perhaps they're still in Northamptonshire or a county still less northerly. Very likely: one thing you can say for the blisteringly cold north, there's a lot of it. His sense of distance, geography, time and place, it's all messed up, unsurprisingly given his emotional state. He wants to know, and frankly he can't stand not knowing for much longer.

When the air rocks and vibrates with a gunshot, maybe he wants to know a little less. Even inside the van, the air smells of gunpowder, cordite, bitter and stinging with it. And Penn falls back from the doors, his hands falling to his sides. There are another two shots, three, and then more feet – human feet – running around the van.

The doors slam again, and the motor starts up. Penn remembers the conversation in the cab of the van. He remembers Parrin taking out his firearm, and fooling around with it in an entirely unsafe manner. Mostly, he remembers the discussion about the bullets, the ones that are treated, hexed, something or other. Something that makes them actually still effective against wolves.

He feels so, so sick. As the van takes off like a cannonball, rumbling and used far beyond its capacity, he hears – dim, and still far away – a single howl. Maybe he's just imagining it, but it sounds like anguish, like pain. (Maybe he's just imagining it, but it sounds like Ree.)

Sam is jubilant, of course. "They got 'em! You heard that? They got 'em, the bastards, they won't be coming after me now! That'll show 'em!" And, bite or no, it puts him in a good mood for the next half hour, sets him off chattering, jittery and pleased and excited. It's good that he's so happy, that he keeps himself amused with his own excitable chatter. It helps him not to notice the fact that Penn's sunk back down in a corner, cold all through and not just bodily, and is barely responding.

Because maybe that was Sam's owner-pack, silenced and discouraged in their pursuit. Maybe, or maybe it was Ree. Maybe it's Ree with a bullet in him, now, maybe it's Ree's howl silent and gone forever. It could be. Those bullets can kill even a werewolf.

It's possible that no-one's coming for him, now. That he has no-one to love him, in the most irritating, blindly oblivious, condescending way possible. To search him out through hopeless years and never give up hope despite that, to own him in a way that isn't just about paperwork, and pounds shillings and pence. No-one to offer devotion to – to remember being devoted to – to follow around like the human runt of the litter, tolerated and offered scraps of tenderness, and finally sneaking and tantrumming and stealing away the larger segment of his heart. Ree knows who Penn is – he bloody ought to. They have owned each other for a good segment of forever, and how can that change now?

Well. Death could change it, obviously.

Now, perhaps no-one is coming. No Ree, no true independent proud creative liberty, no temperate climate in a beautiful green drizzling land. No-one to belong to, and with, who's also his.

Lettice, she might be dead too – if she has followed? Would Parrin shoot his own sister if she was in pursuit?

Freedom could be absolutely all that's awaiting him at the end of this long, rickety, bumpy, bucketing journey. A very cold kind of a freedom indeed. Penn hunches down in the corner, with Sam chuntering and blathering on happily. However long it is, and how winding or straight the journey proves, he doesn't notice any more, and doesn't care.

When he awakes, it's the first time that he properly realises that he's been asleep. It's a useful refuge from misery, after all, and he has experience to tell him that it's so. It's not so surprising that he was able to sleep in the first place: just like a soldier, for a slave sleep becomes a willed function, a pet dog that comes when it's called. Otherwise survival, probably, and rest, certainly, would become impossible.

It's less surprising, in that although he's still chilled, he's not as cold as all that, as cold as he might be. That's because he has one blanket over him, and another over the top of that. It isn't enough, still, but it's better than nothing. (Penn can't feign surprise, that abolitionist wolves would think a cold biting hell of tundra and moss and glaciers, with few even of the amenities it possessed back when only humans could call themselves the dominant race of earth, is a good-enough freedom for humans. After all, they think paper-thin tunics and a couple of raw rough blankets sufficient in the perishing kind of northern early morning, to keep a human body warm, or at least not stiff with the rigours of death. Very careless in their bountiful gestures, they are, considering not everyone has a pelt to rely on in a pinch. Thoughtless.)

The source of the blankets is Sam. And Sam himself has shuffled close by, peering at Penn. Probably that gaze is what's woken him in the first place. That or the wind and the rain, the rumbling of water... Is that rain? In the first moment of waking, Penn isn't quite sure. "I think we're stopping," Sam says, leaping up onto the bench to grab what jolting uninformative glance he can, then leaping down onto the jolting floor, back to Penn's side. And he's right, they're slowing as they're pulling a left, and Penn's heart is broken, but it still manages to stop for a second time.

Because this is it. Isn't it? They must surely have reached wherever it is they're heading, before beginning the second phase of a miserable liberation. This must be Scotland, end of the line for their dear captors/rescuers, and a whole new beginning for their guests. Penn rubs anxiously at his wrists – where he was bound up until shortly before Sam woke up. If they notice straight away, or care, then he'll be bound again and that's goodbye to any chance of getting away. If they're slack and casual enough to miss it, or to let it go with a shrug if they do see, then perhaps – well, it's the entire extent of any possibility for him. So he's relying on it, a bit. Now that they're in Scotland, and the mad run from Ree's pursuit is over. Now they're in Scotland. Now they're—

It's not Scotland. The front doors go, and heavy booted feet run around them in half-circles, and the doors behind them bang open to let excruciating blinding light in. And Penn's heart is eager and leaping as a bird, as he shuffles out, helped by hands that are a bit too eager. He keeps his arms unobtrusively down, avoids the eyes of the wolves, and takes a quick shifty cast of the eyes around–.

"Beautiful Cumbria," Parrin says, the one standing head on in front of Penn, as Sam drops out of the van behind him. Dismissive and derisory don't, as adjectives, really quite cover his tone. "Thought you lads might appreciate a break, since we've been going a fair while now. Bite to eat, take a leak, stretch your legs, eh? I'd say we can afford it. I don't think the friends who were so eager to join us a little while back, are liable to be with us for the rest of the journey. Not after the welcome we gave 'em. Eh, Pennorth?" he questions, head tipped to one side, and a wry grin on his face.

Oh, how very dearly Penn would like to knock his block off. It would almost be worth taking the bite, if it meant having the muscle and speed to do it. But even if the putdown from Parrin wouldn't probably concuss him at minimum, he can't afford to make it so obvious that he's been having adventures with a cigarette and the bindings about his hands – that he's got 'em free.

Perhaps they'll forget that they even bound him in the first place: if he keeps his eyes down, if he keeps his body language submissive and inconspicuous, if he's as close to invisible as a hundred and fifty pounds of healthy young human male can be. And it seems to be working: or at least, he answers a call of nature, (under more observation than is comfortable, but privacy's a luxury he knows better than to expect), accepts tea and more sandwiches from Gus, and stands hovering behind Sam for what must be scanty cover and camouflage. But it's the best he can do, as the wolves stand a little apart, smoking and chatting and seeming pretty damn relaxed, considering the last time they stopped they had to see off other wolves in pursuit, with the aid of usefully activated buckshot.

How can they be so confident that there'll be no further pursuit, though, Penn thinks, and he's too stirred up to know if it's wishful thinking or simple logic, at this point. But he gets some kind of response without asking, when Gus casts a glance their way, and notices that Sam's shivering, as he finishes telling Penn all about what he'll wear as a free working man in Alaska, none of these tunics, he'll have fur-lined boots and a seal jacket, you'll see! "Hoi, are you all right there, lad?" he calls over. And, wouldn't you know it, steps closer, to examine Sam more thoroughly. (Penn shrinks back, and tries as subtly as he can manage it to hide his hands behind his arse.) "No, of course you're not – you're bloody freezing," he continues – and then pulls off his own heavy sheepskin jacket, and hangs it over Sam's shoulders.

Chapter 5

(**P**enn is a little amazed. Freeing a slave is one thing. But such a kind gesture is different. For a very fleeting moment, he could almost like Gus, arrogant big thick-headed brute that he seems.) "What's the matter, kid?" he asks, and it seems like genuine concern and interest.

And Sam's eyes are dropped, and his voice a lot softer, talking to a wolf, than when he was holding forth to Pennorth not a minute back. But he still manages to stutter it out, shyly, as he says, "Not the cold, sir – or not only the cold. I was only worried – well, concerned – do you think they'll catch us again?" He'd been trembling, then, Penn thinks, even as he'd been yarning on at Penn. Penn hadn't realised. The boy puts on a good front.

And so does the wolf, unless he's genuinely unconcerned, completely blithe about the issue. He pats Sam on the shoulder, and it's only a little bit patronising. "Don't worry yourself, son," he assures Sam. "We gave 'em a thorough discouraging, with a spot of silver. Amazing how well it'll do that, against wolves. Haven't seen a sign of 'em since, and it's not like they can keep up with a motor vehicle in any case, not realistically. We'll be in Scotland by morning, and I doubt we'll see hide nor hair of 'em from now until then."

"Do you – do you think it was my pack?" Sam says, and his voice shakes a little bit as he does say it. "Coming after me?"

"Hard to say, my lad," Parrin interjects dismissively. "Hard to say, at that distance, and I didn't catch a distinctive howl. But don't worry yourself: they'll not be wanting another dose, and they'd be doing bloody well to catch a scent or keep up, with us going via wheels and them via paws. No trail to follow, and even a wolf has limits! Gus, Harry, let's be off, now – get these two back in the back, and we'll be moving on."

And he discards his cigarette, and makes for the driver's seat of the van. Gus pats Sam's shoulder, again, and steers him towards the open mouth of the van back doors. But not before He's muttered – perhaps in Parrin's hearing, perhaps not, if the wind's just so - "Well, they managed somehow, eh, first time? Did bloody well, too, if it was Hotstaat."

Parrin doesn't show any sign of hearing, as he swings into the driver's seat. All that he shouts back, in their direction, is on another subject entirely. "And Harry, don't forget to pay attention to Penn, getting him in the van. He needs his wrists tying back up, eh, isn't that right, Pennorth?" It's loud and clear, and possibly a bit vindictive. And Penn could bite his lip off with rage, because surely that was deliberate. Parrin's let him think he was getting away with it, and all the time he hasn't missed a trick, and now he's to be bound again? Damn it. How is he going to seize any chance he gets, this way?

He has no chance right now, that's for sure. It's Harry on him, guiding and keeping an eye on him carefully. No doubt that's why Parrin's left it until now, besides for the sake of amusement and allowing Penn to think he'd got away with something. What escape did he have to fear, with three wolves to give chase should Penn make a break for it? But now he won't be directly under Parrn's eye, and it seems that means he needs muzzling and disabling from any pesky shenanigans he might get up to. Well, it seems that Parrin knows him fairly well.

As Gus passes him, having boosted poor Sam up into the back of the van with great vigour and reasonable good humour, Penn schools his face, and even offers a smile to the great bull's admonition of, "Cheerful, Pennorth! You'll be free before you know it!" A smile, and all the charm and warmth he has for him to command, as he obediently submits to Harry's shepherding and moves towards the doors.

Which is where Harry stops him, a long tan hand catching him by the shoulder and spinning him around. Sam has disappeared into the dim depths of the llittle mobile cell, and the two other wolves are in the front, and really it feels pretty much like him and Harry alone in the world together, standing in a layby with green hills around.

It isn't what Penn had in mind, but considering how poor his chances are currently looking, it's an unimpressive fragment of opportunity, that he'd better capitalise on while the going's good. It's not as if he hasn't already noticed that Harry is quite easily smitten, and has his hands upon Penn right this minute, in fact. If only in order to tie him up nice and tight and render him inoffensive and harmless for the rest of the journey.

And judging by the look on Harry's face, he likes that idea quite a lot. If, perhaps, not for strictly utilitarian and platonic reasons. His breathing certainly seems to catch a bit, as he whips a small ball of leather twine out of his jacket pocket, and takes a hold of one of Penn's hands, quite gently. "Give me your other hand, Penn," he requests, and though there's no please to it, it's quite civil, from a wolf to a slave.

Penn takes his chance. He offers his other hand as asked, and as he does it, he notes that Harry's fairish eyelashes are downcast – as if he can't quite meet Penn's eyes, and there are so few reasons for that, in a wolf. There's a flush on his normally pale cheeks, too, and the diagnosis is easy.

Well. Penn lets himself drift a little forward, and they're practically brushing against each other, now, as Harry fumbles with the twine, his fingers straying over Penn's wrists to no real effect. A kiss from him, an approach, or even too flagrantly tipping his head and offering his lips, that would be a mistake. This is a wolf who likes to give chase, a little, probably literally half the time. But offering something just a little out of reach will probably suffice, with so little time and comfort on offer. Sam may poke his head out of the van doors at any moment, after all.

He refuses to believe that he can't draw an advance out of this susceptible predator, and so it proves, fortunately for his amour-propre. For a second, or maybe a second and a half, Harry focuses on Penn's wrists, looping twine and re-positioning them surely a lot more ineptly than usual. And then he looks up at Penn, and blinks hard, and then there's a little sigh that sounds a lot like surrender, to Penn. They're so damn close, here, that Harry barely has to lean at all to be kissing him. Oh, the bad boy, Penn thinks, smug.

As kisses go, it's a kiss, so. Unremarkable, and with Harry a lot more caught up in it that Penn allows himself to be. Honestly, perish the thought. He's cooperative, but beyond that he's busy carefully flexing his wrists and forearms, subtly re-positioning his hands, and other than that remaining still, so still. So that the twine that Harry's so laxly looped around them to bind him doesn't just fall off, and prompt him to begin the whole chore again. And perhaps, to do it right, this time.

Maybe Harry would stand and kiss him for ten minutes or so, or longer. But that can't be allowed: and Penn eases himself free, gently but decidedly. "Oops," he says, which seems to cover the risk and romance of the situation, at least from Harry's point of view. The poor lad looks distinctly dazed and glazed. But he recovers in a moment, and now he's really blushing. He's having more trouble than ever meeting Penn's eye, and seems to find a haven in concentrating on tying knots to secure Penn's bonds.

"I, er – well, I'm sorry, and I hope–" he's saying, at the same time. He's a lot too focused on the job in hand, now, and it's clear where his thoughts are going. So that Penn cranes his head, downwards and eyes up, to catch his eye, and draw his attention as he does it.

"I won't say a word to Parrin. Don't worry," he reassures the idiot softly. And it's true, he won't. But the actual aim in view is to distract him from the job he's doing: and as Harry ties the last knot – not even looking at it, but gazing vacantly into Penn's eyes – Penn could gasp with relief. Harry drops his hands, and Penn does too. Carefully positioned, flexed and pulled just a fraction apart, the better to disguise just what an incompetent job he's had Harry make of it.

Of course, if he takes it into his head to re-examine the fastenings, then there'll be no purpose served in any case. But bless the lad, this is the moment that Sam chooses to emerge from the shadows, and peer out of the opening of the van doors. "Are you all right out there, Penn?" he asks, cautiously. And Penn takes his cue, sets one foot effortfully on the step before the doors, and heaves himself up into the innards of the van. (Not without a bit of unasked, perhaps wistful assistance from Harry. And indeed those hands, so unskilled at securing bonds a moment ago, seem handy enough at simultaneously assisting Penn in his upward ascent, and getting a feel of his hip and arm and arse, at the same time.

Penn doesn't grudge him it, either. Turn and turn about, and he's got something out of the deal, it must be said. But he's careful to disappear quick, off into the hidden shadows up near the cab, so that Harry still can't get a decent look at him, nor call him back out for more kissing and fondling. There could still be disaster. And he feels, without looking, how Harry lingers a moment at the open doors, how Sam is looking curiously between them. But after all, he can't say much – not without risking it being reported back to Parrin, which would be unfortunate for him, after the dressing-downs it sounds as if he's had now and then.

"I'll see you in a couple of hours, then, Pennorth," is all he risks. But Penn gives him no answer back, but just settles crouching down, far out of his hands and gloating about his little triumph. As the doors close he tests how close and secure his bonds actually are, in the darkness before his eyes and Sam's acclimatise. It's a very poor bind indeed, that Harry's put him in. He grins to himself, and takes it as a tribute to his charms.

But he doesn't even think of actually breaking them and releasing himself. He was too precipitous about it the last time, cigarette in hand and burning his way through rope. They could be a long way off their final stop of the journey yet, and he's learnt his lesson from this time around. He'll save it, until he's a lot more sure, with his feet on earth and rock, that the wolves are distracted and he has a real chance to get away.

Who knows when that will be, and he's just wondering and speculating, when Sam edges to sit a little closer to him, and says, "What time do you think it is, now? I forgot to ask, while we were out. Does it look darker out there, to you, now?" And he nods at the far high little window-strips. It does look a little dimmer than noon-day daylight, out there, to Penn's eyes. But that could as easy be oncoming storm, as the day edging on.

"Mid-afternoon," he guesses, squinting up at it. "I'd say. Or maybe later."

"We've been on the road a long time," Sam says. "How long do you think, before we get there?"

Scotland, Penn thinks. Probably some remote spot on the west coast: could be hours, yet. Hours and hours, for them, and for the wolves, and for Ree. Hours of running, and possible injury, and how many stops for water and food, and no trail to follow? None, and how can Ree find him, with no trail? Probably it was no more than luck the first time, if that time was Ree at all and not Sam's pack. Ree may have given up. Maybe Parrin's right. At some point it's insanity, to persist and pursue. "Long enough that you'd be better off sleeping through of much as it as you can," he says, heavily. "See if you can get some kip, lad. Get your head down."

If it spares him an hour or two of Sam's inane chatter, well, that is also an admissible bonus.

Except that Sam would sooner chat, of course. Always, it's beginning to seem like. And gives a pointed look down at Penn's hands – as their eyes begin to adjust to the dim light. He whispers even with no-one to conceal it from, "They tied you up? I saw Mr Harry tie you up, out there..." He doesn't mention having seen anything else. Although presumably he was having a good gawp, the nosy little bugger. "They didn't tie *me* up," he says, clearly puzzled, holding his own wrists and free hands up for Penn's inspection and his own, as if he thinks that Penn might not believe him otherwise.

"Don't worry about it, Sam," Penn says, vaguely. "I'm just an untrustworthy suspicious character, that's all. And I think Mr Harry may have a fancy that way, for bonds and ropes." And with that thoroughgoing non-answer, he puts his own head down, on a scrunched-up blanket that's his, with the other going to Sam. If Sam won't sleep, and shut up, then Penn can at least pretend to, and resolutely ignore any questions.

It's imperfectly successful, and Sam still attempts to talk to him off and on. But that's the next few hours, light dimming outside as wind buffets past the walls of the van, dozing as far as he can, worrying when he can't, monosyllabic with Sam. It has to be early evening, the next stop. It's almost too dark to identify where they are, and the wolves seem moody and not inclined to chat. Except for Harry, who stares at him with burning eyes, and tries to get up a little closer, and has Parrin bark at him, rough and admonitory. They watch a damn sight too closely, and he shrinks in close to the van, and keeps his hands down and unobtrusive. He's almost glad to get back in the van.

The next time it's almost night, and the time beyond that it *is* night. He's always watched too close, and the country's too wild and even if he had a chance to run, what would his odds be? His hope dries up, and time's running out. Sleep is very welcome. The next time he wakes up, it's dimly light again, outside the window. Perhaps twenty or twenty-four hours, they've been running, driving, and the wolves must have been sleeping in shifts to keep driving all this way.

He can hear water. He's aware of it before he consciously notices it, and then it's annoying.

"I think we must be close," is what Sam whispers, ridiculously. There's Sam, awake and talking, since the two are synonymous. And who is he afraid will overhear him? "D'you hear that? I think it's the sea. Do you think it's the sea?"

Penn struggles to sit up straight, stiff from sleeping in such un-promising circumstances. He cranes his head, and he's sure. Sam's right. "Yes, the sea," he agrees. He feels utterly wiped out and ex-hausted, saying it. It could have been an airfield, but the abolitionists probably don't have the resources for that. Or if they do, it would be a sight too conspicuous, and require co-operation and conspiracy from too many people at both ends of a journey. This is probably the end of Penn's journey, and the end of the life he'd planned. It begins nothing.

The slowing of the van is a hint, anyway. Gravel is rattling and hissing under the tyres, but quieter and quieter. A hard swerve to the right, up over a softer trail that's probably grass or a sandbank, per-haps, and the van comes to a halt, hissing softly. This is it, then, most probably, and Penn's heart sinks. There's not a sound barring waves and wind, no-one rushing to his rescue. And if he puts his hand to his heart then he did think – he did think so. He thought that some-one would rescue him, from being rescued.

He thought Ree would. Deep inside, he'd thought that Ree would always come for him. Some things can't be argued with, though, Possibly a bullet is one of them. It's so stupid that his face is wet from tears, when the doors up front slam and the doors behind them open up.

It's only a pity that he doesn't have bullets and a firearm of his own, when Parrin – with Gus and Harry behind him, flushed and muscular and looking pink but pleased with themselves – opens up the doors. Penn thinks he's smiling, but it's a little hard to tell, because he's wearing the most ridiculous balaclava. Which he fortunately pulls off his head before he speaks, and it's a mercy. Even a grieving and solitary slave may have aesthetic sensibilities to yet be offended. "Come on, lads," he cries, beaming as if it's a happy occasion, as if he's inviting them to a party, a rout, the most exciting social event that the calendar offers. "After me! It's been a rough ride some of the way, but here we are, and your adventure's before you!" He's still waving that bloody gun about, Penn observes: and Sam leaps up and jumps eagerly out of the open doors, to be slapped on the shoulders and congratulated by Harry, and a Gus seemingly reconciled with his motor of a mouth. Just as long as he's departing shortly, and Gus isn't going to have to put up with it for long.

And Parrin waves the gun about some more – and Penn would so much rather not have his head blown off *by accident*, damn it. If anyone is going to do it, could they at least not pay him the courtesy of having intended it beforehand? "Come on, Pennorth," Parrin repeats, grinning at him directly. And – much more slowly – he waggles the point of his revolver, up in the air, side to side. The same gun, possibly, that he or one of the others shot earlier in the journey.

Maybe it's the gun that did the damage. That's the reason he's alone here now with no-one to pull him out of it. "Come and play. It's time to go," Parrin says – and although his expression is just as friendly and benevolent and only slightly creepy as ever, the way that he stands a little aside to make room for Penn, and beckons him with a free hand, says so clearly that he means it.

It's the end of the journey, he's outnumbered by immensely strong supernatural creatures, and if he ran, now, he'd only be a runaway slave, perhaps running back to an estate with... His brain tries to tell him something about what the options are for Ree, what could have happened and what might await him if he tried to return, now. But he just shuts it down, bloody sharp. He can't live with that, and can't allow himself to consider it.

They'd only come after him if he ran, anyhow. It's not as if he has a chance of getting anywhere, running from wolves, and armed wolves into the bargain. Penn walks forward, and almost drops off the lip of the van doorway, half-stumbles on the step. Parrin catches him as he almost goes over on his arse, steadies him on his feet. (The bastard.) With the hand that isn't carrying a nice little handgun, of course.

He could ask, he thinks. He supposes that he could ask, but for that he'd have to be sure he could deal with the answer. He doesn't want to stand and chat with someone who might have – might have – with someone who'd shoot at Ree. So he just nods, brief and stiff, and makes to follow Sam and the other two wolves, where they're making good progress down a narrow little chalk-white footpath. It leads down a slope and onwards to the sagging, levelled off edge of a steeper cliff-face, more of a ledge where it winds down to almost meet the grey sand of a dull, private little beach, with the tide coming in.

it's not a beautiful scenic view, not an obvious tourist spot or anything like that. It looks, as beaches go, strictly utilitarian, a place for sea and land to meet and get the business over and done with. About what he'd have expected of the Scottish seaside, in fact. And Parrin is following him close behind, taking the rear, so that Penn's covered fore and aft. He couldn't get away. There's no cover, and he has no speed and no gun, and possibly no hope. "We had a little trouble, along the way," he hears from over his shoulder, close behind him.

It makes Penn jump a little, and he thinks that it's reasonable for him to be a little jumpy. As well as miserable, and bitter. He looks back, sharply. And Parrin smiles at him some more – the morning light glinting off teeth that are a little unnecessarily extended. He looks exhilarated. He looks like he's enjoying this. Of course he is. This is just a hobby to him, Penn thinks. It's fun. It's what he does instead of gambling, or horse-racing. All of his nobility, his supposed idealism, it's a *sport* to him, in essence.

He isn't going to ask. Does the idiot think he's going to ask? (If he asks he can't be sure that he won't cry, or cry *more*. Or perhaps hit Parrin, depending on the answer. And even if he's going to wind up free in somewhere that's practically Siberia, and free all alone with no-one who gives a damn about him, and free when Ree is dead – it's a fact that he'd still rather not get mauled, here, on a freezing cold drizzling beach in the middle of nowhere, or the middle of Scotland or its northernmost tip. Might as well be the same thing. It's not the way he wants to go, if he's going.

And he doesn't know for sure that Parrin killed Ree – all he has is his suspicions. He doesn't want to know, because as long as he doesn't know for sure then there's some shade of hope. "Yep, one of you had some eager friends who were just so sad that you were planning to leave town. It appeared that they were planning to do something about it, too – or at least they wanted to wish you a very fond farewell." Smooth, just so damned smooth, Parrin is, as he slides a hand down the barrel of his gun. He looks up with a bright pleased eager face through long dark lashes, up at Penn as he comes level with him, as he puts a hand through Penn's arm, to walk arm in arm with him.

Penn feels a little sick, and faint, and there's a grey edge tipping his field of vision. His legs pause, his feet falter, and he doesn't quite stop walking but he slows up a lot. "But I put a stop to that," Parrin says cheerfully: and he mimes a gunslinger's gesture, blowing non-existent smoke from the barrel of his gun. His eyes meet Penn's again, and he smiles fiercer. "Don't you wonder which it was, Penn? Your people – your owners – or poor Sam's, over there?" And he nods ahead. To where Sam is still walking and talking – mostly talking – to the two wolves flanking him at either side, tight together on the narrow path.

"No," Penn says, but he can't say it clear and steady as if it means nothing, the way that he'd like to. It comes out as halfway between a whisper and a croak. And he knows, and Parrin knows that there are tears and horror in it. That he just doesn't want to know, because he's had enough to bear, because he's that much of a coward in the end.

It seems to annoy Parrin, anyhow. He stops dead on the path, and turns ninety degrees to face Penn head on. "Damn all gods, Penn, why are you such a fool? For him? You should be glad to be here, you're supposed to be glad to be here, we shouldn't have had to dope you up and cart you off in the middle of the night! In any case," he says, his narrow handsome face marred with clear disgust, "I've dealt with him and he won't be around to confuse you any further. It's having been kids together that's the trouble, isn't it? It confuses you, because you can remember a time when he didn't hold papers that say you're his property, and when he didn't use those to drag you into his bed and get you so you don't know which way is rightly up or down, or what your name is. He's got your head all stirred up and confused, Pennorth." Penn hates him, for that comforting smile most of all, for that conviction that he's Penn's saviour.

"But that's all over now, Penn," he says. "I've dealt with him for you." He's utterly, utterly pleased with himself. Unshakeable in his conviction that he's done Penn the most immense favour.

Penn doesn't know beforehand that he's going to do it, so he's probably as surprised as Parrin when he fists up his hand and uses it. He's not a brawler, normally – even in a fair fight, with a human opponent his size and weight and build, not over-matched to a ridiculous degree by wolf strength and skill. But he's not some effete sissy either: disputes amongst the disaffected and abused and owned are inevitable, and sometimes he's had to use his fists to stop worse things, like a long sour low-level feud dragging on, with jealous rivals for a master's attention and favour.

Fighting a wolf, though, that's either suicide or madness. He doesn't stop to think about it – absolutely the story of his life, really – and at least he has the element of surprise giving him a minute advantage. Vanishingly minute, of course, against a wolf. In a second, Benedict Parrin has him on the ground – which is pretty uncomfortable in itself, on a chalky gravelly footpath with a low slope in the rain. It's almost worth it, to watch the trickle of blood out of his fine refined perfectly-modelled nose, that Penn's responsible for. His face is close enough, though, that he could bite Penn's nose in turn, and that's a lot less pleasing.

He isn't happy: no. The faint flash of silver fire in his eyes, the very slight glint of diamond-sharpness at the ends of his incisors, it's enough to tell Penn that. How the ripple of taut muscle shudders across his chest, as Penn does his human best to hold him off, has an inhuman violence. How lucky Penn is, really, that this particular wolf prides himself upon his alliance with the interests of humans, his humanitarian and compassionate ideals. With another wolf he'd practically expect his throat ripped out, for such a flagrant act of disrespect. But with this one, he's only wrangled and wrestled to the ground, put out of action and held down until he gives way and submits. It's merciful, compared to what it might have been.

Parrin's allies and confederates have turned on the path and are watching, half-amused and half-stunned, with poor Sam between them looking a lot more like real terror. He must know very well what the consequences of defying or of laying a hand on a wolf can be, and cannot rely – any more than Penn can, really – on a self-styled hero, espousing resistance and liberation, to be really any different from the general run of wolves, not deep down and at his heart.

(But perhaps he's been judging Parrin ill, to an extent. After all, he isn't lying here savaged and bleeding. The wolf's control is excellent, and perhaps his principles are sincerely held, even if tissue-thin in conviction and experience, in Penn's opinion.)

He can only applaud Parrin's control. He is certainly an odd kind of wolf, but then the Parrin clan are oddballs altogether, as he has reason to know. It's still unnerving to have a wolf's face up close – not to kiss him, as Ree's would be, there's no amorous intent in that taut angry face – even with teeth only a little bared, and control quickly regained. Parrin even manages a grin, after a second, then laughs right in Penn's face. "That's one to you, Penn," he says, breath a little hot and fast. "Well done. I do like your spirit, and I'll say it again – you were never meant to be a slave. It only makes me certain that I'm doing right. I'll make you free if it takes buckshot and brawling to do it. And Ree can't come on his white horse and take you back to your gilded shackles now, you little idiot."

His grin is feral and smug, it's the grin of total triumph. And if he had a hand free, then Penn would hit him again and not give a damn for any consequence. His fist clenches, and he wants to wipe the smile off that handsome face, wants to leave it taut and white and stricken and bleeding, to shock his little cadre.

And he does, and he has. Except, no, not him. It isn't Penn that's managed to do that, to put a whitely shocked look on his face as he starts, and pushes himself up on taut tanned forearms, leaving Penn enough room to wriggle away. It's the howl of a wolf – then multiple howls, the howls of wolves, of a pack – that has blackened his eyes and put a look of shock on his face, has robbed his attention completely away from Penn. Penn might as well not exist now, his offence forgotten. And he scrambles out from under quickly.

He moves past, and Parrin stands slower than he does, still looking a little dazed, appalled. The other wolves move back up the pathway, pulling Sam along with them, and it's not as if either of them look much happier, either. "I thought you'd done for him, put 'em off," Gus hisses, and the pointing of his ears and the sudden darkening of the shadow of his beard, foreshadowing a much darker, healthier pelt, expresses clearly just how little he cares for this new development. "I recognise that howl: you can't mistake the Hotstaat Alpha. Nor his pack, neither, and that's the bleeding lot of them following on from him. How in hell alone's name have they found us? We've crossed water multiple times, you put a bullet through him at least – one that should do some good – and they should never have been able to track us travelling in a motor vehicle with that kind of head start in the first place!"

Well, Penn hasn't wolf ears, and can't identify Renally Hotstaat's wolf-voice with anything like the same degree of certainty. Definitely not at this distance, which sounds to still be a fair way off. It's a chancy business even up close, lingering about the grounds and estate of the Hotstaat great house. But he's willing to trust another wolf's ears, and if Gus says it's Ree, then it is.

Of course, he's quite stupid enough to get a surge of relief, even of joy at the words. His eyes aren't dry, and that's humiliating by itself. But it's his idiot heart that he'd like to pulp through a mincer. He can't stop the urgent innocent flood of happiness and acidic relief: but that's a long chalk from being all that he feels, and his second reaction, judged and considered, is the important one.

He's just hovering to the far edges of the group: not edging away, because that would only attract notice. He quietly observes as the wolves come together, Parrin wiping at his bloody nose as if it's an afterthought that he has no time for now. It is. Sam hovers at their edges like a child hovering at mamma's skirts, and no-one has a speck of attention to spare for Penn. It's fine by Penn.

"I thought so too," Parrin agrees, with a rough manly flatness that Penn hadn't thought him capable of. He's a lot less the charming fop, suddenly, the flirtatious dilettante. This wolf, that comes out in trouble, is much more, well, a wolf. Dangerous, confrontational, ready for trouble. "But if Hotstaat's still on our trail, close enough for trouble, we can't continue as planned. Time for a rapid revision, lads. Our boys here," and he nods in Sam's direction, and Penn thinks that he's probably included in that gesture without even being explicitly included, "are going to have to take the boat over to the island by themselves. Sorry, lads," he adds, and now he does half-glance in Penn and Sam's directions, both, before directing his attention back to his associates even as he continues to talk to the humans. "We were meaning to accompany you to the island. There's a natural harbour on the other side, and a contact of ours with a better equipped boat – one that can take you all the way to where you need to go. But now you're going to have to make your way on your own cognizance. We can't stay and wait for our furry lupine friends to catch up with us."

"Too damn right," Harry agrees, screwing his face up and wincing at the idea. "My pack would tear me apart if they had an inkling I was mixed up with this. That's assuming that these bastards don't do the job and spare 'em the trouble." And he turns his eyes on Sam, with a hard-faced squint. Because Sam is nervously edging a little forward, trying for attention, but not sure that he can cope with it when he gets it. Here in the bleak northern early morning, the bruising on his face is more evident. It's easier for Penn to forgive his deference, his inculcated servility, seeing what the kid's suffered. Doesn't he do a pretty good fake facsimile of servility himself, anyhow? The wind is bitter, and although the howling is thin and lonely and distant, it isn't letting up at all. "What is it, young 'un?" Harry asks, quite pleasantly. Sam ventures to speak.

"Alone?" he asks, and from the wideness of his eyes and the goose-pimples on his uncovered arms, that aren't all down to the ambient temperature, it's clear he's not relishing the prospect. "You mean, for us to go – to sail by ourselves? You're just going to abandon us? Where are you going to go?" He understands that this, this incredible thing, is in fact yes, exactly what the wolves mean and intend, as he speaks. Penn can see it in his broad young face, the disbelief and then the pinkening, the beginnings of outrage. He likes Sam so much better, for the outrage.

Benedict Parrin gives him a casual, patronising ruffle to the hair. Which surely means that he's either not a great observer of people – or humans, at least – or that he doesn't care in the least about how the actions of the great philanthropist come across to the little people buffeted about by the consequences of his whims, his mad schemes and ruthless idealism. Otherwise he'd know better, much better, looking at young Sam's face. "Don't you worry about it, young Sam," he says carelessly. "You'll be fine. We were only going to accompany you as far as the island, after all," he says. And, saying it, he flings an arm out to indicate the lumpen green-grey mass on the very horizon, that cannot be as far away as it looks, but is still plenty far, for a novice sailor with no experience of the area and wolves on his trail. And without the protection of the wolf escort that he's been promised, and was relying upon. What, Penn wonders, putting a hand over his brow to block out non-existent sun and very-existent rain – if they're at the northern tip of Scotland – surely they must be – then what island is that, in any case? Sark? No, that's the Channel, he thinks, and curses his sketchy geographical knowledge of the area. It's scant and sketchy indeed, up this far north, and not based on any personal experience.

"You see that outcrop, just there?" Parrin asks, indicating a great hulking mass of gleaming black rock, possibly granite, out a half-mile, perhaps, along the beach and prominently jutting. "Just beyond there where you can't see, it obscures the view," and he flaps his hand at it airily, "there's an inlet channel for a river-mouth, hidden in a deep fissure in the rocks. It's narrow, but deep: and you'll find a small motorboat tied up at a hook in the wall, just inside it. Take it to the other side of the island, and in the harbour around there you'll find our old friend – your new friend – and a better boat still, one that will take you as far as you need to go."

Evidently he thinks that with that, the two human encumbrances are dealt with and dismissed. Because he turns to his comrades, with significant looks between them flying about thick and fast, and is clearly ready to move on to the next thing, the next bit of business on the meeting's agenda. Except that Sam's mouth has fallen open in distress – or anger, because his bright eyes and red face could be taken more than one way – and he spurts out speech as if he just can't hold it in. "But I can't sail a boat?" he says, as one bewildered but also determined to carry his point. "I've never done it. I can't navigate, I wouldn't know where to begin! You're just going to leave us, to flounder about, with wolves coming? It could be my pack too, as well as the Hotstaats! You don't know what they'll do to me!" His voice is increasing in both despair and volume: and he's abandoned all attempt at servility and tact. Good boy, Penn approves: because how will it serve him, now? It's a good lesson to learn, when to feign it and when to dispense with it. Sometimes it serves, and sometimes it's the last thing a slave needs.

The wolves don't want to hear it though, and Penn can read the instinctive disdain and rage and guilt in every line of their beautiful lithe bodies. They're taut with the urge to change, to savage a lesser being for impertinence. And considering their conscious beliefs and secret activities, what a continual effort it must take to repress that unconscious reaction on a regular basis. "You'll be fine," Harry says impatiently. "It's not even fifteen miles out, you can hardly go wrong. Gus – Ben – you hear that?" And he cocks his head with urgency and meaning, and yes, those howls are a little clearer, a fair bit nearer surely. "Go – we need to go," he says, pointed and fierce, as if no human is even present, and certainly of no importance if they are. He begins to strip off his fine jacket, highly tailored with a nap that gleams softly even in this dim cold light, quite eager in preparation for the change, for flight and running over moors and crags and hills with disdain for fences and obstacles. "Let 'em sink or swim–" – charming, Penn thinks bitterly – "they can either get themselves there and barrel over the Atlantic and make their own way – if they really want it. Or stop and give themselves up, throw themselves on Hotstaat's mercy. Personally I'm not even considering trying that. I'm putting on my pelt and getting the hell out, finding the nearest water to cross and running a roundabout route for home. After all, they haven't seen our faces and they can't prove a damn thing, as long as we're not here when they come for those two. What does a slave's word count for, nothing, in fact a quarter of nothing."

Damn, Penn thinks. It's not that he doesn't expect a brutal lack of concern for human well-being from wolves of any stripe. But just the same it's a bit of a choker, from this crew. He'd reasonably expect a little *shame*. Perhaps they take account of their success by statistical methods: enough 'rescues' and successful escapes, to outweigh the odd breaking-out gone bad, and they needn't feel too bad about the occasional loss, a slave caught and made an example of. And Harry, with all his wistful fancies for pretty humans and inappropriate warmth, appears to have dispensed with all of that now, not to mention forgotten the fact that Penn never signed up for this, didn't 'want' this enforced brutal stripped-down version of liberation at all. But why would wolves care for that, a small detail overlooked in their overarching grand plan? And of course, if they volunteer for protection and get caught themselves, then that's another branch of the abolitionist network shut down, and fewer slaves overall with a chance to get out and get free.

Or, at least, Penn thinks that that's most likely how they manage to rationalise it to themselves. The absolute arseholes.

"Right, you're right," Parrin is agreeing, nodding, and beckons at the both of them, as if he just can't wait to be off. "And anyway, I'm pretty sure that Pennorth can sail. You can sail, Pennorth, isn't that so?" But even in the moment that he calls it out, he's already throwing off his greatcoat, kicking at his heavy boots in readiness to pull them off and make way for claws and paws. He's gone already, or might as well be, in his mind if not in body. Penn's dismissed, after all the persuasion, after the kidnap and the forcible attempt at conversion, the conviction imposed on him roughshod, that a benevolent wolf knows better what's good for an owned human than that human himself.

"Oh, yes, I can sail," Penn agrees, loud and clear, so that none can miss it. "I can sail quite well. But you're not going to need to worry about it." No-one's paying much attention, though, not even Sam. He's too busy looking red-cheeked and emotional, piteous and infuriated at the same time, stunned into a clearly uncharacteristic speechlessness. But at least he's observant enough that he notices Penn. He does, but not the wolves: Parrin's pulled the shirt over his head, and Harry's still swiftly disrobing, and Gus is feeling rapidly around in his pockets for something or other, perhaps paper evidence of their plans that he needs to destroy before he removes and hides evidence of his presence and their illicit activities. But Sam sees.

He's the one who notices, when Penn begins to tool and toy with the gun – Benedict Parrin's gun – that went skittering off anyhow over shale and marsh-grass, when Penn smacked him in the nose and Parrin was otherwise occupied and too busy and careless to track where his lousy firearm was. Or, once he'd heard the wolves – more distinct on the breeze now, more unmistakable – had the presence of mind to remember it, and to check where it had spun, to retrieve it. (Penn does take a moment – even now – to distantly disapprove such a scattered and horribly disorganised habit of mind, that allows such dangerous, unfettered gun-play and poor safety practices, such irresponsible disregard for system and order. His disdain is practically regal, for these mental minions. Surely advanced education is wasted on wolves. They don't appear to benefit from it, as someone with more incentive might. He thinks about what he might do with un-limited time and training, and he could despair, or he might weep.)

All these minutes – perhaps four, or four and a half, and that's plenty. Minutes in which he's lingered on the edges of a distracted group, quietly waiting to be noticed. It's taken them long enough, and even then it's the human that's picked up on it. In the meantime Penn has slyly – unobtrusively – and finally, irritably, ostentatiously – been making comments designed to be incendiary, while playing with a weapon lethal to wolves as well as humans. He even pops the damn barrel, to check what he's working with, what ammo he has. Sam's mouth hangs open for just a moment. And then he has a moment of his own, which excuses all of his missteps in Penn's eyes, and wins him an enduring respect. His mouth tightens, and his eyes flicker over the still-disrobing wolves a moment, in quite visible calculations. Penn can virtually see him thinking about what they've promised him, versus what's actually materialised, and balancing and judging risks, rewards and just deserts.

And as unobtrusively as he may be able, he steps away from the wolves, and closer to Penn. Then a lot closer, looking him straight in the eyes every minute. He keeps going until he's well out of reach of a quick grab, and then they turn, and stand together. Parrin's down to briefs and socks, and he's stretching in that painfully body-aware way that suggests that the wolf isn't that far off, is being invited up from where it steams and bubbles under the surface. They're all but ready to be off, to abandon their two human charges to run or give themselves up to the mercy of wolves, such as it is. Penn clears his throat. Parrin looks his way, finally.

"No, Pennorth," is his response, those pretty hazel eyes sucking down the details of the situation without delay. He may be many things, Benedict Parrin – and Penn would happily list a few of them – but dim is surely not one of them. His smile is winning, delightful. Well, Penn might be delighted by it, if it wasn't for the fact that Parrin's dragged him along on an unwelcome adventure ending in snowy lonely wastes and the extinguishing of his dreams and schemes. And, not content with that insult, he's then cut the offer off, if you could call it that, and dumped Penn and his hapless fellow slave to survive as best they can in very unpromising, even malign circumstances.

"You're not going to shoot me, Pennorth," Benedict Parrin says. And he doesn't even trouble to sound soothing. He isn't attempting to coax Penn, to sweeten him up before a grab. He's perfectly confident. The bastard is even amused, Penn thinks, and rage wells up in him that must stink acrid to a wolf's delicate snout.

Of course his companions are alerted now, by his response, by the alert stillness of Parrin and the two humans. A fine trio they make, now, standing half-naked in the grey mist and the soft rain, with the plashy hiss of the waves hushing close, close in, as the tide encroaches upon them. Harry is wide-eyed and still – and not stupid, having been around in the cab for that discussion about the bullets, and their effectiveness on wolves. Gus, on the other hand – the biggest wolf present, and Penn would probably bet a small amount of money the least intellectually gifted – and the most beefcake handsome, to be fair, but then life is unfair and it's not so bad if it gives with the hand that's not taking away, for some, Penn supposes. Really not the sharpest tool, however, and he lunges forward fast enough that Penn thinks for a moment he'll actually have to shoot him.

The thought doesn't trouble him that much, considering how desperate their situation is already. His arm swings up automatically, and he has the trigger cocked before he even knows it, no matter good practice. Wolves have so little to fear from bullets, usually. Many an owner's a damn sight too casual about training a slave up in firearms and target practice for defence purposes, and if they're dealing with stock rustlers, burglars and rival packs. At least Penn's found it so, and old Jay Parrin was a case in point. Old Jay, he'd liked a rabbit stew, wild and a little earthy with plenty of dandelion leaves and purslane and other bitter herbs in it. He'd taken a pride in training Penn as a crack shot, and amongst a host of other reasons, Penn blesses old cousin Jay for it now.

He's ready, so ready, on the verge of pulling the trigger. But Parrin must see the readiness in his face, and he has a grip on Gus, half by the back of his trews, his torso gleaming with the dew, and half with an arm about his shoulders, before he can be on Penn and with a silver bullet through his gut at the same time. His face shows just the beginnings of the change, slower than the romancings of those who've never seen it would suggest, but the raw darkness unmistakable just the same. His fangs are elongated enough to cut at soft human lips when he digs them in, and snarls at Penn. But a fat lot of good that does him. "Really not a good idea, Gus, my lad," Parrin soothes and urges him at the same time. And he has cheek enough, even now, to flash a quick grin Penn's way. Gus subsides, and humanizes, however reluctantly – damn reluctantly, judging by his face, too.

And once he's satisfied, that his underling isn't going to court death and dismemberment at the hands of a disaffected runaway, then Parrin leaves go of Gus. And he steps forward himself, that much closer to Penn and to Sam, saying, "Seriously, Pennorth, you know you're not going to shoot me, so can we just cut out this infantile play-acting and–."

It's true that Penn doesn't shoot him, as he takes that second step. But it's also true that he makes the bullet fly and dance, makes it almost provide the wolf with a pedicure for the bare feet that are still all human, no trace of claw or sprouting pelt as yet. Penn is an excellent shot. He understands much of the trajectory of a bullet and the engineering of a gun. He has been well taught. "Surprised you only brought this little toy out to play with," he drawls, and feels all the sharp satisfaction of having the upper hand, for once. "Aren't there rifles, in the cab?"

It's a matter of credit to Parrin, that he doesn't bluster, express outrage, or continue to question Penn's seriousness regarding his intent to use the tools he has at hand and not to tolerate any nonsense from anyone, no matter if they're in possession of a bowed head and a tunic, or pelt, claws and fangs. "All right," Parrin says steadily, and quite cheerfully considering, as his fellow wolves blanch and tremor. (They're only a little freaked by a slave having the fire-power to fire on them, and what's more, having the balls or the complete bloody recklessness to actually do it. Penn doesn't kid himself for a moment that there's actual fear involved. Either of these two henchmen, he's darned certain, would tear him apart with guts and eyeballs flying, quite happily. Abolitionist sympathies notwithstanding, he's a human who's dared to make them back down, and it goes against every lupine instinct to allow him to dominate, or perhaps even to suffer him to survive such a challenge to their authority. Even sweet flirty randy Harry, with his fondness for pretty humans, is growling softly. The silver-blackness of his eyes and the hunch as his back begs to expand and take on position on all fours, tells plenty of how near the wolf is, and how much he'd like to give it free rein.

"I didn't think they were likely to prove necessary. We should have had much more time than this, with a compromised trail and pursuers in pelt and paw. Hours more, at minimum," Parrin says, quite calm. "And anyway, I hadn't enough silver ammo left for them too. They wouldn't have done us much good."

"Not against *wolves*," Penn points out. "Not exactly a tight ship that you're running, here, Parrin." Slack, in fact, he thinks. Very slack, indeed. If it was him in charge, it'd be an extraordinarily different tale.

"What do you want, then, Pennorth?" Parrin asks, equable and urbane. And he, too, has the wolf lurking close up in his mind, visible in his eyes. He's not safer than the others, just better controlled. "I do hope that the answer isn't our hearts on a slab served with sauce tartare and a little garnish, perhaps a frilled cutlet to accompany. Because that isn't going to happen, you know. You might – with a lucky hit – manage to get one of us. But you won't be quick enough for the other two, and they'll take you out. It doesn't matter what those bullets are made of, then. You'll be done for. So be reasonable, my love. Make your requests modest, and we'll see what we can do to satisfy you."

Penn waves the gun around a little, just like Parrin has been doing on and off for hours now. Let him be the one worrying about a random misfire taking his leg off, or ripping the back of his skull off, and they'll see how he likes it. "I want what you promised this kid here," he says then, and his voice has a roughness that he's never heard in it before. No more pleasing the master, then, not for Penn. "Companions on the journey, and protection, and a guide from people who know how to handle themselves on a boat, and can navigate us to where we're going. You're not running off the moment the wolves that own us catch up, saving your own hides – pelts – and sacrificing us to your own safety. You're coming with us."

It's enough to leave Parrin stunned, and both his companions red-faced with disbelief, and fury too. Not speechless, though: it would take a lot to leave Parrin speechless, he thinks. Perhaps almost as much as with Sam. He struggles a little with the initial protest. But then he gets out, "That wasn't the agreement! We were going to go with you, yes: but only as far as the island, and then we were to turn you over to our contacts and they'd escort you the rest of the way! You're having a little fun with me, surely. And why would you want it, even, Pennorth? You've been protesting being dumped in a sack and brought along for the ride for the entire journey so far. Shouldn't you be pleased at the prospect of being picked up by your ever-loving owner, and carried back home on the back of his white charger? Provided my darling sister allows him, of course. She's a feisty one, you might have noticed." The smirk on his face is quite infuriating, and if a bullet would wipe it off, then Penn would be very sorely tempted. But even Parrin's corpse would probably still have a sickening smirk on its face.

This is the crucial point, that's festered in him since the wolves identified that they were being followed not by a lone Ree, nor perhaps Lettice or a couple of trusted betas accompanying him. No, but a pack, the whole Hotstaat pack. That makes it different. A small group, subdued by Ree's influence, could enforce discretion and silence regarding this little venture. It would mean that Penn's story of how the supposed 'escape' came to be was accepted, by Ree and by everyone else, as far as it was known at all.

That was what Ree would have done, if he'd had faith in Penn and believed that he wouldn't run of his own accord, wouldn't put his trust in Benjamin Parrin. That's if he has any idea that his lady's brother is the wolf responsible, or is aware that wolves are involved at all. But he hasn't done that. Instead he's alerted the whole howling pack of Hotstaats and related and allied wolves, to come after Penn and to bring him back to justice. Well, to some version of justice, as wolf notions of it go. This can't go other than horribly badly for Penn. Ree thinks he's a runaway, has stolen away in the night after a hand-fasting and a consummation that would surely bind anyone with a heart to the other party, or parties, involved. Unless they were as cold-hearted, clear-sighted and sensible as Penn, of course.

Ree never has trusted him, he knows it. Oh, he's wanted to. But deep down he's always known that Penn's soft words and caresses are about as deep as the skin of a peach, and mean as much as soft words in morning breath. He's always been keeping a weather eye out, for the moment that Penn would run. It's not as if Penn's surprised. It's completely justified.

It's just breaking his heart a little bit, even so. Just enough to make him steaming fuming mad, mad enough to spit and cuss. So he's decided. He's not waiting to be run down by a howling pack, and he refuses to be prey. And if he's honest, he expected more from Ree than this. He expected sincerity, at the least.

Certainly he isn't going to wait to be demoted from childhood sweetheart and secret hand-fasted mate, to a runaway slave handed over to the authorities at best, or dealt with summarily by the Hot-staat clan, at worst. He's not going to fall to less than his zenith, to fall before the eyes of every other slave and servant on the clan's property, from pampered pet to scapegoat and runaway criminal. So, the plan has gone into reverse. Parrin had him kidnapped, and all this time he's been resisting, and planning his return to his former glory, his role as petted property and triumphant favourite. For the sake of the opportunities it affords him, of course. For the sake of the future it could open up, and that's the truth (or part of it).

But now Parrin's abandoning him like a used up food wrapper – along with his pals – and not just him, but also Sam. Sam would probably fare even worse than Penn, returned to the hands of wolves for whom he's not even a once-valued pet, who might still merit some gentle handling and tolerance. Sam is a fellow-slave. He owes Sam something, for his own soft treatment and the harsh existence that Sam's endured, in the same time.

So plans are topsy-turvy, now. Parrin wants out, of his grand scheme of abolitionism, the self-admiring ego-petting of coming to the rescue of the helpless and the captive. Maybe it doesn't look quite so attractive, when it's suddenly liable to rebound on you, and there could be extremely serious and possibly even fatal consequences. The Parrins may be as eccentric as they please, and abolitionist, egalitari-an sympathies are fashionable and turned a blind eye to, in a certain segment of the stylish young set of wolf society. But it's quite a differ-ent thing, to actually get caught doing something about it, red-hand-ed and with slaves not your own, heading for a motorboat and the frozen north.

Parrin wants out, but that doesn't mean he's getting it. Penn's changed his mind. He's all for escape, suddenly. And not too fussy about where or how. In fact Parrin's plan will do, and he'll take Parrin and co., as well as Sam, along with him. Whether they like it or not. "Do you want me to take a toe off, sir?" he enquires. And that is possibly the greatest quantity of sarcasm that anyone has ever managed to pack into the last word. "Or I could do some real damage, instead. Some mortal real damage, even." He looks Parrin dead in the eye, and doesn't flinch an inch at the flickering growl that Parrin lets rumble softly, tic-toc-ticking, through several seconds and the granite-like wall of his nicely-modelled, less-than bull-like chest. He's a slight, lithe, slip of a fellow, for a wolf. But he's still a wolf, and he's saying so, not quite in so many words.

Much earthly good may it do him, the fool. Sam is alert and looming closer at Penn's side, and hisses, "Shouldn't we check they haven't got any more guns? Or weapons? Want me to frisk them?" It's a wide-eyed and sincere enquiry, from a kid who's seen too many gangster films, and how has he seen them, even? Given his shady, cultish, violent pack-owners, by everything he's barely said. Or if it's just straight out of his own head, or the pages of a detective novel, then still more credit goes to him.

Penn only laughs – because if the other two wolves were armed, he'd have seen some evidence of it by now, with three of them against the one of him. And barely counting Sam, for all the kid clearly has a good heart and enough balls for six or seven. Gus opens his mouth readily enough, though. "You ungrateful little shit," he hisses,"after everything we've done for you, to give you your freedom. I ought to rip your heart and lungs out." And he's much on the verge, eyes wildening, red in the face, dark enough around the gills to be suggestive that his control is weak. Penn mislikes that, significantly.

But the risk of a loss of control of the situation is enough for him to waste another bullet, a hostage given up for the sake of regaining mastery. And he doesn't only give it up for the show of the thing, because he's done it once and the effect can only be diminished with each successive threat. Instead – as the enraged wolf lunges at Sam, and his face stretches closer to being wolf, Penn puts that bullet in the bastard's calf, with thought and care and good aim.

And quick smart, he steps back, and drags Sam well out of harm's way too, as Gus shifts abruptly halfway to wolf, ripping at fabric and stitching, a furious roar ripping itself out of his broad throat and cutting off to a pathetic whine, as the pain and the mess of a real wound, that won't heal with ease and speed, cuts into his consciousness just like a human would experience it.

His face slips back to human, over a few seconds of whining panting gasps, the two other wolves stilled and horrified. And now, perhaps, properly respectful, and understanding of the seriousness of Penn's intentions, his willingness to do what will put him in place as master of the situation. They're quiet, watching him intently. Not that he doubts any one wouldn't take his arm off with teeth like ivory knives, watchful for the opportunity. Penn gestures with the gun again, down the sandy gravel track, towards the bulwark, towards the cave and the boat that Parrin's promised. "Yes," he says drily, "all that you've done for us. And now you're going to do a little more. Come on, get moving. You hear that on the air? We've not got all day, nothing like it."

He has successfully communicated the seriousness of his intentions, it seems. They actually grab at clothes and move ahead of him, a little slow except when he barks out a reminder that he has wolves to the rear of him as well as before him, and they'd all be best off making good time and getting as much of a head start regained as humanly – wolfishly – possible. It puts a bit of a zing in their step, for certain. But it doesn't prevent a half-naked Parrin from shooting off behind him the rejoinder, "Good work, Penn. I can only applaud – you pulled that off beautifully. But how far do you think you can keep it up? Do you think you can keep three wolves under control, for the whole of a transatlantic voyage?" He delivers it with a sneer, and considerable emphasis.

It's true that Penn had thought that exactly, for about a minute. Or at least that it had been unconsciously behind his first impulse in picking up the gun. With a whole pack of the Hotstaats baying after him, what he considered a betrayal from Ree burning in his gut and the sudden overturning of his assumptions, the determination that he wasn't going back, would suddenly rather die than go back... He hadn't thought it out. He isn't naive, or unaware of his own responses. There was only a deep conviction, an instantly born determination that if he was dispensing with Ree – and he was, and he is, no matter that the thought makes him choke and something twists and hurts in his chest – then Parrin would be useful after all. And since Parrin's a volunteer, then Parrin was damned well going to make himself useful, whatever excuse-laden yellow-bellied second thoughts he might be having on the matter.

On second thoughts, though, Parrin's observations and objections are completely valid, and Penn will concede that limited truth. "In that case, you can go for a dip when we hit the island," he snaps, sharp, crisp, watching every move and every step. "I imagine it'll count as well as crossing water for covering your tracks. You'll just have to shift your arses a bit quicker making your getaway, that's all, and take a bit more trouble to avoid being spotted and hunted." Perhaps there's a smirk on his face, as he says it.

"Why don't you just put three of those bullets through our backs and have done with it?" Parrin asks sourly, still stepping smartly as they head for the inlet, but no happier about it. "You might as well, with that kind of head start on Hotstaat and his crew."

"I give you better odds than Sam and I would've had, alone and unarmed against them if they caught up with us," Penn says sharply.

And miraculously, Parrin is quiet in response. Although his back is stiff, for a wolf, as he walks, his jaw quite rigid too.

The boat is tied up in the inlet channel, discreetly inside the fissure in the rocks, under cover. It's a neat little twenty-footer, a natural go-between's vessel. It's small, with a tiny hold and still smaller engine, but no space for extra fuel or supplies, no sleeping room, no nothing much. If they were relying on this to get themselves across an ocean – even leaving out Sam's complete absence of sailing experience, and the fact that even Penn's is extremely scanty, restricted to assisting on a sailboat on one owner's summer cruises – then they'd be done for. It'd go under in the first storm. They could never bail out or stay afloat long enough, even if they didn't starve or drown first.

That is the reason why he's insisting on a party of wolf outriders to accompany them to the island – or, at least, it's the objective rationalization that he comes up with on the spur of the moment. Because the real reason, transparently, is for the hell of it. Because he can, to assert his power over Parrin, over his consorts, over the race of wolves in general. (Over Ree, even, symbolically. See, Ree? This is how much protection I need, really, from wolves. This is how much I need you. Who needs you? I can take care of myself, you're the one who'd better watch out. Quite childish, obviously.)

He doesn't need to yell, threaten, wave a gun loaded with silver around or put a bullet in anyone else, to get them moving, the boat loaded and manned and afloat, heading in the island's direction. It seems they've got the message thoroughly, and godspeed isn't half speedy enough. No doubt it's self-interest that motivates them, but that's not surprising. Even human ears can hear the high thin wail of wolves on the wind, now, though Penn still can't distinguish between one voice and another, nor identify Ree's voice amongst the rest. (He'd like to, would like to be able to say he could. It would add that extra little fillip of rage and zest and fury, that splash of romance that makes his bitterness all the tastier.) Even over the sulky honks of seagulls and the noisy splashing of the sea, even louder than the heartbeat in Penn's ears, the wolves can be heard.

It's certainly a motivation for an abolitionist caught in the act, to get his arse moving like a motor and get the hell out of town.

Chapter 6

They're out easing through the narrow route through the sand-banks, carefully parsing the way to avoid getting beached and marooned, when the tone of the howling begins to alter: more raucous, louder, more gleeful. Closer.

Definitely closer. Penn and Sam, now the masters, now with the whip-hand, are at the head of the boat, and Penn's set Sam on to watch the wolves' every move as closely as he is himself. They're so busy watching each other, the tiller and the sea, that even as the howls grow loud, louder, they're not watching the cliff. It's not so very high, not a dramatic looming physical presence.

But it's still an ominous vision, when Penn turns his head from examining the graceful muscle interplay as Parrin tears his shirt off again to gun the motor – a pretty boy, certainly, Penn wouldn't trouble to argue the issue – and there they are. Or there it is, at least: a single wolf. The sun in the east, and looking from the west, it's no more than a silhouette. Penn couldn't say if it's Ree, or not. He thinks that it looks perhaps too small, slight and lithe, but at this distance he could be wrong. It's silent, not joining the howls of the rest, which is enough to make hackles rise even if you're not a wolf. It's ominous.

"Well done, Penn, well done," Parrin says caustically, as he and the other two fight to beat the hell out of the motor to get that extra knot out of it. "Those extra minutes spent enjoying your natural dominion – being the stroppy little slave-boy that you are – and haranguing us at the arse-end of that gun, might just be the thing that means we all go down together. You suppose he's going to go any easier on you than us, just because he's been used to indulging you since you couldn't run without falling over and rolling like a ball? For the sake of your pretty eyes, and the pout you put on when you don't get your way? I don't think so, Pennorth. You've been replaced."

Maybe it's true. Ree hasn't come alone, on a white steed, to save him in secret and privacy, and keep his slave good name pristine, free from doubt, accusation and danger. It's true that Penn's being hunted down like any fox. (And he feels much kinship with foxes.) He doesn't feel sure enough of his ground to come up with a snide reply. Even though his mind goes back to what seems days ago, certainly more than twenty-four hours, perhaps: to being teased and toyed and played with, to a long slow love-making that might have left him feeling disorientated and put somewhere between his head and his heels and not steady with respect to either, but also touched him somewhere about the heart, as well as in less socially mentionable parts. To a raw, simple, extemporized hand-fasting, that had very little of the ceremony or ceremonial about it, and much more of the holding hands, and holding each other, all three.

He's not sure, though. Not that it meant anything, and the proof's against it now. He remembers that he's angry, and he's running, and he's done with Ree, and by extension Lettice Parrin too.

So he doesn't say anything. Only glares, and slides one fingertip down the cold wet barrel of the gun, in grey misty rain, with the island closer but not close enough in the unceasing rain, on a relatively calm sea that's still hard enough to push through. It's not so very necessary now, not now that they're irrevocably committed and must run and run fast in the direction they've set, threatened or no. It's just a reminder, that's all. He notices that none of the wolves are looking up at the cliff, even in glances. They keep their faces turned away, and their heads down as far as possible. Of course, identification could be a problem. Where's Parrin's ridiculous balaclava, now?

Then there's even more reason for discretion. The single wolf is joined by the rest – minutes in, ten or five? There, at the top of the cliff, leaning out from the very edge, crowding and massing together in a black, grey, brown horde that moves like one black shadow, sinuous and constantly moving.

It's too far for Penn's weak human eyes to discern Ree, or any other wolf, from the rest of the pack. But he knows he has to be there just the same, and he knows also that he'll be at the very front, almost leaning over the edge of the cliff, paws and claws straining at the rubble and grass tussocks on the edge. And he feels a bit distant and far away – and restores his attention to the wolves more closely at hand, quickly, considering they present a more imminent danger – when he hears Parrin, and Gus too, swear softly, beneath the breath.

It's Harry, the quieter, more amenable, more sexually harassing wolf associate – still quite likely enough to tear his throat out, in Penn's opinion, in these unfavourable circumstances – who breaks a harsh uncomfortable silence, while looping up thick rope around his shoulder.

"There, there they go," he says, flatly, yet it's a tone of doom. "They're in."

The flicker of his eyes gives Penn the direction, because he's heard nothing. The wolves, Harry means, of course. The tide is fully in, now. And the first has leapt, from the height of the cliff – nothing death-defying, unless you were human, perhaps, but still to watch it is to feel the heart rock up into the throat and the stomach pulse with bile.

Another follows, a malignant black shadow that becomes a shade whistling through the air and then a v-shaped sharp prow of foam, as it pushes through the water like it was born to swim as much as to run.

Penn turns away, because he feels sick enough at the pursuit. He doesn't need to see the rest. "Zeus damn it," he snarls. "Can't we make better time than this? I'd like to end this journey in one piece: even if it has to end in the snowy north, for Pete's sake."

There's a discomfited silence, that follows, since no-one knows the answer to that one. And the wolves, the great heroes who've got them into this situation, seem much less gasbags than they were when they were proudly boasting of their heroism and white-knights deeds, less inclined to own their plans and intentions. He gets a glower from Parrin, and that's it: and Sam pats him on the back, awkward. He's white-faced, and frightened, and if Sam has no words to offer him, then they're probably all done for. But Penn isn't giving up, not with a hand to play still left in the game. It's against his nature, and that's as deeply ingrained as any wolf's.

They're turning an angle on the mass of the island – which is small, and not so far from the coast, so that its turning angle is pretty sharp and obscures vision rapidly. From there, very quickly, they'll not be able to see what the wolves are up to, to follow the path of their pursuit and know how close they are, their long lethal jaws snapping, saliva drooling, after Penn's hide and the rest of them too. But Penn takes a swift look back, before they're obscured from view of the boat. It's a vision that has some beauty to it, but Penn isn't of a mind, right now, to judge it on its aesthetic merits. Three wolves are swimming towards them, jaws up out of the water, eyes gleaming with a wild yearning and intent. Their fur must be heavy as bricks, sodden with the seawater, and yet as far as Penn can judge they're making good time, are perhaps as fast as this little boat and its struggling motor even. He's human with human perceptions, and he cannot say for sure.

But he eyes these liberationist wolves carefully, and cocks the gun in his hand a little more meaningfully. If they choose to get any ideas in their heads about abandoning ship, leaving two poor hapless slaves to carry the can while they swim for their lives and trust to their native supernatural strength and speed in the water, well, they'd better think twice, is all. Gus and Harry, though, at least, seem to have all their attention magnetised by the wolves, grim concern on their faces. "That's Hotstaat, the one in the lead. I'd swear to it, the size and the colouring. Pretty sure, at any rate. I thought you'd taken care of him," Gus remarks. And it's pretty probable that he's talking to Parrin, though his face is facing south. It's not the first time he's said something of the type, Penn thinks.

And Parrin, Parrin has his back to the wolves, even as they round the island. The set and stiffness of the angle of his shoulders is probably a warning, but not one that Gus seems to heed. "I did," he says, quiet enough that only Penn may be listening carefully enough to catch it. Except, *wolves*, of course. "I did."

"Yep," Harry says, relatively breezy in comparison to his fellow lieutenant. And he points out into the water, the mist and the grey, at where the wolves are swimming, swimming with fixed wild eyes that Penn, even Penn, can faintly make out. "You winged him, Ben, I can tell that much. See how he's favouring the right side? His rhythm and gait are all out: and yet he's still ahead of the pack, still the closest one behind us. Damn, but you have to half-admire the bastard. He's a tough son of an alpha bitch, you can't withhold the tribute. There must be blood in the water – he can't have healed in this time, not from a treated silver bullet. If only a nice friendly shark would come along and solve the whole problem for us. But I suppose that only happens when it's the last thing you want to happen. What do you think, Pennorth, do you reckon your master's the kind of monster who can bounce back from silver injury, or does he have a bit of weakness in him? Can we take him, if it turns out to be necessary?"

He isn't a monster, is what Penn wants, dearly, to snap back to that. *No more than you lot are yourselves, at any rate.* But he isn't looking to provoke them: his control of the situation is very tenuous, and he's very aware of the fact. He turns away to the horizon, and then to the island. And in his last glimpse of the cliffs, the beach – the wolves

– he sees the mass of them, barring the three already in the water, still teeming and writhing in an inky mass at the edge of the cliff. Perhaps waiting for the howled word from Ree, or just getting their courage up. Penn doesn't care. He's trying not to. It's not hard to turn away. In fact it's much easier.

"Shut up, Harry," Parrin says quietly, eyes down as he steers, hunkered as far down in the boat as he can go, much like the other two now. No doubt they'd as soon not be recognised by the wolves following, given their druthers. Though Parrin has now had the sense to don his balaclava again, maybe too late. There's a white strain at the hinge of his jaw, a clench. "That's my sister, second behind him in the water."

So, Penn thinks. Lettice here too, chasing him down. Well, well, there's a reversal of fortune all right. He turns away, and then they're around the furthest point and out of sight of the wolves. And Penn concentrates on the gun and his four companions, and on not caring about the wolf in the water behind him, or the other two swimming wolves, or the pack who'll surely plunge in *en masse* and bring up the rear. Why should he care? As long as they're fast enough, that's the thing, the only thing that matters.

Or there's the other thing. The thing of not caring that Ree's hurt, wounded, quite possibly seriously. Possibly seriously enough to be life-threatening. Penn doesn't know, how would he know? It's not like he's ever known a wolf shot with a real treated silver bullet. It's not exactly a common occurrence, not least because they're strictly illegal, and practically unobtainable even besides that. Penn doesn't care, though. And the not caring is taking up all of his energy and attention, with only a very little left over for keeping a weather eye on Parrin and co.

Those things *aren't* important. Penn does get a grip on himself, and perceive that even in the instant before they round the island, and get a first glimpse of the bay, the natural harbour where Parrin and his pals have arranged to meet up with their freedman contact, for a better boat and some supplies and a chance. A chance at not expiring completely in an attempt to cross the water into Canada. He reminds himself that – now – with the decisions he's made, including the ones that he's been all but forced into – this is the important thing. The only important thing – getting to the harbour, and meeting up with the contact and getting the boat.

Getting away, getting out, and getting to freedom. That's what counts. Not Ree, not a binding and a ceremony that clearly meant nothing, if this is what it comes to not a day later. Not Ree and Lettice, not his whole life and what he thought it might be, if he pushed and plotted and angled for long enough. (It feels as if his heart is weeping, and he's genuinely shocked at his own softness. If he could cane himself for it, if he had time or agility, then he would. This isn't how a slave survives, by allowing himself such dangerous indulgences. Penn's hard, has always been hard, has had to be hard as a stone, a pretty diamond. It's too late to change that now, to let the cliff-face crumble into soft damp chalk.)

It's what he remembers and reminds himself of, as they round the bulk of the island, head into the bay, Parrin gunning the engine to keep still ahead of the wolves at their backs. The island, the harbour, the boat are what matter. The wolves, whether at their backs or in the boat with them – with himself and Sam – they don't. Sam, who's gone quiet and sullen and worried, who isn't at all himself even going by the tiny blink of time that Penn has known him.

It's a hell of a problem, then, that as the harbour opens up to their view, it's empty, open wide. There's no sign of a boat, nor a helpful local contact. Only the rocks and the splashing grey waters, splashing up against the built-up supports and the wooden pier, where the boat that isn't there for them should be at anchor and moored to the rails.

Parrin swears, quite mild and quiet, still gentlemanly even under such duress. It's that that really makes Penn's heart sink. He's not missing anything, it's not a subtle detail that's escaped him. He hasn't misunderstood the arrangements. The contact simply hasn't turned up, and that leaves them about as exposed as a surly band of knaves, wolves and runaways can be. This little tub that they're steering to hell isn't going to get them over an ocean, and safely landed on a different continent. It'll hardly get them to shore here, even.

"Where the hell is the boat, then?" Gus demands. Which makes it official, now that he's gone to the trouble of stating something so obvious.

"Don't worry about it," Parrin says, tinkering with the controls, trying to squeeze an instant's greater speed out. "Just stay down, get out of my way and pray. Any gods you have lying about handy will do." His face is set, rather calm. However reluctantly, Penn has to rather admire how cool he is in the face of disaster.

"Don't worry about it?" Gus roars. It's very nearly an actual roar, and Penn can only pray that he retains control over the animal inside. He's certainly lost control as far as addressing a senior officer is concerned, or however the structure works in their informal little organisation. Pelted wolves are the last thing they need on board this tiny tub. It might result in having to break out his last bullets, and battle for control of an uncontrollable situation. It would be disaster. If this isn't disaster already, of course. It probably qualifies. "What do you mean, don't worry?"

Briefly, Parrin turns his face to the other wolf, and doesn't even look impatient, or anything but completely impassive. "I mean, don't worry about it, and shut your mouth. Because it's a bad development, and he'll either arrive shortly, or he won't. And that means that we have two useful choices: head out to sea in this tiny tub that we're currently sitting in, which I'd estimate has around a ninety percent chance of resulting in every one of us expiring of natural causes or natural disaster. Or alternatively, to get to shore as quick as may be, and scramble to either find my man and stick to the original plan, or to take cover in the hills of this little rock – what cover it affords, which isn't too generous – and escape as best we can, every man and every wolf for himself, devil take the hindmost. And I'm favouring the latter, because while we may all still wind up segmented into a few bloody pieces, it's at least possible that some of us might survive the next twenty-four hours. With our reputations intact, even, given a bit of lying our heads off and calling in favours. So – Augustus – I strongly recommend that you shut your bloody mouth, help where you can, and get out of the way where you can't. You comprehend, I'm sure?"

There is a third option, of course, or there was. These wolf rebels could take a flying leap off the boat and swim for their own lives, bet themselves and their prowess against a head start and a wounded, slowed-up alpha of the Hotstaats. They could, or they could have, but it's a little late now, fortunately. The island is so much closer, and he has the gun still trained upon them, besides. And they've lost a part of whatever head-start they had to begin with. Penn turns to regard the pursuing wolves in the water again, to confirm that they're making headway, slow but impressive, just the same as heading out from the mainland shore. (And how can Ree do it, with a wound that can actually burn and fester, that in a different spot might have ripped apart an organ, his brain, and killed him, is real and potentially mortal, and Penn–. And Penn, damn him, Penn thinks, bitter and wry, is a teenage wolf-girl with a fervent idiotic infatuation. Or he might as well be, the way he carries on, pining over the heroics of his lost love.

Lost, yes. He concentrates on that: that he's just a mislaid item of property to Ree, now, clearly. That he is on a mission to re-appropriate, with appropriate punishments witnessed and properly carried out by a formal and furious pack. They're all here, aren't they? He finds he's closed his eyes tight and lightless – very careless indeed, with surly wolves under his eye, but it was only a moment, and the terror of the situation commands all of their attention, very fortunately. A tear or two has not escaped the lids that cover them, no. He's not that weak. Not yet. Perish the damn thought. But as he opens his eyes, he does look for Ree, and all the rest. For safety's sake, to confirm the necessity of their current hashed-together plans, to assess all relevant information and modify if necessary. And also, yes, to get one last look at a Ree who has loved him.

If he's captured as a runaway, after all, he might see another face of Ree altogether, one he's never known before. He wants to remember this one, man or wolf, as long as may be possible.

They're still just far enough off – closing rapidly, cleaving with furiously pedalling limbs and speed through the grey waves and the grey rain – that Penn's eyes aren't equal to the job of discerning one wolf or another, only perhaps judging by muscle mass and shade the likelihood of one furry bright-eyed wave-swamped beast being one particular wolf. That one ahead, nearest, a great hulking beast but fast, is listing a little, asymmetrical and having to exert more force for the same forward progress as a result. Ree, then. But behind him, only two more are pursuing him, and pursuing Penn and the rest of them into the bargain. Behind the one with the list and sway, Penn struggles and squints his eyes, and tries to discern. Is that Lettice? Is it? He can't be sure. And the third, he cannot say at all.

Behind them, there's only heaving waves and the open sea, and nothing else, nothing. Well, no doubt the rest of the bastards are on their way and just rounding the island now: or else waiting for the appropriate instructed howl of permission. Penn turns away: from Ree, and all the rest. And he feels that he's turning his back on his past and his history and the documentation of his ownership. On his slave status and all of the love he has left in the world, every little iota of warm affection he can bank up and trust, on every slave friend and servant companion. On every wolf who's ever claimed a resented affection for him: Lettice and the Dam, and Gerald and Pinks, old Jay Parrin, and perhaps even sodding Benedict Parrin here. On Ree, most of all, of course. Ree full-grown, with a wolf that owns everything it sees, and a man he mistrusts, and misses horribly, right this minute. Child Ree, whose wolf was his playmate and the boy he'd have followed to the wildest ends of the earth, or at the least the outer limits of the Hotstaat estate.

And right now, on the shot, physically damaged, no-doubt enraged Ree, cutting a swathe of waves through the boiling water of the sea.

He hates that his eyes are dry, although it's a mercy. One ought to cry, at a moment like this one. Everything's so rotten and grey and spoilt forever that he can't. It's rotten leaves in autumn and sour compost that won't give life to anything. He wouldn't have the wherewithal and the interest in life to kill himself, even, now that any possibility of anything beautiful has been sucked out of his future. A slave should always be ready to die: at a master's hand, or by his own if life as a slave becomes beyond toleration. So said some old Roman philosopher, or so Pennorth seems to remember. And the wolves do love their Romans.

But Penn isn't going to be a slave any more, so it doesn't apply.

Sam is a very good thing, because with thoughts as dark as these, he just might find the impetus to pitch himself overboard and let the wolves savage him, right now. Except that Sam presses in close, his head right by Penn's, and whispers, "Five minutes, sir–." And he hesitates, but he's no usage to using Penn's given name, and Penn's used to a bit of respect from younger slaves in any case. With the duties he's had to perform, and everything he's seen in his time, he's earned it. "We'll be there, in less than five minutes. What – what the hell are we going to do?"

Penn gives him a bleak look: and a bleaker one, surveying the wolves. Parrin, the most seamanlike of them, basically doing the job of steering and powering, the other two miserably and disbelievingly huddled at the bow. They're close together and staring out, furtively and heads down, at their fellow wolves in relentless pursuit, following them in the name of the law of the land and the pack, and retrieval of property, and punishment of theft. That's what it is, abolitionism, ask any right-thinking wolf. The purest theft. No doubt it must be difficult to believe that they're in this position. Ignominious flight and the imminent possibility of capture and disgrace, and maybe worse than disgrace, has no doubt not formed part of their plans at any point. It must be splendid, to paint oneself as the liberating hero in one's own head, puffed up with ideals and magnanimity, and to foment all kinds of strife and rebellion with a few like-minded cronies, to seek to make the world into a better place. It's a bit less splendid, no doubt, when it all fails to come good, and you're left with a bill to pay that your wallet and the pack trust fund can't cover.

They look sick. Penn can't much care. And he doesn't have any cheerful answer for Sam. He keeps his voice low, though, but it's more to comfort Sam with the pretence of privacy, than that he fancies that if he's discreet enough they won't hear it. "Run with 'em, first," he says, sketching the faintest, most vestigial nod at Parrin, that the bastard's quite alert enough to pick up on. "Make sure they don't forget we still have the upper hand – after a fashion." And he lets the barrel of the gun twitch, little as he expects it to actually motivate those three, at this desperate juncture. It's only their insurance against being completely abandoned, really. He doesn't doubt that if they were on the mainland, then the wolves would be up and off in any case, devil take the hindmost and risking that it would be one of the others, not their own hide with an active silver bullet in it. But with a fast little boat in view – perhaps, if they can locate this errant freedman with anything like adequate speed – then that's of more advantage to them than trusting to their own strength and speed, supernatural as it is. The internal combustion engine generally has the edge, even if just slightly, sometimes.

And, provided that humans can keep up, then they may as well take the two slaves with them, as planned. Especially with the incentive of the four silver bullets that Penn still has remaining. They may be his only ace left, but he'll play them if he has to. "But if they can't find their pal, and they can't find the boat," he adds to Sam, still quiet and as soothing as he can make such brutal advice, "then we'll all just have to run. Every man, and wolf, for his own hide."

Oh, Sam's still young, though. Penn isn't sure just how young, but however old it is, it's still too young for this. His wide grey eyes pop and gleam with disbelief, and his too-thin frame is goose-pimpled even with the damp blankets clutched around him. Penn knows it was too harsh. "But me and you... Pennorth?" he says. It might as well be a plea, for all the shortage of actual words.

Oh, Penn's heart sinks. He knows it doesn't make sense, that as a matter purely of numbers, a strict calculation, they'd do better to split up. Maybe then at least one of them would have a chance to get away. (And, no doubt, to live a brutal, horrible and quite possibly short life, on the run, and eventually caught up with, no doubt. But still, to get away, for a bit.) He can't enforce it, though, can't do the sensible and sane thing. "Don't worry about it," he says, giving in, with a tight, forced smile. "If it comes to that, we'll stick together." And he's rewarded, because Sam's face lightens completely in a sick relief. Just as long as it *doesn't* come to that, Penn thinks, and refrains from actually saying. There's very little hope for them, if it does.

And they might as well not have been whispering at all, because Parrin isn't prepared to play along – unsurprisingly, really, and what difference does it make? "That's so sweet. But we have more pressing concerns, right now," he says, brusquely, looking Penn right in the eye. "Get ready to jump, get ready to run. Have you seen how close they are behind us?"

It's the truth. Penn grabs a look. Wet and large and untiring, unceasing, their pursuers are closer than Penn would have believed possible even a minute, a minute and a half ago. Well, to say that: it'd be a fair old distance to a human, and Penn still has to squint to see them. But they're not human. Damn good thing, then, how close the boat is, too, to the rickety little wooden jetty built on to the outcrop of rock and into the depth of the bay where a boat can lay anchor and wait. They don't really stand a chance – no observer would possibly give them good odds. But it's still worth running, at least. Or maybe it's just instinct.

And maybe they'd stand a better chance, maybe even odds, if some signal didn't pass between Parrin and his pals. They're wolves, blast them. They're so much better at that kind of thing than any human: perceiving practically inaudible communications, getting the message across via the least physical cue in the chase, so that you'd almost reckon them telepathic. He had the upper hand only a moment back – he should have the upper hand still, but it's too bloody quick. The boat's not docked, stable, tied up at the rails – it's not even within range for beginning any procedures for that. Not when they move as one, like a beautiful great orchestrated wave. He could describe it after, if there was anyone to ask, but it's too quick while it's actually happening. The elegantly shod feet – on half-naked man-wolves – up on the boat rails, the graceful stag-like leaps through the air that carry them further than any human leap could do, further than physics can explain.

Carry them onto the jetty, and it's not like they pause and turn and wave goodbye. They bloody ought to, their slave charges are owed some apology and explanation at the very minimum. But they hit rickety wooden planking, instead of the heaving, wave-like motion of the boat-deck, and they don't look back and they don't stop, not once. Their heels and their haunches working like engine parts, their nude backs glistening under raindrops and rippling under the beginnings of the change, they run.

Of course they're going to change on the run. Quicker, and it'll speed them up past all catching, by Penn and Sam or by what's chasing them. Penn yells, furious, incoherent, as a surprisingly efficient and tight-lipped, red-faced Sam ties up the boat at great speed. Penn lifts the gun, cocks it. And then he thinks they're already a bit far and moving, and he can't waste a bullet. And then they've got the boat close enough, tied up and stable, to leap off and run themselves. It's sweaty and wet with the rain, and Harry up ahead, in the lead, is already halfway wolf, kicking off human shoes and human tailoring tearing and ripping of its own accord off wolf haunches as he goes, up stony ridges. It's at a sudden sharp sideways bent. And that suggests to Penn that the wolves have a second potential meeting place arranged as a failsafe for disaster, and some idea of where to find their pal.

He's running himself now, following in clumsy slave's sandals, and Sam's struggling to keep up. They're into the brush and light woodland themselves, now, with a little cover from the pursuing wolves, and too much for the escaping ones. He sees that Gus is halfway to wolf too, and Parrin – the one who was so intent on saving him, absolutely dead set on it and look at him *now* – is just beginning the change, bringing up the rear. He was the last off the boat, but even then he'd spared no look or word for Penn. So much for his heroic schemes, his insistence on playing the white knight for poor beleaguered enslaved Pennorth. It all evaporates, when a question of self-interest and survival comes up, or something threatens his ability to carry on with his grand schemes of liberation for the great mass of slaves. A single one, a brace, they're quite dispensable it seems, if it means a utilitarian service to the greater good.

At least, Penn is pretty sure that that is how Parrin justifies his current betrayal to himself. There's always a justification, for everyone, no matter what. Parrin'll only be faster once changed, and even in these much less than ideal circumstances, Penn has to take what opportunity he has. Injury might persuade one of them to linger enough to take them along, still. He's a good shot, he's been trained. He prays, and tries for a moment's steadiness, pauses, shoots. Misses, tries again and swears, with the recoil still leaving his hand numb and vibrating, and lifts his hand again anyway.

Then he runs, and he keeps running, and only prays that poor Sam's keeping up. They're losing their quarry with every step, being left behind in these scrubby woods to be caught. He can't get a proper glimpse even of Parrin, now, and he can't waste another bullet. His sandals are ill-equipped for running, and his legs and chest hurt, he's too damn slow.

But he's been too much focused on what's before him, and too little on what's behind. How can he have forgotten that he's prey as well as hunter? When he feels the ground under the soles of his feet shake, he knows then in that instant. There isn't much else, barring an actual earthquake, that can make the soil and the stones of the earth tremble. And he hasn't time to turn, to lift a fist, to point the gun in the opposite direction, or any of those suicidally foolish things. Which is without doubt all to the good.

He's down before he can take another step, but not before he registers that the thunder of the footfalls behind him – in retroactive sensed memory – were oddly uneven, heavy and light, heavy and light, someone favouring one side over the other, someone with a paw or haunch wounded–. Of course it was, of course.

You'd think he was stupid, or something along those lines. He goes down as if a hod-carrier has dropped a hod full of bricks on his back, and in fact the cause is not so far different. Ree's built like a brick shit-house, after all, and probably the effect of him leaping and falling, hard, on Penn's shoulder-blades, is much the same. For a minute Penn can't breathe at all, and it's not even from panic but purely physical, crushed under the weight and mass of Renally Hotstaat.

The daylight is full and clear, now, even if the grim drizzle lends a grey silvery cast to the light. But now the edges of his vision are much greyer, darker, and he's possibly about to pass out. He wonders if Ree will do it like that, will just smother him, casually cut off his windpipe as a punishment for being a disgrace to the pack, a runaway slave who's been unfairly favoured and repaid that not with gratitude but with an insult to the whole pack. And an unacknowledged mate who's eminently discardable, unworthy, has proved himself a foolish choice and no loss. It's more dishonourable an end than being savaged to death, with blood spilt. Perhaps Ree will think that that's what he's merited.

He wonders it, with little coloured stars lighting up the edges of his vision that are probably something to do with absence of oxygen and reduced blood-flow, but it's not as if he's worrying. It's peaceful, really. He's extremely tired of struggling to put his life right and make it something valuable, and being frustrated at every turn, of cherishing every bitterness to keep the wounds open forever – for the sake of justice – and of not loving Ree.

He has mostly succeeded. What softness is there has been strictly regulated, limited, cramped up in tiny quarters with no room to breathe or grow, not watered nor fed even. But it gives him nothing to struggle for, and he doesn't. So that he's barely conscious, hardly moving when he becomes vaguely aware that in fact Ree isn't holding him down any more. That in fact, he has got up, and is crouched at Penn's side, tapping at his cheeks, shaking him a little, then dropping him suddenly and yelling off into the trees and the long trail they're on, after running wolves. "Let them go! For the sake of gods unknown, there are more important things! Come and help!"

And then he drops back to his knees by Penn's side. He's human again, of course, has shifted back again so quickly, quicker than any regular pack wolf and quicker than most alphas, even. (His lover has very remarkable abilities, Penn thinks, and is used to quashing the sudden surge of pride that it stimulates for him. No need for that, and certainly not now.) There's a wave of dizziness that has him closing his eyes fully for a second. But he's brought back to full awareness by Ree shaking him again urgently, and snapping, "Penn, come, wake up, I'll not have this. I won't tolerate you dying on me, not after the trouble and sweat we've had to find you, to catch up with you. And there's not a mark on you that could kill you, so stop fooling with me, Penn, when I tell you!" It's accompanied with another shake, and it's blunt and rude and rough. But Penn can hear the panicked note in his voice, and he knows that it's because the damn fool has never taken the trouble to learn basic resuscitation techniques, not even the simplest first aid or formalized safety precautions. (Just as wolves in general – brilliantly intellectually gifted as many of them are, excelling in all directions – disdain and hand off the sweat and labour of engineering, inventing, building, to humans. All the monkey-cleverness and trickery that humans excel in through necessity, and these being often enough the only fields open to them. It's an area of dominion due to the field left clear by wolves, in a world where so little dominion is open to humans.)

That he is in fact in some respects a babe in arms dependent upon slaves and servants for every other basic competency, and his life would grind to a halt and him be left helpless in the face of mass manumission or revolution, and a slaves' labour strike.

Not that that excuses him for not freeing every slave he holds the papers for, not in Penn's book. It's only an observation he's made many a time. Possibly he should play possum, should make as if unconscious or dead for the longest time possible, just in order to punish the bastard. But there are more important issues at stake, and he's come to himself, so he opens his eyes. It gets him a tight and bitter embrace that's distinctly uncomfortable, as Ree gasps out in a way that sounds distinctly more like a sob. (And for that matter, the embrace might as well be a punishing battering to the ribs, and Penn isn't sure it isn't intended as such.)

And he struggles, scrabbles to make himself uncooperative and spikey enough an armful that Ree lets him go, a few inches distance until Penn pushes him away fully. And looking around, Penn takes in a scene that disturbs. Sam's no more got away clean than he has himself: he's flat out amongst the brush and the ferns, a little way up into the thin growth of trees on the hill that the mud track he's laid on himself lies on. And he's flat out because a wolf – a wet, panting, irritable looking small grey wolf – has her paw in the small of his back, and is pressing down, hard.

He isn't arguing, and he isn't moving, because he's a smart kid. But even when she lets him go, he stays still – slumped, flat and defeated looking. It jabs a corkscrew of guilt in Penn's gut, but it's no use. Their bid for freedom is done: and Sam may pay the price worse than himself. This is the reason a slave should be careful about attachments, about doing more than acceding to demands, about getting too close. He's known the kid a few hours, that's all, and he's failed him already. It's a terrible thing to fail someone, with consequences like these. At least he doesn't leap up and try to run. That would constitute a death-wish.

The little wolf – in relative terms, since she could still flatten a human with one paw – pads over, to Penn where he lies, propping himself up warily on his elbows, Ree still crouched over him looking half-furious, half passionately relieved. (Naked as a jay, of course. It means surprisingly little. Modesty means nothing to a wolf, of course, not in circumstances like these.)

The wolf is Lettice. Even never having seen her wolf before, it's not hard to recognise her in it, in there. He can hardly miss it, as she pushes up against him, with a faint insistent little growl that demands his attention, banging the top of her head against his wet damp-tunic'ed shoulder. The expression of her displeasure is perfectly clear, and he doesn't even need for her to shift back to human, in order to translate it. To them, he's a runaway, an ungrateful lout of a slave who's rejected the honour of the hand-fasting, who has rejected them as mates and the sharing of intimacy, the gifts and privileges and status it would almost certainly lead to.

(And half of him feels the wound of it too, wants to say *but I didn't choose it, you don't understand, Benedict Parrin took me – and if you know your brother then you damn well ought to understand. I didn't choose it, I didn't want it, you're the ones who gave up on me and came after me with a punishing horde, I would never have gone of my own accord.* On the other hand, the other half of him would rather like to say *choke on it, stick your gifts and your honouring and your hand-fasting where you wouldn't expect it. Give me inalienable rights, the right to stand free and look you in the eye, or leave me to serve and stew and don't pretend I'm an equal.* But that's just Penn, and it's not as if he's changing his essential nature for anyone.)

He doesn't and can't say anything – because, for one, he fears his voice might break. And he's stupidly moved against his will, to be welcomed back, even in a way half-angry. And for two, he doesn't trust himself – not in the heat of this moment – not to say something bitterly impolitic that might ruin what looks like it could still be a retrievable situation – possibly, possibly. He's relying on nothing. There's only two wolves on the scene, true enough, right here and right now. But it's a situation that could change any minute, with them lying in wait down on the jetty, lurking in the water, swimming towards the island. He's not giving up his jealously-guarded suspicion and self-protection, not on so flimsy a basis.

He just keeps his head down – properly submissive and respectful – and lets Lettice buffet him without protest. It's without heat, a mild reproach, but to them he's earned it, and he knows quite well it's better to show himself contrite and accept their reproof. Ree has allowed him a measure of distance, but now his hands steal over Penn's hair, his torso and arse – half grooming, half checking again for injury or ailment. And he says, "Was it so bad, to be hand-fasted to me, Penn? To us? Bad enough that you'd run off and risk being caught by a sheriff's pack? Do you know all of the terrible things that could have happened, if you'd drawn attention to yourself, if you'd been tracked down by anyone other than us?"

His voice is angry, and it makes Penn twitch with a repressed flinch. (Because he won't flinch, he won't. Not unless it's by his own choice, to placate, to manipulate.) But Ree's hands are gentle, and Penn trusts them more, as indication of his mood, than anything he might say. He hesitates over what to respond, and it might be any one of a thousand inflammatory and unwise things. Foremost of all, that he knows very well about all of those terrible things. And that it's been the thought of them visited upon him by the Hotstaat pack, by Ree himself, that had him changing his mind about resisting Benedict Parrin's escape plans, and colluding in his own kidnap, his own perfunctory, brutal, forced escape. He doesn't think it would be anything like well received, now.

He pushes the head of Lettice's wolf away from him, where he lies cold, and wet and rather miserable (and secretly happy). Not that it does any good, and she takes not the least bit of notice, just evades his hands and continues to worry and grizzle at him, wilfully unhelpful, since that's her way. He considers actually trying a response, perhaps something conciliatory that will solidify the benign intent of these two wolves. Who – possibly – have come for him without the intent of punishment, but rather to rescue and to protect, or at least to restrain in an escape attempt with discretion and persuasion, instead of violence and chastisement. These two wolves, he thinks, except that that's wrong. Wrong because there were three wolves, in the water, pursuing, if he discounts the rest of the pack left slavering and palpitating on the edge of that miniature cliff. Obediently and resentfully palpitating, perhaps, if they've been left behind at Ree's instruction, an order to hold back, while he retrieves his stolen property and keeps things dark that are better left dark.

Or that may be how it went. For now, Penn can only speculate. But certainly, three wolves, not two, followed them into the water, and yet there's only two fully accounted for, now beside him. Also there are three scurvy abolitionist wolves currently missing from the ledger, and really, you'd think he'd be quicker at adding up this interesting list of missing persons and coming to a conclusion. But it's only when there's the first crash of thunder in the ferns and the undergrowth of the copses surrounding, that he realises. The third wolf went off in pursuit of Parrin and co. – and here it is, back on the scene.

Faster than he can think it, it bounds out from behind deep foliage, lithe and smoothly dark grey. Not a hulking great brute of a creature like Ree, but bigger than delicate, elegant Lettice. And he's the only one who jumps and trembles a bit, as it regains perfect balance and poise on the level ground, and prowls up close to them. To them, but mostly to him: and it slinks forward, lets its snout quiver around his jaw, his collarbone, his nape, mouth hanging open and one delicate trail of saliva hanging down. It hits his wet naked knee where it pokes out of his tunic, where he's hunched up and surrounded by wolves. Its breath feels like there's a furnace down deep in its chest.

There's no sign of Parrin, or his crew, that's what Penn mostly notices. Well, apart from the fact that he's surrounded by wolves.

"Well, Mother?" Ree asks softly. But his voice is quite matter of fact: a general, waiting on a report back by an underling.

The new wolf on the scene steps back, and shifts. Not quite at the speed that Ree makes nothing of, but fast enough for Penn's head to split, to feel sick. He knows what it costs most wolves, that type of speed. He's an old hand at this game, and he can even hear faintly the grind and gravelly re-shaping of bone and sinew.

But the great grey bitch makes no sign of discomfort, only forces herself through it, and in under a minute she's back in human form. Naked, mature, rather magnificent too, with her rain-speckled thighs standing sturdy as she straightens to stand upright. Of course, it's the Dam: and she gives Penn exactly the same unimpressed, faintly savage look as if she was wearing rose-coloured silk and a lorgnette, at a dinner-dance where he'd upended the soup on a local dignitary's lap. "Pennorth," she says coolly, by way of greeting. "Never anything but trouble. What a fool my son is on the subject."

And Penn – beyond a quick upward flash of the eyes, to take in her magnificence and her disdain – drops his head that little bit further. He knows better than to expect anything other than this from her, after all. Except at the most startling moments, when it's the most likely to surprise him when he's off-guard. It's not the most pressing question or the foremost priority in his mind right at this moment, after all.

"And the wolves who were with this pair, ma'am?" Ree asks. He's still crouched on the ground beside Penn, still has a heavy arm across his shoulders, holding him in place where he's hunched up with his arms around his knobbly knees, not adequately covered by a dirty damp tunic. (Never his best feature, and for all Ree's frequent observations on how beautifully he's grown up, Penn sometimes thinks that it's his flaws and imperfections that Ree finds the most endearing. It always seems to be some display of his carefully hidden weaknesses – his knees, his temper, his absence of ability to hide his own vanity, his duckling's lack of grace when challenged with a fencing feint or trying to follow a partner in a dance – that brings out the most intense and tender display of feeling from Ree. As if it takes them back to days when Penn was a tubby follower and adorer, and

Ree was his protector, exasperated and tender, reaching for maturity and leadership qualities.

The Dam smiles back at her son, not fazed one bit by their shared state of undress any more than she could have been back in the days when her lightly fallen dugs gave him suck. She replies, "You are my alpha, Renally. Now," she adds, with light emphasis. "And as you instructed, I gave them chase. Until, at your howl, I returned. I can tell you that they double-backed as I gave chase, and that two have split off and one is closer than the others. But at your command, I returned, and here I am – Alpha Hotstaat," she adds gracefully, with a slight inclination of the head. There's no resentment in it: the Dam gave her son the pack and the status of Alpha to it, after all. Only the slightest reminder that it was a gift, and that the Dam used to be Alpha to the Hotstaat pack, and might still be, were it not for certain promises and undertakings offered her by her son, in exchange for the succession. "And I can tell you that there's something familiar about their trail and their stink," she adds, the faint smile sliding off her face and being replaced by a fierce expression. "But it's so covered over with that bloody treated-silver stink that I couldn't make it out. My love," she adds, with a slightly softer tone in her voice to her eldest child and her only son, than any she's used thus far, "how is your leg?"

And damn it, it's only now that Penn remembers – though he thinks he might be excused, what with everything he's dealt with in the last twenty-four hours, and even going back beyond that, well beyond that – that Ree's injured. And not just injured, the kind of inches-deep gouged rip that a werewolf would normally walk away from and be healed of in hours. But properly wounded, by the only means known – or known to Penn, at least – to mortally wound or at least seriously injure a wolf.

It must make him insane, addle his wits for a minute. How else? That's how he accounts for it, for dragging Ree's arm from around his shoulders, and gripping his hand tight enough that if Ree was human he'd cry out from the startling pressure, the possible lacerations. Not just that, but he's up on his knees and shuffling forward to lean over Ree's legs, to examine every inch of them and search out the wound, the bullet. Numerous deities alone know what his intent is, for although he's well-trained in many aspects of first-aid and emergency treatment himself, he's far from being any kind of true sawbones, and certainly it's difficult even for a freedman to gain admission to a real medical school. (In fact he knows full well his intent, or at least the first wave of instinct and fury. He's searching for the wound, so that he can cut out the bullet and suck out the poison and then perhaps shove the bullet up Benedict Parrin's arse, and that, that is how temperate and indifferent and detached he is, in relation to Ree, really and deep, deep down.)

He still holds Ree's hand, though, as he despairingly thinks it, and it might be a lot more accurate to express it as Ree having *his* hand, now. He holds it tight enough to mark it and to cut the circulation, even as Penn finds the bloody gash, high up on his far thigh, and presses forward to examine it. "It's going to be all right, Penn," he says softly. But Penn's not an idiot. He knows quite well that there's as much triumph as comfort for Penn in his voice – triumph that Penn cares in the first place, has given himself away so much. "Lettice got it out with her little claws," he adds. And the affection in his voice – for Lettice Parrin – would be enough to make Penn spit, if he had the attention to spare. "And then the Dam sucked it clean. Those abolitionist bastards you ran off with did it in the hills on the Pennine Way. We were getting a bit too close for their comfort, and one of them got a lucky shot in from up on the moors. Have to admit the bastard could shoot, even though his other tries went wide. I suppose I have to admit moving targets must have made it a challenge."

"Such drama," the Dam herself says with some disdain, her eyes on Penn. But he can feel the curiosity and the intrigue in them.

She's always thought him a leech, a bad influence, a seductive chancer who's led her only son astray and used his old affections against him. (At the same time as thinking him a little fool whose hero-worship elicited Ree's affection in the first place, against his better judgement. But it's possible to hold contrary opinions at the same time, especially for a wolf.)

Lettice, the only wolf present pelted and clawed still, leans in against Ree's legs on the far side, perhaps not quite careful enough not to press against the wound a little. Ree sucks in a sharp little breath, because even wolves feel pain. "It's active silver – the kind that can hurt you," Penn says, staring down at the ugly torn bloody mess of thigh muscle, and his heart's rhythm is odd, is following some dancehall jazz beat that isn't regular at all.

"Don't worry, baby," Ree says. There's a big hand weaving gently through his hair, and his smile is so pleased. Penn is utterly given away, has given himself away, more thoroughly than ownership papers ever could. "I won't heal like I would from a regular wound – nothing like as fast – and there'll be a scar. Which will be interesting for you. But I will heal, and that's the main thing. They didn't manage to get a headshot, or any vital organs, which is what they would have needed to snuff me out. Not such good shots after all, eh, your friends?"

"They're not my friends," Penn says, quietly. Lettice is very quiet, pressed up against Ree's side with her silvery eyes looking up at him rather devotedly. The effect of the hand-fasting, he supposes. For himself, he didn't need it. He's been concentrating rather more on *not* gazing up at Ree with that exact shade of devotion and longing, these past many months. Bad enough that he was the one going chasing around and after him back when they were kids, apparently.

He's a little troubled by Lettice, so present and attentive. It's not going to be pleasant news for her, about her brother and his illegal rebellion-fomenting ways. Not exactly a surprise, perhaps: he doesn't make as much of a secret as he should of his sympathies, and she's his sister, after all. He probably troubles less with discretion in her company than with anyone. And they're both Parrins, after all. Unwise political sympathies, rebellion and seditious opinions are largely meat and drink to them, in a dabbling, boho style. Still, it's a long way from having fashionably shocking opinions, to actually doing something about them, and it's not the kind of news she's liable to relish. Still less getting it in front of an audience, and even an audience of her hand-fasted betrothed, and his dam. It's not as if Ree has ever favoured Parrin much, or at all. It's not as if the Dam cares much for Lettice, as a mate for Ree, in the first place.

Lettice Parrin is, after some secretive fashion, his mate – Penn's. Penn supposes that means something – to wolves. More than that, she's been – in some ways, and largely unasked – a friend to him, off and on. As far as wolves understand such things, in any case. Certainly she's been an ally, and Penn counts that as sufficient of a mark in her favour.

He shivers in the dank cold. The heat of Ree's body up against him helps, but only so much. And out of the corner of his eye he sees Sam stir, from where he still lies on wet grass and squashed ferns, and gives him a quelling look. For him to run, now, would be a very bad thing indeed. "They took me," Penn says, and he finds that however true it is, somehow he can't lift his eyes and look Ree in the eye to say it, to mark it as true with one moment of communion. Ree would understand, wouldn't take it as a challenge. But Penn has wanted to be free for so long, has wanted to escape. It's true, but it doesn't feel that way. "I didn't run with them. They kidnapped me." And now he manages it, looks up and glares at Ree, where he's wet with the rain and messy-haired and beautiful, even with his thigh a bloody mess, and bruised and scratched and sweaty from running and swimming and never stopping, never, not even for a bullet, not when he's coming to get Penn back.

It's not as if he expects to be believed, really. Isn't it every runaway slave's tale, once caught? 'I didn't want to go, they were illegal slavers, they were going to re-sell me, it's the truth'? If anything, it's a challenge to Ree, to accept him on his own terms and at his own word, or to have done with it and drop this pretence of being lovers, meant for each other, devoted since they were little 'uns with no real understanding of what *wolf* and *slave* meant in their lives.

It doesn't work out too well, though, his challenge, because Ree isn't even looking at him. He's a damn sight too busy with a challenge of his own. He's staring up at his mother, with a look on his face that Penn would never direct at a formerly alpha wolf, not to a wolf who was his mother, not even if he was a wolf himself. (Not even if he was an alpha wolf, to be frank.) And he'd have cheerfully bet ten shillings, in every second leading up to this one, that Ree would never look that way at the Dam, either. They may have had their disagreements and perhaps even bad feeling – Penn's had the distinct impression of it, at points, especially regarding the whole 'getting mated and producing a few kits' issue – but still, Ree has never referred to his mother, in Penn's hearing, with anything but a very great respect.

(Well, except when he refers to the day that he and Penn were parted, back in childhood. When she'd plucked Penn out of his own mother's arms, the better to keep him out of Ree's reach, and had a furiously wailing Ree dragged off to the nursery to keep him out of the way, while Penn and his mother were removed from the estate forever. Well, forever up until the present day, at least. In reference to that incident, Ree has referred to his esteemed dam as 'that old bitch' in Penn's hearing, at least once. But except for that, yes, the greatest esteem and respect.)

Now, though, he's staring at her with a defiance that... isn't really necessary. Not between an alpha, and a wolf of technically lesser status. Even a former pack Alpha, a very strong and powerful former pack Alpha, who is the other wolf's dam. "You see?" he says now, and his tone is a bit less than respectful. Quite a distinct bit less. "I told you. Didn't I tell you? I told you he wouldn't just run off in the middle of the night, not with abolitionists, not with anyone who came by and strung him some tale of promised lands and liberty who'd just end up selling him on illegally or, in the best case possible, dumping him in one of the human lands like a parcel or a bag of trash. Because he's too smart. Because he wants more than that. Because he needs what I can give him." Ree's voice is getting thicker, more wetly undisciplined and incoherent. It's neither angry nor pleading, but some combination of both. "Because he might hate us – he might hate me. But he has a loyalty to us, too. He was ours first, and he remembers that, and he'll always remember that. He belongs to us, and we belong to him, and nowhere else is ever going to be home for him." He's flushed as he finishes what he has to say, and Penn thinks there's a little bit of angry triumph in it. As if he thinks his logic and reasoning are inescapable, irrefutable. And although it would be an indulgence, unwise, and an admission that he's not about to make, Penn rather wants to press in close to that stubbled, dazzlingly sculpted cheek and kiss it. For Ree being such an idiot, mostly.

"Well, I'm glad you've convinced yourself so thoroughly, my love," his dam replies, looking – with rain running down her still rather-lovely breasts and hips, a faint blue chill even on her milky-marble wolf-human skin – magnificent, and violently bored. "And the rest of us have finally established that there's officially no limit to the amount of fool this boy can make of you." She doesn't vouchsafe Penn a glance, not a single one. He's quite used to that, though.

He doesn't give a damn, what's more, not one. Ree believes him – or wants to believe him – which is about ninety percent of what really counts in this situation. And Lettice, too – who rolls her lupine head over Ree's knees, to brush her snout up against Penn, his thighs, his own knees blue and wet and chilled. She whines a little, and rolls her eyes up soulfully at him, like at least a second person here who is glad to see him, who wanted to believe for the best in him, who cares where he is and what he does and will have arms open to welcome him, taking him to a place called home. (And by the devil, he must get this folly reined in. All very well as a tool, to pull closer the ones who can advantage him. But a salesman who begins to fall for his own spiel is liable to wind up very greatly in debt, more than his pockets can afford. The Dam might malign him, disparage him, do him wrong. But the thing is, if Penn had any sense at all, then she ought to be right.)

"How did you find me?" he asks, though. Because it seems that his folly is unceasing, and he has no control at all over his damn fool mouth. If he wants to know something, then he doesn't care how much it gives away everything that he thinks and feels. (There's also his scholarly curiosity to take into account. It's a damn good, reasonable question. A wolf – a werewolf – might have extraordinary tracking powers, and a whole pack still more so, to a supernatural degree. But even so, there's a reasonable limit. And following an internal combustion engine powered vehicle across hundreds of miles of country, on stone and mud tracks and cobbles and tarmac'd roads, over water more than once, and with the lead wolf lamed and halted by a treated silver bullet for at least part of the time... Well, there is a limit, and that surpasses it by a mile and more. It's a very small wonder that Parrin and his company were poorly prepared for such an eventuality, little as it excuses them being caught hopping, in Penn's opinion. A good general should be prepared for the unlikely as well as the obvious, he'd say.) "There was no way to find me," he adds, breathless, wide-eyed. "We had a head-start – they had a head-start," he corrects himself at speed. "We were too far gone, too far..." And he stops talking. Because with the best will in the world, he realises that he's sounding less and less trustworthy as he continues, putting his foot in it like it's his primary objective in view. However much

Ree must want to give him the benefit of the doubt – and it's surely a significant, considerable amount – there's still a limit to that, too.

Ree's smile is limitless and lovely, as he gazes at Penn, his hand resting lightly on Lettice's head as he speaks. You might think he'd never heard a word of what his mother had to say, as she stands with her arms folded and her lip curled up like a sceptical headmistress with a tardy pupil. "Darling," he says, soft as butter, like a warm wrap, a blanket. And Penn only wishes he could fold himself up in that warmth. (Especially right now. Or a towel. A fur rug would also be useful.) "Did you not feel it? After the ceremony? No... I suppose you wouldn't. That's a little bit sad, my love." He reaches to push the strands of wet hair out of Penn's eyes, that are a lot closer to ginger than they'd normally be, dry. He shivers with what a sight he must look, and how strong Ree's devotion must be to withstand it.

He doesn't understand a word, though. Which is fair enough, because it makes no sense. Evidently his uncomprehending-mutt expression must be fairly amusing, however, because the Dam cracks out a sharp cynical laugh, her eyes bright and fierce on him now. Oh, *now* he's worth a look.

"Oh, isn't it?" she agrees. It's mock-agreement, though, Penn is pretty sure. "Now that you've hand-fasted yourself – bound yourself – to a slave, isn't it sad that he's not wolf enough to feel the bond? Oh, not only enough that I let him choose your bride and he has to wilfully, obstinately choose the only one I indicated clearly was off-limits and out of bounds. But then to go and make it a threesome, to conduct a ceremony and pull him into the mate bond along with you! Of course," she adds coldly, giving Penn a look up and down that could excoriate the flesh right off his bones, "the bond probably wouldn't have taken at all, not without him being somewhere there in the mixture. And better if it hadn't, if you ask me. Every other pack's alpha is content enough with a lukewarm formal marriage like any human. They have some tricks and ways that are useful and canny: why else would we have parroted and mimicked them in so many ways? But no, you have to go and track down a human childhood sweetheart, and half-wed him in secret, and now you're stuck with him and with her for life. For life!"

To be fair, she looks more exasperated than furious. "I'd damn well better get some grand-kits out of this," she adds, snappy. She says it much as if she's already addressing children, anyway.

All of what she says seems to skirt around making some kind of sense, to Penn. And yet he can't quite get there with it. He's almost too tired to actually ask – and he'd be pretty damned wary about asking the Dam anything, in any case, even not in her present mood and under present circumstances. But the question asks itself, because something in his brain that won't ever let him rest and shut up and do the wiser thing, just needs to know. "I don't understand," he says, softly, but to Ree, not to the Dam. Not even Penn is that foolhardy, given her present expression. "What does it mean?" (His wording is careful, because 'what does *she* mean' seems less than diplomatic.)

Chapter 7

Ree turns eyes on him that are – amused, yes, very distinctly amused. But that's all right, because Penn is used to being a source of entertainment, for Ree. It started long ago, after all. "Darling," he sighs, and Penn can feel it, the warm breath on his face. "You don't feel it. But we do, eh, Letty?" he enquires, patting at the head of the wolfish hound with her head, still pelted, still lupine, in his naked lap. She whines a bit, eyes large and bright and winsomely liquid, and it seems mild enough to be intended as confirmation. "Not straight off. Perhaps it takes enough distance established, to start up. But before the morning, anyhow, before the daylight. I woke first, and you weren't there. Letty here was out cold," he adds, and he strokes her head. Her large, slavery jaws snuffle and sigh against his thigh, a pretty and diminutive wolf, but only by comparison. A huge and terrifying predator, compared to any other creature in the forest. "And," Ree continues softly – with the Dam tutting and derisive, not five feet away – "I felt it hit me then. Like something in me was manacled and chained, and something on the other end of that chain was pulling. Pulling and pulling, and I'd slid out of bed and crawled along the floor – it didn't exactly hurt, not physically, but it was so painful even so, it didn't even occur to me to try to stand up – and I could hardly see with it. My eyes were watering and my muscles were cramping and darling, you've no idea – you should have, but you clearly don't – and then I knocked over a lamp and it woke up Letty, here."

Letty looks up, and snuffles at Ree's fingers when he trails them over her snout. She's still wolf, with no sign of any inclination to shift to human. But she's not wounded anywhere, and for all it's warmer that way, no doubt – lucky wolves – Penn does wonder faintly at it. On the other hand, perhaps she only prefers to stay tongue-bound and silently civil in the face of her putative mother-in-law, her future pack dam. That, Penn can well understand. Even the angle of her head and the look in her eyes seems assent, though, or Ree takes it as such. He looks back at Penn, eyes glinting, fierce, passionate.

"It was the bond, you bloody fool. Of course it was, what did you think? We didn't need tracks, or scent, or so much as a signpost to follow. Miles, and water, and rain and new-fangled engines, none of it made the least blind iota of difference. How should it? The hand-fasting bond took, and we didn't need to choose direction or wonder or so much as try to track you. I helped Letty, we helped each other understand it, and then we ran out into the night and ran and ran, howling for the pack across country, to force them to join us. And the pack heard us howling across country, howling for you, to you, and they ran miles and miles across country to join us and–. And, we followed you, and found you. I knew you'd not run away of your own accord, I knew someone had taken you, Penn, my Penn–." Oh, he's exultant, as his hand closes behind Penn's head, and he presses a kiss to Penn's cheek, irrepressible even in the presence of his mother.

(Who seemingly knows about the hand-fasting, about the three of them coming together for the ceremony. Damn Ree for a transparent fool, Penn thinks, despairing. Has he no discretion at all?) "I don't understand, at all," he says, exhausted and perhaps a bit irritable. Unwisely irritable, with wolves, but then this has gone a long way beyond wise and circumspect etiquette. "I don't feel anything, I don't, I didn't. There was nothing. How can there be a bond, and I feel nothing?"

"Because you're not a wolf, little dummy," the Dam says – with such distance and hauteur, it near freezes Penn where he sits, the chill of it. "Honestly, my son – the times you've assured me of his intellect, as justification for your raving infatuation. I won't dispute that when it comes to book-learning he's clever enough – but for even the most basic wit and common sense he seems halfway to a halfwit, at times. It's probably a good thing that you never did give him the bite – a lunatic wolf is really the last thing we'd want in the pack."

Ree closes his eyes. And looks slightly away, in the opposite direction, before answering. Penn can see how his jaw flexes, how he counts before replying. But all that he says is, "Thank you, Mother." Then he squeezes Penn's hand, and grins at him, rain running down his nose, his chin. "But she's right. Letty, poor girl, and I, we were knocked sideways by it. We can feel it, leading to you, binding us to you, as well as to each other. And if you were wolf, then you could feel it too, my love."

Oh. Penn can see the hesitation, the thoughts and the suggestion hanging at the very forefront of Ree's brain, the way it's just waiting to leap into life in the air and be spoken. He feels afraid, at the thought of letting those words be spoken. (He feels afraid that exhaustion might overtake him, and relief, at not being shut out and punished and disbelieved. Perhaps he's afraid that he might give in: and he can't have that. Not after he's held out and resisted the very idea for so long.) "I'm cold," he says. And if it's a little bit petulant, then he's surely earned it, after everything. After everything. "And tired, and it's raining. And I'm not a wolf," he adds, but it's different, coming from his own lips. He knows it's clear what he means: that he doesn't have wolf resistance, or stamina or strength – or resistance to bacteria and viruses and infection, for that matter. "I'll be dead of influenza or pneumonia in a couple of days," he adds, pettish, and aware of it. "I hope you greatly enjoy two-thirds of a bond with Miss Lettice, here. I will watch and look down on you from on high in a slave's heaven, where sofas beckon eternally and no bells ring to demand service, and my poor frozen feet can–."

There's a tight, repressed snort of a laugh, somewhere behind him. But it can't be Ree, because Ree is busy trying to pick Penn up – to carry him away – and Penn is busy too, not letting him. "I can perfectly well stand," he hisses, because he has his pride, still. Doesn't he? At least, he has some scraps of it. "And I can perfectly well walk, too. What about Sam? What are you going to do about him?" he asks. He looks over at the other slave-boy, and the wolves look, too, scrutinizing the poor human with rather less interest than they've given to their own home-grown runaway. "If you're taking me back – back home," he says, cautiously, because what else is he going to call it, now? "It's not the same, for Sam," he finishes, bleakly. And he finishes picking himself up, painfully and feeling the numbness of his extremities, how deficient and dank his outerwear is. "He was voluntary – he had something to run away from. You can't just take him back." And his voice is worn and unsteady on the last words. Because what say does he have, even now? What weight, what influence really? It makes him feel sick with guilt, as Sam gets up on his own two feet at the beckoning of Dam Charity, and looks afraid and guilty and bloody cold and uncomfortable. The both of them probably will be dead of exposure or a virus within the week, at this rate. It's probably a futile affair to bother to feel guilt, even, considering that. But he still feels lousy, can almost feel Sam's fear as well as his own guilt. If he'd done a better job at chasing after Parrin and his cronies, if they'd caught up and evaded capture, then... He doesn't know. Even if they'd made it all the way to the liberty territory, it would still have been a brutal life out there. And even with Parrin's aid, they might still have been caught. Almost certainly would, in truth.

He feels terrible anyway.

Ree's close to Sam, now, and puts a hand out to the lad's chin, turns his face about this way and that. It's gentle: but it's still being manipulated by an alpha wolf, and he can only imagine how Sam feels about it. His eyes are downcast, and Penn almost doesn't need to be a wolf, to smell his fear. But he knows, too, that a close examination shows the old bruises, marks and scars that are plentiful on Sam's poor body. And maybe it's the deciding factor, when Ree says – short, and without expression - "What pack are you from, my lad?"

And Sam answers, eyes still dancing everywhere but not on Ree's face, "The Holmford pack, sir. In Nottinghamshire."

Ree nods, and the thin set of his mouth is very resolved. "Well, my, my. Is that so? Don't worry, lad. We'll have intensive discussion with your pack, before handing you over. And before negotiations are done, we'll make them an offer they'd do well to accept for you. I think you may rely upon it that they will accept. I have some influence in that area, geographically: and there are certain territory disputes my word would hold sway in, that it would be inconvenient for them to lose. You'll be better off with us."

Actually it makes Penn a little sick, to see the relief stand out clear on Sam's face, the lighting up of it as he risks a quick glance up at a strange alpha with a cautious little twinge of a smile, as he nods. No-one should look that happy, that relieved, to be going from one slavery, one owner to another. No man, human or wolf, should be afforded, and credit themselves, with that little dignity. (No woman, either, for that matter, Penn thinks. And he doesn't think of his mother, so happy and proud to be singled out for attention, to be adored by a wolf. He doesn't.)

Not that he can't understand it, in a way. He knows that the Hotstaat clan has a 'good' reputation amongst slaves and servants. As these things go, which in Penn's book, doesn't count for much. But still, it has to be accounted as counting for something, after all, or such pack reputations would be useless on the grapevine, and no-one would bother to whisper in hushed tones in the slaves' halls that *so-and-so has been bought by such-and-such a clan, and who would have thought such a stroke of bad luck would befall him when he thought himself safely ensconced with the so-and-sos, quite indispensable until the elder son married and had no further use for him?*

There's a kernel of truth in every pack reputation. It's accreted by word-of-mouth recollection of one incident after another after another, stretching back over years and decades. And it gradually becomes cast in one direction or another, this light or that, to settle a pack in the unofficial annals of the slave community as 'good' or 'bad' to belong to. (With a few extra qualifiers and modifications, qualities relevant or not depending on what interests and ambitions a slave may have. For example, a pack might be accounted cultured, artistic, and be much desired as a settled final resting place by a slave with such interests. Or they might be accounted political, oddly religiose, a little fanatical about some things, bookish, obsessive, eccentric and frankly bad hats who might get a good slave into trouble purely by association. Like the Parrins.)

Slaves – as a whole, and generation upon generation – have long memories. They know and remember more than wolves might think. Wolves would be surprised, if they knew how much.

Penn knows quite well that the Hotstaats are a 'good' clan to belong to, after all. He's known it since before he was bought for the second time by them, or by Ree's agent, Parribee Parribee. It offered him little comfort, since he knows how little it means for a particular slave at a particular time. Historically, a pack might be accounted lenient and fair with its slaves. Does this mean that a particular slave, during the reign of a particular alpha, might not have the living daylights beaten out of him on a regular basis? It doesn't, no. Does it mean that a slave belonging to a pack accounted to feed and clothe and shoe its slaves well might not go cold or hungry or dry, if he crosses the wrong master or even a subservient wolf? Well. Penn knows his opinion.

The Hotstaats are... mild, in their treatment of their possessions. That doesn't mean that Penn has ever felt comfortably sure that the next week wouldn't bring a beating, or being sold off, or public reprimand. It doesn't make his time, or his life, or his body any more his own. And no, it will never reconcile him to being owned. (Never.)

But Sam is relieved – looks happier, in fact, than when he thought himself bound for snowy wastes and a very chilly freedom. Which no doubt was better than constant beatings and the fear of what the future might bring, in a pack where he was so much walking meat and a dispensable asset. It's evidently not better, at all, than a warm bed and a welcome in a pack reckoned relatively benign and well-disposed to human property. His thanks are almost inaudible, but Penn can hear how heartfelt they are, in every word. He tries to shut his ears, because rage is going to rile up every instinct of the wolves about him, and that doesn't serve his purpose.

Ree's a little dismissive, probably embarrassed by the effusiveness. And the Dam is still less impressed by effusion. She clicks her tongue in obtrusive impatience, and Ree – a good son – looks around at Penn, and smiles. Soft fool, Penn thinks, as he smiles back. In truth it's done him good to have the reminder of human servility, of wolf patronage, casual kindness, still more offhand cruelty. It's good to have his life and his ambitions back on track, to be returned to the life he's intended, planned and worked for. Liberty is a wonderful thing: at the right time, and to serve his own purpose, not a condescending gift bestowed from on high by a lordly master. But he's been allowing his relief at not being abruptly swept away to a snowy and despairing outpost like the wildest spot of Alaska, to soften him. Penn's not made to be soft. Now he feels cleansed and refreshed, his normal bile and cynicism restored. Ree is all very well, and very useful: as a tool. He serves his purpose in Penn's plans. And Penn is tired of his own lies and fudging of the truth, regarding his feelings. He has a certain affection for the bastard, and he won't embarrass his own wincing reflection in the mirror, in future, trying to deny it. But that affection's a tool to be used, too. It isn't that he hasn't realised this, before now.

But now, he must *remember* it.

So he thinks pretty thoughts, recites odd bits of poetry in his head, and controls his heartbeat, his limbs, his breathing, and his expression. When Ree smiles at him he gives him a pretty smile back, and smooths his hands through his hair, only wishing for a little eyeliner and a comb to present a better picture. But it's good enough. It doesn't take a lot, for Ree. And that's a good thing, that his almost worn-out charms are still irresistible to the important audience.

"Come, we've done enough dilly-dallying about and procrastinating," Ree says, decisive, though the authority's a bit undercut by the fact that he's still smiling into Penn's eyes. "Let's get you down to the jetty and that rickety little soup-bowl of a boat. Damned considerate kidnappers, then: at least they left us the means to get the both of you back to the mainland, without having to carry you on our backs. Not that I couldn't still manage it: but it'd be bloody cold and uncomfortable for the pair of you, and I'm sure you've had enough of that already."

And although he naturally falls into step with the Dam, the dominant wolves present taking the forefront and leading the way down the winding barely-trodden path to the jetty, Penn knows quite well that Ree is deeply conscious of his presence, almost twitching around to take a look or two behind himself and at Penn, as Penn follows on with obedient grace, meek and seemly as a well-trained pet, obedient and adoring. Of course.

(And he shoots a careful look at Sam, a quarter step behind him as is only seemly, what with him being only the – putative – latest addition to the slave staff of the Hotstaat household. Because Sam has demonstrated himself able and bright enough. And certainly, so far since their recapture – or retrieval, or rescue, depending on how you look at it – he's demonstrated also that he has an excellent grasp of one of the most important tenets of slavehood. That being, to never once volunteer information unasked. Not unless you're damn sure that you'll be called to account for having withheld it later, and that the consequences of not volunteering would be worse than offering the information freely.

Sam could offer all kinds of exciting and unwise tidbits here, especially regarding the identity of their liberators, or their captors depending on your perspective. And if he does, then that in turn would raise a good many questions in Hotstaat minds. Foremost amongst them, the issue of why he hasn't immediately brought up an extremely pertinent fact, that fact being that Benedict Parrin is the ringleader of the little group of insurrectionists who've tried to rob the Hotstaat estate of a useful pair of human hands.

Penn doesn't feel guilty, any more than he would if he'd run for the border and run for real. But he flinches from revealing Parrin's role. He remembers old Jay Parrin, and that he owes him a little loyalty, especially considering that he perhaps didn't appreciate just how much old Parrin appreciated him in turn. Even an intent at manumission foiled by death, is still more than he's ever got from any other owner. From any other owner, including Renally Hotstaat.

He thinks of Lettice, too. She's an odd duck, and a loose cannon, and a naughty girl too. But she's his mate, and she stands in his corner. And besides, damn hand-fastings, mates, and even friends. A slave can't afford to alienate an ally. He will wait, he resolves, until a private moment, to share a bit of private information with Miss Lettice, about her brother. Certainly he owes her that much: and especially if Parrin hasn't the sense to get out of England and head for states where werewolf jurisdiction is moot, and wolf connections and diplomatic relations are not influential. Considering how much sense Parrin usually displays, it's unlikely in the highest degree that Penn won't be seeing him again before long, just as blithe and confident as previously. The presence of at least two individuals – himself and Sam – even barring his own confederates, who can confidently identify him as one of the cohort of slave-liberators – or kidnappers – responsible for this particular little adventure, isn't liable to trouble him enough to disrupt his plans.

He'd only confidently dismiss the word of slaves, as unreliable and probably nothing but lies, Penn muses. Just the same as any non-abolitionist, and with at least a fraction of a chance of having his word taken over theirs. That is the world they live in, and that he assumes it immediately is symptomatic of just how much trust he has in Parrin, or wolves in general including even the most well-meaning.

And he keeps his mouth shut, the same as Sam does, and hangs back submissive and dutiful, walking down to the jetty. Every muscle he has groans with relief at the thought of a warm, stuffy little cabin, of someone to run the tiller who he doesn't need to keep a gun trained on, at the possibility of rest and sleep and food. Of home, really, however much he resists speaking and even thinking of it as that. It's enough just to listen in to Ree's conversation with the Dam, down the little path and over the jetty to the boat. Now that he's watching Ree walk before him, instead of running from him and from Lettice and the Dam, it's more evident that he's wounded in a way that Penn's never seen before. Not enough not to be able to walk, although any human with that level of damage to muscle and tendon would have to be stretchered to move the shortest distance. But Penn has never seen him physically impaired to this degree. Though he's still beautiful, naked and strong in the thin grey light of early-morning, with the rain just barely dried up in the sky, he's limping, unarguably. Lamed, torn at, slowed and half the fearsome creature he usually presents as. Even though Penn is pretty sure that, without any significant organs damaged or a headshot, even this silvered wound will heal in a wolf in time. In a wolf. It would probably have killed

Penn himself, from blood loss and shock. But Penn's busy listening, and he can neither worry about nor gloat over Ree forever. He's listening.

Especially when the Dam asks Ree, "Are you sure you don't want me to go back and scout for the wolves who took them?" She nods back at Penn and Sam. "We can't let them just carry on their merry way and try it again, go happily rustling property from every pack they see as vulnerable and can get access to."

"No," Ree rumbles with a great peaceful calm. He's listing to the side like a great ocean liner, the H.M.S. Renally, but it doesn't seem to impair his mind, his thinking, nor does he betray any pain in his speech. "We can send the pack after them, when we get back to the mainland. It's not as if they can swim or sail back without attracting attention, or they'd be doing a damn good job if they managed it. Come with me and look after our lost little lambs, madam. They've been through enough: I don't want them to come to harm." And he shoots a soft look back at Penn – just the slightest flicker. Penn thinks that he will never lose Ree's affections, will never allow it to happen. That this will set the course for his life to be put right, and on the course he's always intended. (He thinks that his heart is softened dangerously, and that he could cry, would like to nestle into the corner of Ree's chest and pet him possessively till he's healed and he – he shuts that down.)

"Bloody fool," rumbles the Dam, her great white haunches working powerfully, and that's true too.

Sam casts a quick look Penn's way, and it's not so unintelligible, not so hard to read. He's wondering – it's transparent to Penn – how exactly one comes to have the master of a pack in one's pocket that way, as a mere slave, as property. If only you knew, poor kid, Penn thinks, regretfully. Just how hard it can be, how much prior preparation it takes, and just how dependent it is on a million chance vagaries of fate and luck. You might as well just run for the liberated territories with no support: the odds are about the same.

But just the same, he drifts a little faster, further forward as he walks, and homes a little closer in to gravitate nearer to Ree. It is, in full honesty, much as if he can't help it. Ree sucks him in like a great massy dark planet pulling in a little satellite, and hasn't it always been that way, by all accounts of those qualified to know and present at the time? But Lettice, trotting demure and self-possessed at Ree's side, tacitly accepted but half-ignored by the Dam, and maintaining the mysterious silence of her pelted form, ducks sideways a little. And she brushes against his side as if to comfort or joke with him.

(He ducks away quick, though, perhaps a little aloof. Perhaps it hurts her feelings: she trots faster forward, and regains her former privileged position. It gives him a little pang, but it's better. She might catch a whiff of Parrin on him, after all, above the stink of the petrol of the boat and his own sweat, over water and mould and over the silver-stink that their liberators must have been laden with. Anything could be perceived, could happen. Letty's alert, and a clever little bitch.)

And then, here they are, on the jetty, walking from pebbled dust and muck path onto wooden boards, a few steps forward, half way along the jetty... The Dam stops walking, at this point, and both Penn and Sam stumble a little, and stop with a little effort. Ree stops a couple of steps along, turning back with a questioning look. To his mother, who's also the one who gifted him power and authority. Who's also the one calling in debts of flesh and genes, who's also the one who serves in his pack alongside every other beta, technical or physiological, and on downwards.

"Mama?" Ree asks. It's more gentle and solicitous than Penn's heard him towards her, times before. Perhaps it's that he thinks time is exacting an onerous price, wearing down on her prodigious supernatural gifts and intellect. (Or merely a wise and measured wariness, of the wolf who's been Alpha and Dam and Mother, and who, for all she's his mother, is still an adversary to respect and to fear.)

The Dam waves a hand at him, irritable. And she cocks her head up as if she hears distant music, but it's not music that she hears. She lifts a finger up, as if she's about to start conducting music, in fact. "Do you hear that, my darling?" she enquires, a sweet little smile that's not at all amused on her beautiful, patrician face. "Wolves, on the wind. The very wolves we're after, I'd wager." She's not wrong. She's only the first to hear them, the most alert, the most on the ball and the least infatuated. She might as well accuse Ree here and now of being too busy spooning and sighing over his pretty darling to be keeping a scanning eye out and maintaining security.

She doesn't trouble to wait for permission or instruction to pelt up and go chasing prey. She only smiles at her son, and says, "I'll deal with that for you, my love." And she leans forward, to give Ree a quick peck on the cheek, before she drops to all fours. Even as she drops, she's changing. And her change is quick: not as quick as Ree can change, but it's still impressive. There's something to be said for the matrilineal line and careful breeding, after all.

Even before she's fully pelted, before her skeleton is fully extended and lupine, she's executing a hairpin turn on the jetty, and loping off, to the end of the wooden slats and up the muddy track, up the hill towards trees and the skyline. Penn can hear a faint ululation of wolves, too: dim and persistent, carefully quiet, not the hunting howl that's designed to be heard. Perhaps they imagine they're subtle enough to evade detection. Or perhaps they think that surely the wolves in pursuit and the slaves they were so set upon freeing, are gone from the island by now. (Or perhaps they're a little bit dim, and haven't fully calculated the options. It's a distinct possibility.)

She's gone, moving at a cracking pace, and almost out of sight before Penn can even track her with his eyes. Wolves, damn them. All three of them watch, for a moment, the big-haunched grey wolf move like a blade or a bullet, remorseless and confident in pursuit of the source and direction where those howls have emanated from. There's nothing good that the Dam intends, for those she's after.

The feel of fingers at his nape makes Penn shiver: a fact he rapidly represses and tries to conceal, from young Sam, who doesn't need a bad example set him even before he's officially a member of the staff of the Hotstaat clan and household. But there's not much use to trying to conceal it, when Ree leans in over his shoulder – and never mind the fact that they have a very inappropriate witness to this – and whispers, "Let me take you home, my love. I'll take you for a spin in a boat, we'll crack open a bottle of bubbly and enjoy the waves and the scenery. Quite different to this little scene."

To which – because this is clearly a flagrant piece of soothing and comfort – Penn is much inclined to respond that a) the weather is not at all conducive to such jamborees, whatever Ree's fantasies might involve, and also that b), what about his mother? (Once she's done gutting the prey she has in view, of course. But then, who knows how long that is going to take?) And not only that, but six heavy blankets and hot soup would answer the issue a damn sight better. He would open his mouth and make these civil, orderly, politely respectful observations, he fully has the intent and coherence to say them. He doesn't get to, though.

There's a splash, a great smacking plunge and a sudden roaring upsurge of water, off to one side of the jetty behind them. And if Penn was a mite quicker, then he'd be turned to face what's behind them as quick as Ree is. But he's not a wolf, of course... So he's only almost as quick, but still a damn sight more agile than Sam.

Ohh, it's Parrin. Benedict Parrin, who must have doubled back from his pursuit by a Penn armed with treated silver, mislaid by careless wolves. (Or by the Dam, who he's probably in more fear of.) And then – now – again by an angry, moon-fuelled, righteous Dam Charity Hotstaat, taking him on as prey in the name of the Hotstaat pack, of the dignity of her injured son, and of Hotstaat family property misappropriated by filthy abolitionist wolves. (Penn has never, in fact, heard her express opinions on the matter in quite that way. But in his mind, that's the way she'd carry on, at Benedict Parrin. Perhaps his own feelings on the matter lend a little colour to his mental script-writing on her behalf.)

And of course, if Parrin had the slightest sense, or sense of self-preservation, then he'd have taken that pursuit as a hint – just a little, mild, gentle suggestion – that he should shift his arse and get the hell out of town, and never return. That there are considerations more pressing than defending his good name and returning to the defence of his property and reputation. Or, still worse, returning to the scene of his crime and practically bearing a sign identifying himself, shouting to the rooftops that he's the one responsible.

What an idiot. Penn has no sympathy. Or he shouldn't have, at least.

Parrin's naked as Ree is, of course, and about as conscious or mortified as he is too, which is to say not at all. Also dripping wet, though, from where he's swung himself up out of the water. He doesn't shiver, because it takes a lot for a wolf, even human form, to feel cold deep in the bones and disagreeable the way a human does. But the streamlining of the water emphasizes how narrow and lean and lithe he is. Ree has a good fifty pounds on him or more, and all of it muscle, not that most wolves ever run to fat without considerable effort and dedication to gluttony and greed. Parrin's hale and healthy and hasn't run three hundred miles in the last twenty-four hours, which even a wolf would feel, somewhat.

And he hasn't had a bullet – a treated silver bullet – in his thigh, what's more. It puts him at about evens in any match with him opposite Ree, in Penn's estimation. Maybe it even gives him a slight advantage, which isn't something he'd have under normal circumstances. And he has to be aware of it, because Penn can't think of anything else about this situation that would put the smug, pleased-with-him-self grin on his face that it's wearing, this minute. You'd think he had an army at his back, to see that face, rather than it being Ree who has an entire pack's worth of wolves waiting. Spitting fangs on the edge of a cliff, and waiting, just waiting for the word to leap off and swim for the chance of sinking their teeth into Parrin's furry flesh.

"Hotstaat," he says, lightly, now, nodding at Ree. "Small world, eh? Fancy running into *you* here, eh? Now, I wasn't expecting for you to catch up with me quite so quickly – or at all, for that matter. Nor my dear sis, either, for that matter," he adds, nodding down to where Lettice Parrin stands tense and wild-eyed at Ree's hip. She's taut as a bow-string, Penn notices: you could snap her with a little hammer. Except that, for a small wolf, she's pure muscle and terrifyingly lethal, and could certainly break wolves twice her size without excessive ex-ertion. All the biological alpha in her is coming to the fore, close up under the surface and straining to escape, and the pretence of defer-ence and sweet submission to Ree has to be half-killing her. She looks on the very edge of launching herself at her brother and giving him an excellent mauling, of savagery, and only the most rigid self-con-trol exerted can be preventing her. And perhaps a mite more sense and sanity than her sibling possesses.

Silver-stink may cover a lot, to a wolf. But how can Ree not know that she's alpha, at this point?

"But, still, how pleasant to see you," Parrin adds, smiling like the maniac he is, straightening up from the labour of the clamber out of the water, the surge. "Now, I'll just pick up the young human friends I appear to have temporarily mislaid – you might know them as slaves, an uncouth term, so ugly, I prefer not to use it – and we'll be on our way. Thank you so much for taking care of them for me, but you needn't trouble yourself any further."

It's provocation in a grand style, and Penn knows Ree well enough to see how effective it is. Ree's still listing port-ward, though he's upright, strong enough to take the pain and the injury and function through it as if it wasn't there. But he's trembling with a wild silver-eyed fury, at Parrin's insolence. And his voice trembles with it too, when he says, "You'll take nothing, Parrin. You'll not lay a hand on what belongs to me, nor on what you've come by dishonestly from other packs, neither of them. Why am I not surprised, that you'd be behind this?" And he pushes a hand back angrily, to either side, to push and shepherd and gather both Penn and Sam closer in behind him, as if merely being sheltered in his shadow would be protection enough. It sets Penn's hackles all awry, although he allows himself to be shepherded in meekly enough, out of his own choice. And Sam, poor timid Sam with his violent history, jumps to obey, head bowed and a cowed look on his face, dread at the promise of imminent violence even not done to himself.

(Penn likes to see wolves rip each other apart. If only their rages were directed at each other more frequently. And he could stomach Ree's righteous fury, at Parrin's overstepping and his incursions, if it wasn't over his property being stolen from him, and from others. At least, however he feels, that's how he's expressing it, and perhaps it's telling, Penn thinks. Perhaps it says more than Ree knows, whatever his declarations and his promises.)

Parrin isn't one whit disturbed. His smile is still brilliant and pleasant, on that surface level. And he takes a step closer, too. "You shouldn't be," he agrees sunnily. "You knew what to expect, from Parrins, when you hand-fasted my lovely sister. It's not as if our reputation doesn't precede us, far and wide, up and down the country. And yet you've taken her on anyway, haven't you, and I wonder why? Oh, no, no, there's no need for me to wonder, is there? Everyone knows why: because you let young Pennorth, there," and he nods at Penn while his eyes are still trained on Ree, and never does Penn the courtesy of actually, explicitly acknowledging his existence person to person, "make the decision for you. And in so many things, you let him lead, so that it gives him the illusion that he's actually important, that you actually regard him as an equal."

Oh, this is dangerous ground. Penn knows what it is that Parrin's referring to, with that smug look on his face. Even if Ree doesn't. "Even to the point of bending over for him and letting him think getting a crack at that fine arse of yours translates into any kind of dominance, eh, Hotstaat?" Oh, it's a bombshell. Or it ought to be, at any rate, and by Parrin's expression he clearly expects it to be, with a quick outrageous sideways wink in Penn's direction.

But Ree manages to stun both of them, with his reaction. Which is to grin at Parrin, as if he's not displeased at all. And then – making Penn's heart thunder and try to arrest itself – to drop to his knees a moment, by Penn's side, and push his face into Penn's thighs. For all the world an obedient lupe at the heels of its master, by Zeus. The silence is utter, from all of them: and then Ree leaps up to his feet once more, with the widest grin, more satisfied with himself than is less than obscene. He doesn't trouble with an actual answer, even: just smiles and smiles, fiercely, at Parrin, as if he thinks the act speaks for itself.

It's true that Parrin's voice wobbles a little in response, and he's clearly a bit shaken at the blatancy of Ree's uxurious satisfaction of submission, even in play. But he goes on and lets his voice become hard, become steady and more assured. "Except that you're never going to give that implicit promise any actual legal status, are you? You'll just fob him off, and fob him off, until his youth's gone and he can't catch the fancy of anyone who might actually give him what he wants. What he wants isn't *you*, Hotstaat. He wants what any sane human slave wants: liberty."

(The unpleasant fact is that Penn thinks Parrin is probably right, up to a point. He just hasn't the same faith in Penn's abilities and charms that Penn has. And if he chooses to take his own chances, then that's up to him. It damn well is.)

"Shut up," is what Ree snarls, not all that eloquently. He's not so happy now. "If you're here to try to take him then you can try. I'd like to see it. Yeah, you can try, Parrin, and let's see just how well you get along with that plan." He's still unsteady, still clearly wounded and hurting. But there's also a nascent sprinkle of wolf hair along his jaw, a cracking and warning stretch of the long bones along the thighs and shoulder-blades and arms. The wolf's near enough for another wolf to take it as a warning in itself. And Lettice whines and scrabbles her paws, hunkers down with her great shoulders pressed low to the ground at his side. Angry, not happy, her wolf is, and it's hardly surprising.

"Shall I?" The thing is, it sounds like a genuine question, from Benedict Parrin. He muses, openly, flaunts it, fingering his narrow, elegant jaw. "The thing is, Hotstaat, that normally I wouldn't be such a fool. Normally, you could take me, and I haven't such an ego that I'd deny it for a minute. But we're not in normal circumstances, are we?" he enquires. "No, no no no, not normal at all. Not with that bullet in your leg, and about eighteen hours of solid full-tilt cross-country run to recover from, I'd say. If you even took breaks. Even you could do with a bit of a breather and a nice cup of tea, before getting on with fighting to the death over your pretty little slave-love. Eh? Isn't that so?"

Oh, he's kidding, and he's joking, and this is exactly the kind of thing that goes down very well with Ree. When it comes from Penn, and it's kidding and joking that's conducted largely in his bedroom and dressing room, and followed by a little hanky-panky with gilded handcuffs and blindfolds. Not from Parrin, and not in a situation quite likely to lead to the deaths of one or more parties. He's dancing a risky little dance, that's what Penn could tell him – could tell him that he isn't quite pretty enough for it, and doesn't have the emotional strings to pull on that would enable him to get away clean with it. Not that Parrin seems to care much.

"Try me and see, why don't you," Ree offers back, though. And he makes an uncoordinated, but still powerful lunge Parrin's way. It's really truly a dance, the way that Parrin sways back and eludes him, too. But there's no panic or fear in it. He seems just to be enjoying a graceful little pavane. "Try me, try your sister, see how we protect what's ours." And his fingers move in the elegant little ruff of fur at Lettice Parrin's neck, so that she's prodded and stimulated to offer a growl. A growl that sounds confused, half-hearted, to Penn's ears. But where's the surprise in that, after all? Parrin is still her brother.

That stills Parrin, at least. It seems to give him food for thought: will it cause him second thoughts, too? But then his quieted face breaks out in a second smile, slower than the first, but deeper, seeming truer, more genuinely amused to Penn. Who watches, still, from behind Ree's shoulder, as much to both of them the toy and ornament to be disposed of, played for in games of chance, just like Sam. For both of them, it's the wolf victor who takes his winnings and disposes of his human booty. It's only what they do with the prizes that differs. "Are you sure about that?" he finally asks, his face amused in the dim northern daylight. "Because you, Hotstaat, you look like I could push you over with the toe of my boot, right now, and herd your two little ducklings along with me for an experience of real freedom. Eh, Sam? Just like I promised you." He diverts his attention for a moment to a Sam who blushes and fumbles for words he'd do better to not even try for.

"But my sister?" he says, squinting at Lettice, in her pelted form, very thoughtfully indeed. "I'll confess I'm surprised to see her here at all. But then, really, I'm surprised to see either of you – any of you, you owners, you slave lovers, you *wolves*. You've made damned incredible time, coming after what amounts to two stock items, as far as you're concerned. One might almost think that you actually cared about what happens to them."

And Ree's smile is tight and fierce and perfectly unamused, on his broad handsome face. It looks more like a promise of the pain he'll be gifting Parrin, than amusement. "I care more than you can understand, Parrin," he answers, with a tight intensity. "A cold-blooded intellectual like you," he adds. "Passionless."

And Parrin shrugs. "Perhaps. You may have a point. But the life of the mind, there's some value to it," he suggests. "Ask your clever little darling, there – doesn't he love to stew and pore and fret amongst the books and the papers? Always has, since he belonged to my old cousin, who afforded him that luxury. And as long as he's a slave, he'll be utterly dependent upon the whims and graciousness of any patron and owner, as to whether he flourishes and grows in the life he loves, or lets his mind dry up in meaningless meniality, or works the fields, or is used as a toy for limitless perversion and the kind of duties you probably like to imagine only you have used him for. Ain't it so? I believe that it is, and you can't deny it. Slave owners, wolves, you're all much the same, whether you flog and beat the poor bastards, or flatter and preen yourself on your indulgence, your kindness. It's all the same exploitation under a different guise."

"And you're a wolf yourself," Ree points out, like grit shovelled over his vocal cords.

But Parrin only shrugs. "I'm a Parrin. We're odd ducks, and everybody knows it. And that goes for my sister, just as much. Actually, it goes for my sister, twice." And he grins, now, looking from her, down a little and to the left, and then back up at Ree. "Which is also part of why I'm surprised to see her here." At this Lettice takes a quick step forward, and rumbles out what sounds a lot like a warning to her brother.

He only laughs at her in response. "Good joke, sis," he observes, coolly. "Now, we both know that you can make me jump, if you really mean to. But do you really mean to? It's going to take a bit more than just a threat. She loves me really," he observes, grinning up at Ree, who flinches a bit as he takes a threatening step forward. That flinch is pain, Penn thinks, with slight foreboding, and it explains much. Especially why he hasn't simply clouted Parrin into next week immediately, and taken him out. Ree is putting it off, and hoping that it won't materialise as an absolute necessity. It's rather a shock to realise it. He's hoping for the return of his mother – who would be well equal to the task – or for Lettice to step in, as would be perfectly appropriate, given that Parrin's her dear brother. He's hoping it, because he suspects that Parrin's right, and it would be a much more equal match between them than it ever would be under other circumstances.

In fact, he's thinking that Parrin might be able to do as he threatens, to overcome Ree – just now – and to take Penn and Sam off with him. Barring Lettice's involvement, obviously. Penn has no claims to telepathy, and nor do wolves as far as he's aware. Fortunately, since their abilities are quite extensive enough as it is. But he's pretty damn sure, just the same, that that's what Ree's thinking. He knows the wolf pretty well by now, even this strange unpredictable adult form.

"I mean," Parrin continues pleasantly, "considering that we had this whole little set-up nicely planned... She was supposed to keep you otherwise occupied or dozing off unawares, while I retrieved young Pennorth here and swept him off to an exciting life of liberty and adventure. While the two of you sighed in the bliss of your handfasted togetherness. I have to admit that I'm a bit miffed – miffed and puzzled. I mean, sis, what game are you playing, exactly? When we had it all worked out – get good old Pennorth, loyal to the Parrins in his half-arsed grudging fashion, to influence the Hotstaat Alpha to take you on as a mate, using his highly undue prettyboy influence. And then, the job done, to give him his freedom – not that I expected him to argue so much about it. I've never met a slave so stubborn, so reluctant to embrace liberty – and leave you, sis, a clear field to take over his place, and exert all the power and influence in his place that his approval would automatically give you."

And he stares at the pretty bitch in front of him, at her angry eyes, teeth showing and the pulsing in her throat still warning him, low with a slow rumbling. Penn's own mouth is dropped open, and he can feel that his eyes are wide enough for madness, stunned, quite stunned.

"So what happened? It was perfect, Letty. There's nothing an abolitionist and slave-liberator needs more than a good cover: and what could be a better cover, than a mating to a family as old and powerful and respectable as the Hotstaats, slave-owners for centuries, utterly conservative? I could have gone on for years, quietly detaching one slave after another from vicious owners, dispensing with them to the network and freedom and a better life – the ones with the stomach for it, anyhow. And never a breath of scandal – for who'd suspect a Hotstaat brother-in-law? The cloak of respectability would have covered me – and you into the bargain, with what we all know about your tastes and preferences. It was a perfect plan, designed for everyone's benefit. Including young Pennorth, the hot-headed conservative young fool." His smile is the smile of a cherub who's just farted quietly and then cast blessings upon the populace in apology.

Ree looks a little shocked: and then, just angry. Perhaps he doesn't have so very many more illusions about human and wolf nature than Penn does, after all. Penn himself is close enough to shell-shocked that he couldn't speak even if it was his place. And it's not his place, in the presence of his betters, even if those betters are also his mates, his lovers. But if his tongue wasn't stilled by caution and – yes, and fury, to match anything that Ree can produce – then he'd probably speak out now anyway. Well, he's always been reckless enough for it. Probably it's a good thing he's trembling too much for it, couldn't keep his voice steady at any price. In the absence of words, there's always violence, of course.

He stares at Lettice Parrin's pretty, pelted wolf, his mouth fallen open with horror, and fury. He could lunge at her, claw at her face with a handful of nails that'll never rival a wolf's, but can still do a peck of damage given the motivation. But she's still a wolf, and he's still human, and no matter the rights of the situation, she still has dominance as a counter to any accusation or play he might try. She could rip him apart from breast-bone to belly, with just a quick swipe of one casual paw.

(He still can't believe the facts as laid out by Parrin, however. Lettice, Miss Lettice? That same Miss Lettice who has played games with him, yes, but with a quiet affection at the back of it? Who has reminded him herself that her family owes him freedom, has acknowledged a debt to him over being chosen by Ree, has given him as a gift to Ree and lured him into a ceremony that's designed only and originally for two? Who has bound herself to him with the hand-fasting, not only to Ree, nor herself only to Ree with both of them the supporting legs of a tripod, but all three of them bound to each other. And with a bond that she and Ree, evidently, as wolves who can feel a supernatural aura that's alien to Penn, can feel even without Penn being aware of it.

And yet, still, she's betrayed him, given him over to Parrin to liberate – by his own standards and definition. No doubt that's how she excuses it in her own mind – that they're bestowing upon him a freedom that's more immediate, if also more rough and ready, than anything that he could achieve for himself, labouring for it through working the affections of a powerful patron, gathering gifts and alliances and contacts to himself, hoarded as if a dragon's treasure might buy him what he's after.

It's not for her to decide, he thinks, bitterly. It's still a betrayal, and it's not for her to decide. Except that a wolf always does believe that it knows best. He doesn't say it, though. He keeps his mouth shut, because he's so good at doing that.

"Really?" Ree asks. And though he snaps it out harsh, and cynical, Penn thinks that it's a genuine question. "You plotted this together? You always intended to get rid of Penn – to steal him away? After what he did for you. And all the fuss you make about how special he is for your clan." And in the first moment, he's asking it of Benedict Parrin. But then his face, his gaze drops, and it's pelted Lettice Parrin that he's asking instead. Shock may have worn off quickly, but there's still disbelief and hurt there, on Penn's behalf and perhaps on his own behalf, too. She's his mate, primarily, after all, or supposed to be.

And anger's bound to soon follow, too, if Penn knows Ree. It seems as if Lettice knows them well enough to be aware of that, as she gazes back with wolf-eyes that are, to Penn, frankly shifty and evasive. But she's cornered with a dangerous accusation, and remaining in wolf form is tacitly refusing to answer it. That's not a tenable position for long, not with the wolf pressing the query as her mate, and the hand-fasting between them just barely done, the ink still tacky on the documents. What else is she going to do, run full-pelt into the woods on this little island, barely a rock in the shallow basin of the bay they're in, a pebble in the sea before the harsh blare of the Atlantic. She has to face it, and better now than later.

With a low protesting snarl and a pulling, tearing, glutinous stretch of hide and fur, a shimmering imperceptible liquidity of what should be solid and tangible, she changes. It's not immediate, not as quick as Ree, although still damn quick. The alpha in her coming out, Penn thinks, though he keeps quiet on that score too. Can one wolf and another not sense it, does Ree not know it still, he wonders? Whatever the case between Ree and Lettice, he keeps quiet on that issue. It's hardly the most prominent of the things he has to take umbrage with them about, and she might still prove to be an ally. One he's less likely to trust without question, or at all, in the future, no matter what their collaboration or connection might be, but... Sometimes Penn could wish himself less canny, or more gullible, or a little less willing to be strung along or to string along, in the name of future advantage. For just one time, to let his true feelings show, and his anger to rise and to damn all consequences, for the sake of satisfaction of current furies.

And if that was who he was, then he might do it. But his calculations trump all other considerations, as usual. He keeps silence – well, apart from a glare, perhaps – as she stretches and writhes into her fleshy human form, and gasps and kicks her way into its finalized perfection, narrow and slight, breasts like a couple of small russet apples and no rump to speak of. To see the outlines of her barely-sketched out little form, you'd never suspect her alpha nature nor her lithe, moderately-sized, but lethal wolf. And she stands braced for assault and demands, as she hits full human embodiment, her wide grey-blue eyes almost transparent, with all the swirling confusion and emotion of this stand-off clearly visible behind them.

And now she has human tongue, and human voice of course, and no excuse not to answer Ree, when he steps – almost staggers, in truth – forward. And disdains to notice it, but forces himself to stand straight, to lean forward in an aggressive stance – and says, "Well?"

She's edged away from him, in the progress of this whole scene, of course, for him to have to do it at all. She's halfway between Ree and Parrin, now, and either one of them could reach out to grab her. (Not that Parrin's liable to, Penn thinks, half-amused. He knows his sister too well, by far, and his place in their dynamic. In wolf form, she'd have his hand half-off if he tried it.)

And Lettice doesn't want to answer, clearly. If you could fidget nude, then she fidgets. She looks away – and it's not often she does that, except when she's doing her most blatant impersonation of a seemly modest beta. But in the end, what choice does she have? "It isn't how Ben makes it sound," she says pleadingly, to Ree. And she puts her hand out, as if she'd lay it on his arm. But Ree snorts, and makes as if to throw her hand away from him. It's a clear rebuff, and Lettice's face whitens, angry. "You talk as if it was a plot to do him harm!" she says, indignation in a voice that's too pretty for an alpha. "We're Parrins!" she asserts, as if the bare assertion in itself is sufficient evidence to prove her case. "And Pennorth belonged to Parrins before now! We're not *Hotstaats*," she spits out – and it's very enlightening, the sudden disgust on her face. Penn never realised, until now, perhaps, just how fully Miss Lettice is indeed a Parrin. Of course, he knows she's opposed to slavery, that she's one of the fashionable young crowd who decry it. (But in most cases, without actually doing a damn thing about it.) But up until now, he didn't know that she despises it possibly quite as fiercely as Benedict Parrin and his co-conspirators. That, in fact, she rather despises the Hotstaats, presumably for their casual acceptance of the political *status quo,* and their pragmatic continuance of the practice of owning other sentient beings, even including ones one might have a personal affection for.

Actually, Penn thinks that it's probably worse to own one that one *doesn't* have a personal affection for – so much less incentive for decent treatment and civilized standards – but that's currently by the by. "We – Benedict was only going to make him free," she allows, now. Her face has hardened up, lost the little bit of disarmed uncertainty it was expressing. "The bloody fool," she adds, in a quick aside to her brother. "What'd you have to go and open your mouth for, you idiot? How am I supposed to protect you, when you announce our hand, the first chance that you get?"

And Parrin's mouth twists up in response, a tight thin line that expresses much dissatisfaction and rebellion. "I could say to you, dear sister, in response, why did you have to pursue us – and with insane speed, too – instead of keeping your lover quiet and the pursuit slow, hindered as much as you could? Why show your face at all, and get in my way, when the whole point's to use your push to slide me out of trouble and our name out of actionable proceedings? Or pack executions, for that matter. All of this, for security and to keep us dark, and yet here it is thrown away on chasing after a pretty face."

"For liberty," Miss Lettice reminds him, sharply. "For liberty, too – Pennorth's liberty."

"For your own *advantage*," Ree growls at her, and Penn can feel all of the red rage seething under his words, the readiness to be wolf again, to take his anger out on flesh. He's looming up close to her now. And yet, she's still his mate. It's not likely she's the one he'll turn upon. Penn is less angry than Ree, now. Miss Lettice clearly has her own brand of pragmatism – and while he's unsatisfied with the results, he can understand the principle. He can believe that it's true, that she didn't mean him any harm, or at least consider it harm. "When I thought we'd become united in friendship, at least, if nothing else. That, and by Penn himself. The fool I was, sending you up ahead when I was shot, to keep up and make sure they didn't slip out of our hands while the pack flanked me! And all the time, you must have been so careful to lag behind as much as you dared. All for yourselves, your own ends."

"For the sake of the *cause*," she snaps, sharply correcting him. She's rather beautiful as they lean in fiercely together, she as sharp and fine as a white blade in the cold air, and Ree's whole body practically a vee of muscle and olive-tan skin, beautifully made and terrifyingly vulnerable, his thigh still oozing blood as he leans to one side. It doesn't matter what she has to say in response, though, because that's the moment – it transpires – that Parrin sees his chance, in Ree's momentary distraction. He makes a lunge, swerving around a Ree half-turned away, to grab Penn.

Who, as ever, is an obstreperous and uncooperative subject. Who leaps back, starts backing off at inelegant speed, almost tripping over a loose plank in the jetty. And his declining of the unspoken invitation, to either be free or serve as a hostage, is all that's necessary. Ree's injured, but he's still quite capable of putting up a good fight against the likes of Parrin even so: and all his attention's robbed from Miss Lettice, in order to pay it to Benedict Parrin. He's on the younger, slighter fellow, even as he makes his play. And Penn has the good sense to step back and let them have at it, falling rolling and grunting and wrestling onto the ground. There's another wolf present, after all: let it be up to *her* to make peace, and prevent them from killing each other, since one's her brother and the other her mate.

And she should, certainly she should: but she doesn't make a move to leap in, to physically separate them and prevent the two wolves she's most bound to from making a good fist at ripping one another apart. (Which Parrin, frankly, is making a worryingly good effort at. Not that he'd stand any chance normally. But with a temporarily half-crippled opponent, suffering significant blood loss, then it's an evenly-matched wrestling bout. In fact, he could guess that Ree's a little over-matched. Only temporarily, of course.)

But he'll not fret. Letty will sort it out of course, and she does. Not physically, but with the merest intercession by voice. Although even Penn can feel it – the tingle along the dimples of his spine, the pricking up of every goose-bump on his body – when Letty, truly for perhaps the first time since he's met her, really ceases to pretend that she's anything other than an alpha. "Benedict," she says, and she doesn't even trouble to shout, to raise her voice in the slightest degree. Penn can hear, because he's standing apart, and because, for a human, his hearing is reasonably sharp. But he's not sure that Parrin can actually hear it. And Ree isn't listening to a damn word, and that's for damned sure.

No, he's too busy snorting with fury and trying to snap Parrin's back in half, kicking his legs out from under him and lunging to bite at his ear with teeth that aren't fully lupine – yet, but aren't completely human any more, either. But whether Parrin actually hears, or not, something in him that's wolf even when he wears a human face, responds. He goes abruptly slack in Ree's grasp, ceases to fight or to struggle against him, becomes quite malleable and obedient to Ree's manoeuvrings. It's not that he becomes a celluloid dolly, of a sudden: but he doesn't resist when Ree stands and pushes him away.

Nor does he stand up alongside Ree, but just stays knelt there on the jetty, with his eyes dropped a little, and a mutinous expression on his face. Clearly it's painful for Ree to stand, and it takes him a moment to straighten, his face a little twisted. But then the change wears off, and a faint dark, sardonic amusement takes its place. Looking from Parrin to Miss Lettice – with a quick, wide-eyed glance at Penn, because he always looks for Penn, always – he whistles, and nods his head, with a grin that isn't kind.

But Penn doesn't care too much, about whether Ree's kind, to Parrin. He might have a slight preference for a quick spot of torture, in fact. Well, psychological torture, in any case. "There's a reversal," he observes, looking pleased, looking a little smug. Not looking altogether surprised, though, and that sets something in Penn's mind a-ticking. "The great abolitionist hero and revolutionary, on his knees and doing as he's told, at the bidding of his alpha sister. You look like a little schoolboy, Parrin: and you've been a damn fool. Perhaps I should try that tone of voice on you myself. But maybe it's just that Letty has you well-trained."

It's not difficult to see that Ree's enjoying the sudden easy dominance over a wolf he's never taken to, for one reason and another and mostly because of Parrin's oft-exhibited close interest in Penn. (Much too close. They all know that know.) Or his fiancée's dominance, in which he feels he has a share, at least. But Penn can barely spare a moment's attention for that. His brain's too busy putting all the incomprehensible pieces into place. Well. So Ree knows about Lettice Parrin, her true status, her alpha nature. (And has never seen fit to mention that to Penn, either, when you'd think that pillow-talk would lead inevitably to the subject.) The idea doesn't appear to trouble him too much, either.

Well, Penn thinks. Maybe it's only now that she has him hooked, safely hand-fasted and affianced, that she's chosen to disclose that very pertinent bit of information, for any marriage papers and dowry settlement. Or she must have thought she had him hooked, to let that out, at least. And now? Now he can only wonder, at how this whole mess will play out.

But looking back at Letty, with a bright enquiring, sparky look on his face, Ree doesn't look one whit disturbed. A sapphist, an abolitionist, a proven liar and now an alpha into the bargain – and Ree's still, still looking at his affianced bride, as if she's the brightest, sparkliest, most amusing bauble on the tree. Not in exactly the way he looks at Penn, no, that's true. There's none of the soft tender devotion, the doe-eyed gentleness that Penn is accustomed to drawing out of Ree, to commanding as if it's his natural and inborn right. (No, Benedict Parrin's not the only one well-trained on this jetty, with the arctic breeze whipping a direct path though them.)

But still, he begins to wonder if he hasn't taken Lettice Parrin quite seriously enough – and Izanagi knows, that he's assessed her damn carefully, a bride to Ree and a mistress to himself – as a potential rival. Ree loves Penn, there's no doubt. But he does like his toys, his games and pretty things. And Lettice is a bright and shiny toy, Penn thinks.

It doesn't matter, right now. What matters is foiling Parrin's half-noble attempts at liberating a pair of mis-matched slaves, and making sure he abandons any such plans for the future. Penn watches closely, as Miss Lettice gives him a look that could take the hide off a donkey like quicklime. "I know I've reneged on a deal, here, my brother," she tells him, and her pale, pretty face is regretful. "But you have to understand, I have other responsibilities now, not only to the Parrin pack and name, and to your ideals, Ben. I'm mated – and however much I might disagree with Hotstaat regarding certain fine points of law and ethics, still I'm bound and mated to him, and I have to take his point of view into account. And he does have such very strong opinions on the subject of our Pennorth."

Chapter 8

Here, she even – damned cheek – casts a regretful look Penn's way, as if that's all the apology he's liable to get. A quick glance, and a wry grin. "Doesn't he, love?" she asks. "He won't be parted from you, and I ought to know. So despite our best intentions, I think you and I – Ben – are just going to have to accept that Pennorth is unshiftable and rock-solid in his pole position for my dear fiance's affections. Which I think I can work with, seeing as I'm very fond of him in any case – as I know you are yourself. And what with the three of us now being hand-fasted together – and a true bond formed, into the bargain – I do consider that it would really be an inconvenience for us to find ourselves without him, in any case."

She casts Penn another look, sweet and sparkling, and he – and he – well, he can almost understand Ree's attitude. She's damned annoying, and turbulent, and provocative, and... It's hard to stay mad with her. Getting mad, that's easy. It's just the enduring and steady annoyance part, that has a bit of a trick to it.

Parrin, Parrin looks sick. Perhaps he's got the trick of it, after all. Or perhaps a lifetime of being under her alpha thumb has inured him so much that he's long since acquired the knack. "A bond," he says, terribly flatly. "You hand-fasted with him? You and him and Hotstaat, hand-fasted, and a true three-way mating bond? With a slave? You damn fool, Letty."

There, out it comes, Penn thinks. Damn, he'd like to say it, just once, to take the leash off his tongue. "What a snob you are, Parrin. Even with everything, even with the liberation of slaves and all your political ideals, you're just a snob like any of them." Now he has, and he never meant to. And with the words out and loose in the free cool grey air, it's too late to wish he had a speck of sense in his damp uncombed head.

Which could earn him a backhander across the face, in the company of other wolves, in other times and places. But here? There's a tiny moment of silence. And then Ree cracks out laughing – fierce, loud, manic laughter, uncontrolled and wild. And when Penn snatches a glance at Lettice Parrin, she's twisting her mouth up, much like one trying not to let a cackle escape her lips, into the bargain.

But she keeps it from cracking the surface, just the same, and gives her brother a hard stare, instead. The brother who's glowering at Penn as if he'd like to give him the kind of beating he'd get from the type of wolf Parrin professes to disdain, and as if he's busy coming up with a come-back to Penn's sneer, too. He doesn't rise off the wooden planks, though. And Lettice Parrin says sharply, "He has a point, Ben. And now, you can just stay right where you are – while we load up that little boat. We'll take the poor dears you've had running all over the country back to a safe warm home. Eh?"

She turns, to face a Ree who's also regained sobriety, who has a stern face as he returns her look. "We're taking them back to the mainland?" she asks. But to Ree, instead of her brother, she does the courtesy of phrasing it as a question. "And send the pack back for the others with Ben?"

There's a slight glare from Ree to her, in response, like he thinks she's somehow evading the issue. And of course she is. He jerks his head at an angle, to indicate Parrin, still sitting and sagging against the wooden planks of the jetty, and with his head fallen, eyes down. Is he pouting? Penn thinks that he's probably pouting. "And your brother?" Ree asks, far from unreasonably. "What are we to do with him? I notice you're assuming that I'll take you home, and say nothing. Keep my mouth shut and accept your treachery, swallow it and bury it and marry you anyway?"

Lord, but that's an uncomfortable silence. Miss Lettice's mouth falls open, a little. And is that a nasty little cackle from the direction of her brother? Almost certainly it is, Penn thinks. Not a surprise at all. To her credit, Miss Lettice regains her poise almost instantly, though. Or, at least some simulacrum of poise. "I suppose I am," she concedes, with a breathless little flutter that puts away her alpha nature in a drawer, slides the drawer shut and makes as if it never happened. "Am I wrong?"

Penn wonders that too. Can one mate discard another so easily, so soon, and never have a qualm or a second thought about it? It doesn't augur too well for Penn himself, if so. A break with Lettice Parrin – even if the full truth about her scandalous brother were repressed – would involve hostilities and a break-off of civil relations between the two packs. It would be a serious matter with serious repercussions. Certainly in comparison with discarding a slave lover, a surreptitious bit on the side. Even with a true bond involved in the mixture.

Ree lets the silence linger a moment, tortures her with the possibility. (Oh, Penn knows his man, he knows him all right. The *bastard*.) Then he relents, because of course he always meant to relent with her. "I suppose not," he says, if grudgingly. "And your brother?" He doesn't even look at Parrin as he asks it: it's like the man is a parcel, to be disposed of and apportioned out by the adults in the room, his fate sorted impersonally at their hands. Knowing Parrin, Penn can't see him caring much for that.

Miss Lettice just hesitates. Then, impulsively, she says, "Oh, Ree. Let's just get things sorted, before we thrash this out. The boat, and these boys–." And she affords Penn a quick glance – "And, oh, everything. First?" It's the most blatant bit of manipulation, of pleading and putting off of the inevitable that Penn may ever have witnessed.

It's not as if it's not perfectly transparent, that she's seeking to put the deciding of Benedict Parrin's fate, his unofficial sentencing and the matter of how she and Ree are to deal with him to the very last minute. Now that she's evaded any consequences by virtue of her privileged position. And then – unless Penn is a damn fool with no judgement whatsoever, which he isn't – her intent is to plead, and fudge, and come up with some plea-bargain that involves Ree's silence upon the subject of his ne'er-do-well slave-runner brother-in-law. There'll be some form of attenuated and moderate house-arrest, that will inevitably diminish and lapse here and there, until Parrin is gaily off about his abolitionist, slave-liberating business once again. Except this time, with the Alpha of the Hotstaats at least covertly aware of it, and turning an uncomfortable blind eye until they're all discovered, until disaster hits the house of Hotstaat like a typhoon destroying a little wooden shack.

Of course, it might never happen. But it certainly would render Ree complicit in Parrin's activities, as well as Lettice Parrin. (And as well as Penn.) Not that now's the time to worry: even though, judging by the tight rictus of Ree's face, he's no more a fool on certain subjects than Penn is, and can see through Lettice Parrin's machinations simply enough. Even if he chooses to let her get away with it, for now. His brow's furrowed, his black eyebrows twitching with near-incredulity at the transparency of it. But still, he nods, and says, "I'll check the boat. Keep an eye on things out here." He indicates the jetty, Penn, Parrin and the grim white haze of a winter Highland Scotland day. "I'll be out in a minute."

It's a fair distance down the long, wobbling jetty, but he jogs down it and is inside the cabin, and then disappears out of sight checking the hold, within a minute, graceful, lithe, only a little impeded, visibly, by the wound. (Penn's heart aches a little, but he's used to disregarding that. How is this how it's supposed to be: to be taken such tender care of, forgiven what in a wolf's eyes is betrayal – and yet at the same time, to be treated as if one's a parcel, a trouble to be organised, transported and re-located, with never a moment of consultation and enquiry about one's own ideas and wishes? Ree loves him, Penn can accept that. It's just that he does so in the most infuriating way possible.

Penn loves him back, and can concede it to himself, finally. Sometimes, at least. But love doesn't amount to trust, and doesn't compare to it.

It's only that he's beautiful, and home-like, and a thread back to the past they share. And he cares where Penn is, and if he lives or dies. Oh, it's an excruciating thing to get old, and maudlin, and sentimental in your withered dotage. It's only Lettice Parrin who saves him from such regrettable temptation, in fact. She walks up to her brother – where he's still slumped, and by the looks of him evilly plotting, if Penn's any judge of the matter. (And he has some experience in evil-plot-mongering, himself.) She kicks him, which seems – well, not at all uncalled for, if you care to ask Penn. But still, a little excessive, and without warning.

Parrin doesn't protest verbally, which is probably a good and wise thing, to judge by the look on his sister's face. But he glares up at her in a way that would take the skin off, if he had a witch's powers. "How am I the one in the wrong, here?" he hisses up at her – *sotto voce*, but Penn still makes it out, looking out discreetly at the grey incessant waves of the iron-coloured sea, apparently inattentive. "I'm the one following the plan, and you're the one who's cocked it up and let him follow on after – not just follow on, but you can't have delayed him even five minutes, not for him to catch us on the Snake Pass like that! And now, now look where we are! Not even just us, but the poor bastards we made promises to, as well!"

Oh, ho, you didn't make any promises to *me*, Penn thinks privately. At least, none that I was asking for, just a few I'd have sooner done without. As so often, he buttons his lip, though. He folds his arms, feeling invisible as per, an irrelevance to their little blood-kin spat. Miss Lettice is the one who responds. "Oh, shut up, Ben," she says, tensely. "Did I know that a true bond would kick in with the hand-fasting? What were the odds? And then when we woke up, it wasn't as if there was a hope in hell of keeping it from him – it grabbed a hold of him just the same as me. It had the pair of us by the throat, and it was a miracle we managed to get the rest of his pack alerted without just haring off into the night and following wherever it was leading us. It wasn't as if it was a *choice*. We could feel how he was raging and frightened and angry, and pulling away further and further every second, and we had to follow, we had to–." She pauses, her lips tight and thin. "Well," she adds sniffily, "you haven't got a mate, have you, love? You can't be expected to understand."

Parrin cocks his head back to get a better look at her, and his mouth's set, like he's taking in something he hadn't reckoned with before. "That's what I've got in store, then, is it?" he asks. "Lofty patronage and snooty allowances made, from the mated to the unmated? Well, it's not that I haven't come across it before: except that I'd have thought you'd have more sense, Letty. And especially with a slave-mate."

She lifts a hand to him, then: and Penn is a little ashamed of the glow of satisfaction and relish that sizzles through his belly at the sight, at the sight of Parrin's flinch, too. He's been in that same position often enough, himself. And to see a wolf subjected and cowering, instead, and on his own behalf, standing in his defence, is... If Penn claims it's not satisfying, he'd lie to himself, even if it's a long way from an attractive admission.

But she drops her hand, of course. Perhaps it's enough merely to see her beta brother flinch, and know for sure that he knows his place in the pecking order, and who's actually in charge. If they were humans then it would be funny, the slight, delicate girl and her lithe but muscular, still powerful brother, the reversing of anything you might expect. But wolves are never what you quite expect, and you can rely on nothing. "Anyway," she says, halfway between placatory and still annoyed, "it's a done deal. This is how things have played out, and you're just going to have to accept it. I'm not sacrificing my bond-mate for your sake – not either one of them. And if you could feel the bond yourself, you'd know that how he feels about forced liberation," and here she nods her head in Penn's direction, "is tanta-mount to a sacrifice. So if you could kindly refrain from trying to re-capture him?" And oh, none have ever been so witheringly sarcastic as Miss Lettice, with that final suggestion. "And from aggravating a wolf who's more dominant than you, and has about fifty pounds on you into the bargain, then that would be an excellent idea."

It's a withering summary, for certain: and yet the volley of her relentless sarcasm trails off towards the end. In fact, she's no longer even looking down at her brother. Her gaze has drifted away, in Penn's direction. But no, not quite in Penn's direction. In fact she's looking a little to the side of him, a little beyond him, and... And Penn thinks, and realises that there's something that he's been failing to keep track of, to take account of. And if he was blindfolded this very minute, if someone prodded him in the chest and said, "Hey, where's Sam?" then he would have no answer.

Sam is a chatterbox, judging by their brief acquaintance. Sam, in fact, barely shuts up for one blessed minute, barring if he's deeply up-set, or afraid, or thinking deep. But Sam has been quiet for a good long while, hasn't uttered a peep nor asked a question. Penn turns around, although really and honestly he already has a good idea, a gut feeling of what it is that he's (not) going to see. Even as he turns, though, Miss Lettice is too quick for him. Her narrow pale willow-switch of a body is running right past him and not slowing, as it hits the edge of the jetty, the beginning of the cold grey restless waters.

Because there's no damn sign of Sam, nowhere on the jetty, nowhere back on the island where they've come from. Not until he looks further, lets his eyes skim out over the water, and – there he is. A fair distance out, his reddish head bobbling about above the waves. And it would be impressive, that he's managed to slip into the water so quietly and without even wolves noticing, and get so far out in so short a time. It would, except that he's not doing well, not making good progress any more. He's struggling, and every little bit of progress is clearly hard-won now. Who knows if it's lack of skill and experience at swimming itself, or the sheer perishing bloody cold of the waters. Either way, he's liable to go under before he gets much further, going by current progress.

That's probably a good half of the reason that Lettice Parrin heads into the water like a bullet into soft foam rubber. Her compact and lovely form dives in with barely a splash or displacement of waters, as she disappears beneath its grey welcome. She changes as she leaps, for the sake of the thicker hide and the protective pelt that her wolf will afford her, and it must cost her something to do it, so fast and seamlessly easy. Penn's never known any wolf but Ree, even alphas, who can do that much without suffering a penalty of pain.

The other half of the reason is out at the very furthest visible point of the island, coming around the curve of the slight incline, only just in sight as it hugs the edge of the island shore. It looks to have just come out of the masking cover of the overhang of vegetation and greenery from the well-planted side of the island. It's a motorised sail-boat, neat, sturdy, highly functional: not especially big, only a thirty-footer or so in comparison to the scant twenty-feet of motor-boat that got them here in the first place. Thirty feet is enough, though, and Penn doesn't doubt that it's well-stocked, sturdy and capable of getting a small crew and a few landlubber passengers across the Atlantic in inclement weathers. Mostly whole, hale and in one piece, even.

Parrin wouldn't have picked it, otherwise. He may be an idiot, but he's not a totally incompetent idiot.

And this is why Sam's in the water, then. It's not hard to see the calculation he made, the weighing up of pros and cons with the answer coming up heavily weighted in favour of flight. No matter what assurances and reassurances Ree might offer him, regarding being returned to his old masters and purchased from them, a promise from a strange wolf is hardly a guarantee. Perhaps even when you know the wolf, it's something to eye askance and consider carefully. And on the other hand, there he was, set off dumbly and obediently to one side while the wolves who'd obstructed his escape squabbled amongst themselves. It was hardly a promising augury for the future, and his life under their service.

And then, he must have been the first to spot the appearance of the bigger boat, the one they'd been promised but that had failed to materialise. Until now, of course. Spotted it, wavered, decided where his best interests lay – and slipped into the water, almost admirably sneaky and dedicated to his own vision of his future.

Penn thinks that, on the basis of a rather brief acquaintance, he likes Sam. Not that it does either him or Sam much good now, what with Sam spluttering and half-going under in frigid northern waters, and Lettice cleaving an unforgiving path towards him with clean white spumes of spray spitting up and foaming around her wet dark grey form, wolf shoulders a broad ominous bulk amidst the lighter grey of the water. Sam's doomed – or at least, his second, independently-powered bid for freedom is. Lettice Parrin will have him back in the fold in exceptionally short order, and Penn knows damn well there'll be no arguing or struggling with her, not if Sam has the slightest good sense.

In short order, but perhaps not in short order enough. Penn has his attention fully engaged, what with watching the drama unfold from the safe haven of the jetty. (Well, fairly safe, anyhow. It's shaky as hell and has creaking loose wooden planks galore, shudders under the thunder of a wolf footfall, even at a slow measured walking pace.

But it's better than frozen waters, and Penn's quite happy to leave the heroic rescue of a damn fool to someone else, particularly a wolf.)

Still, it's riveting, and a relief too, to watch Sam struggle but Miss Lettice making good enough time to rescue him, to retrieve him. He hasn't attention to spare to be watching the little motorboat and monitoring what Ree's up to inside it, or to slide careful glances Parrin's way, where he's no doubt casting evil and resentful glances Penn's way in return. It would be characteristic for him, to blame Penn for the outcome of his own insistence on a rescue and liberation that served his own ends so neatly, until it all went vastly wrong.

That's how much attention he's paying Parrin, then, and he should honestly know better. It's not even Parrin's fault, because he should truly blame himself, after twenty-seven years of living in a wolf world and learning wolf ways, of learning always to know what's at your back and how your environment is populated and controlled and navigable, by wolves, by you. It's just – if he's going to try to make excuses for himself – that he knows how a pack structure works, and he knows the control and the authority that an alpha has over a beta wolf or lower, right down to epsilon, and especially in the same pack. By rights, Benedict Parrin must jump at Lettice Parrin's instruction. And from what Penn's seen, he does.

Or, at least, he does when she's right there and enforcing it on him, her attention on him and no wriggling away, no squirmy get-outs. For many wolves, an alpha's instruction is sufficient to enforce permanent obedience to it, even in the absence of the alpha. Except that it seems like Benedict Parrin has something in common with Penn: namely, being an obnoxious little bastard who will wriggle out from under instructions and rebel in any way that comes to mind, any time he can find the possibility. Maybe he just has to be far enough away from Lettice, maybe he just has to be out from under her watchful eye for a moment. But he's not obeying orders any more, and he's not quietly kneeling to the side of the jetty, a safe distance from Penn, minding his manners and staying where Lettice put him.

Bad news for Penn, then. The first that Penn knows of it is an arm clasping in a headlock around his neck, and then he's being man-handled at an awful stumbling speed down the jetty, and back to the island. Which is... dumb, surely. But Parrin seems awfully set on it, gasping with laughter, jerking Penn along, and snarling as he goes, into Penn's ear. And Penn's struggling, but he's no wolf, for all his muscle and brawn from years of field work and service and horse-riding. "I swear to Pluto, Pennorth, you're stupid enough that I don't even know why I'm bothering to try to save you, to put this right. But I am, and I'm going to. Because you're a long sight too stupid, even, it seems, to understand that any promises they make you are only words, and they don't mean a thing. I include my sister in that. Her intentions are fine, I'll give you that, but the only thing she's ever actually done for the liberationist cause is providing me with a bit of necessary cover when an operation's gone awry. And even that's grudging. Never riding along, never running slaves herself or bring-ing anyone in, never a damn thing that might be inconvenient or risky. The clan are very proud of her, in fact. Her opinions are immac-ulately liberal, and she never provides them with a moment's embar-rassment, or does one concrete measurable risky thing for the cause."

Penn is struggling, kicking. If Parrin didn't have a bicep locking the crown of his head down, with his wrist under Penn's chin, then he'd be screaming for help too. Bloody wolves, what use are they? He tries to get a hand free, since Parrin's gripping one and has the other pincered against his body, but he can't, can't – not even to save him-self from the self-satisfied monologue as Parrin goes to walk him off the jetty. As if he was a dolly, as if he was a tailor's dummy. "And Al-pha Hotstaat?" Parrin asks, and the laugh in his voice, Penn tries to kick him for that. "Do you really imagine he's going to publicly ac-knowledge you as a mate? That's strictly for the bedroom, you poor daft gullible love. And it always will be – even if he was going to re-lease you, to sign off your manumission, ever. Which he isn't, sweet-heart! Hotstaat, letting you go, letting you run away from him? Do you think that's ever going to happen?"

Oh, Penn's furious. Furious because Parrin's kidnapping – no, hang on, *re*-kidnapping him. Because he's doing his best to destroy Penn's innocent pleasant dreams about a real bond, about true mates, about Ree truly acknowledging him as an equal and a mate. And, worst of all, Parrin really does think that he's that gullible – that he believes it all without question, that he's the kind of starry-eyed sighing born slave who might swoon for love and believe everything he's told. Instead of enjoying it as a pleasant fairy story, and keeping a wary eye on his lovers and allies, who might turn traitor at who knows what minute. An eye on the main chance is Penn's prime char-acteristic, and he's vastly insulted by any suggestion to the contrary.

He's furious enough to say anything, to do anything. But his fury doesn't distract him half as much, it seems, as Parrin's thoroughgo-ing, full-throttle enjoyment of the sound of his own voice distracts *him*. Otherwise, surely, he'd notice or stop in the middle of his lec-ture, when the rumble of the wooden planks beneath their swiftly moving feet starts getting louder, getting deeper, shaking the planks more perceptibly. Parrin doesn't perceive it, and he's a wolf, for heav-en's sake. But then, he's also an idiot, who's infatuated with his own moral rectitude and the image he sees in the mirror.

But Penn isn't an idiot – most of the time. He doesn't stop strug-gling, and he doesn't stop cursing, and he even starts up – with a little jerk of his chin, getting it free – a little low-grade yelling. Why de-prive Parrin of the extra distraction, the one extra demand for his at-tention that's leading to the inattention that could possibly kill him? "You're an idiot, Parrin! You stupid arsehole! You absolute prick! What are you going to do with me on the island? They'll only come after you and probably rip you apart, for daring to steal me again after being caught at it once!"

Parrin's voice is warm and calm in response. Penn begins to wonder, frankly, if the fellow is more than a little unhinged somewhere in the fine handsomely carven skull. "Oh, Pennorth, Pennorth. Do you have no trust in me at all? What do you think the boat is for? What did you think Gus and Harry were howling for, earlier? My freedman pal knows my howl, and my signals. I'll have him bring her round to a quarter turn round the island coastline, and we'll be away. Ripping motor he's got on her, she can move like a couple of werewolves with fireworks tied to their brushes, arse on fire and pelt alight."

Penn could spit, or swear, or panic. Mostly panic. He's not going to pull it off, is he, Parrin? Even now? Surely not. Fate can't do that to Penn. He fights more desperately, now, to get away, he kicks and he *screams.*

But Penn wouldn't say that it works, not in the sense that he's really contributed. No, Parrin can take the full weight of credit for the outcome all on his own. Just like he takes the weight of a two-hundred pound alpha wolf on his back, when Ree hits him – full-bodied, not in the sense of a blow – a bare split-second later.

Truly, although Penn appreciates the rescue – and had been beginning to worry that it was never coming, that Parrin would actually succeed in re-capturing him and consigning him to a frozen, snowy waste of tundra where all the things, everything that Penn is and has made of himself would be wasted and useless – there's still a real downside to it. The downside involves being on the actual downside of Parrin, as he goes over like a tree being abruptly felled, and hitting the rocky floor of the forest. Penn isn't crushed. He just feels like it. And then he scrambles out from under with the most speed that he can muster together, because he doesn't want to get in the middle of what's coming. It's something he's seen a few times in his lifetime, and he knows better. It's ugly, and he's much attached to his limbs, his delicate soft bits and all of his parts.

An alpha can usually cow a beta without fighting, that's the thing. Even if he's not the other wolf's own pack alpha, the simple discrepancy in status can make the other wolf bow the head, shut up, submit – if necessary. That only necessarily applies in relatively urbane and civilised social situations, however. Even a beta wolf, even a wolf lower in status than that – and the complexities of wolf status can be labyrinthine and subtle, to a true student of the species, more complex than they appear at first glance – will fight, if put to it with no time to prepare and to accept submission, no pause for the human to overmaster the wolf and accept the inevitable. Instinct and training play into each other oddly for the wolves, and what you'd think to be mostly instinct is often mostly civilisation at work, or the reverse.

So Parrin fights, even against an opponent he surely can't hope or expect to beat, because he's a wolf. And Penn – because he has a lot of native caution and the brain he was born with, he veers off to one side, with the jetty bouncing underneath him alarmingly. He looks off into the waters with a bit of desperation. Because for heaven's sake, this is when you need the calming influence of a mate to one wolf who's also a sister to the other. She's needed to broker agreement and demand peace, to impose her will without even needing to change and savage fools into obedience.

But Lettice is still struggling with a panicking and thrashing Sam. He's clearly not a strong enough swimmer for it ever to have been a wise move to trust himself to the water, to strike out on his own for the great boat and freedom. She's not going to get back on the jetty dragging Sam with her, not for the next five minutes at least. And that's not the only problem. Because Penn's done a good deal too much assuming, thinking that it has to be a done deal, any squaring-off between Ree and Parrin.

It would be, normally. These aren't normal conditions. Far, very far from it, indeed. Ree's leg is wounded, and Penn's kept forgetting it, discounting it. That's for good reason, because he's never in his life seen Ree truly seriously wounded, as a wolf would account serious injury. There's been nothing he couldn't recover from in the space of a day, and very often more quickly than that. But this wound is different, and since Penn's already been provided with the information, it shouldn't be so damn difficult to remember that.

Ree's in trouble, that's what he's using so many fancy words for himself for, to cover up. He watches, and sees how Parrin's getting more hits to land effectively, getting the upper hand with a bulk that's not even impressive by wolf standards. He'd barely managed to hold Ree off, in the first minutes, but that was because he was still human-form and Ree had changed to wolf even as he'd cottoned on to something out on the jetty gone wrong, had jumped off the boat and come a-running to help Penn. But Parrin's changed to wolf pretty damn quick, for a beta. And if he wasn't already stronger than Ree, what with the injury, then he'd have been savaged enough during those initial minutes to give up the fight.

Now, as they wrestle and snarl, it's wolf against wolf. And even though Parrin's the smaller wolf, he's whole, and he's giving Ree a pounding the like of which Penn can't believe. Rage has to be the fuel for it: but every minute, Penn thinks, surely now, *now* Ree will turn the balance, and get the upper hand. And if not this moment, then the next.

He keeps waiting, as Parrin forces himself under Ree's whole body to send him bouncing up and slamming back hard enough to crack a wooden plank. He still waits, as a growling Parrin sends a struggling Ree almost into the water with a body charge that has Ree scrabbling and desperate for a scanty unsafe foothold, only saving himself from the icy waters with a crazy ballet-dancer leap around Parrin. It's an evasive move, though Penn knows perfectly well Ree's no physical coward, even against hostile odds. He's just accepting – quicker than Penn can – that he's outmatched. The idea's terrifying.

Ree has been his protector, as dear friends in childhood, and in adulthood as lovers. Penn's talked so much big talk, to himself, about looking out for himself, about not needing anyone, anything, barring as tools for him to use on his path to freedom and agency.

But if Ree's gone, then he has no-one. No-one to protect him, and no-one to care that there's no-one to protect him. (Can he rely on Lettice Parrin, her promises, her mateship? He wouldn't care to rely upon it. She may be a Parrin, but so is her brother Benedict, and he's trying to put an end to the only unfailing support and affection Penn has known in a long, very long time. So was old Jay Parrin, and whatever nice fancy promises and intentions he might have expressed to the rest of his family, he never mentioned one bloody word to Penn himself about eventual manumission. How is Penn to know whether his vaguely benevolent expressed desires might ever have been fulfilled, if his wishes would have come true?)

And... Penn's thinking much too slowly. Even as he struggles with the next thought, the conclusion of his struggles, Parrin jumps half-on Ree's back, and Ree staggers with the weight full on his back leg. Parrin bites him, right over the hulking meat of Ree's shoulder. Parrin's lupine fangs sink in so deep that the whole muscle could be ripped off – and Ree jerks, and staggers, and tries to throw him off. He fails, and it's one of the most frightening things that Penn's ever seen. He's still hesitating a few feet from their moving radius as they wrestle and rumble threats at each other, furious and cursing. The planks tremble underneath him. And Penn trembles, too.

At the second try, Ree does manage to throw Parrin off. But his shoulder is torn to bloody and fluttering ribbons, and he staggers as Parrin closes in tightly once again, and leaps on him a second time.

Ree can't withstand this much longer. Penn knows it. And however quickly Miss Lettice gets her furry arse back onto the jetty, it might not be soon enough, not at the rate of damage that Parrin's inflicting. Penn really has no choice, and he rebels against the idea. But on the other hand, there's no-one more pragmatic than Penn. What is, is the thing that *is*.

The dominant knowledge in his mind now is this: if Ree can't protect him, then he is going to have to protect Ree.

It shouldn't really be so hard. His hand goes to the deep and tight-stitched, double-felted pocket of his tunic, damp and thick-coarse in texture. But well-stitched, hard-wearing, durable: and a good place to put something you don't want anyone else to notice or to find. (Slaves make their own tunics, by tradition: and there's a reason they obey and adhere to the tradition so zealously.)

It isn't as if he'd drawn attention to it, up the sloping hill of the island when they'd been picking themselves up and setting off for the boat. Penn knows so much better than that. Nor had he had any specific reason to pick up the revolver from where it had fallen, after he'd recovered from being brought down and winged by Ree, along with Miss Lettice and the Dam.

He hadn't needed one. A slave needs no incentive nor reason, not to observe, learn and take advantage of any possible opportunity that offers itself, as he navigates his path through ownership and exploitation. He'd been happy, oh, heavens, more than happy, to be found and reclaimed by Ree, and the rest. Well, at least once he knew for sure that he wasn't going to face a punitive pack and severe sanctions as a result. But even if a return to the Hotstaat estate was good news for him, and even if being carried off to Canada and a very tenuous and hard-scrabble freedom was the last thing in the world that he actually wanted, still he wasn't going to turn down the opportunity to acquire an interesting bit of information, a useful bit of tech, a weapon that might at some future point make the difference between survival and being snuffed out, between freedom and captivity. He was too busy thanking many gods that he wasn't being tightly

questioned over it, that the wolves behind him had presumably assumed that the gunshots fired had come from the wolves up ahead
of him. And the silver-stink on their tracks that he can't perceive at
all, that's clearly so pervasive and powerful in the nostrils of a wolf,
covering over the gun's immediate presence, as well as the excitement
and adrenaline of immediate circumstance.

As if it was ever an option, to leave it behind. Penn isn't sure that
he knows any slave who wouldn't have quietly lifted it from where it
had skidded over rough ground, ferns and undergrowth, and pocket-
ed it as discreetly as possible.

That's what he did, and that is the reason that he has a revolver in
his tunic pocket right now.

But it's one thing to have it, and another to use it. Penn feels his
heart race, wobbling in his chest, unsteady as a rickety old wooden
shack, as the rotting softwood planks his feet are struggling to stay
steady on right now. And he takes the revolver out of his pocket, feeling the barrel swivel with the treasure inside, and he spins that barrel. Two bullets, that's all he has, and it's damn all good anyway, of
course.

Because the two wolves are writhing in a wrestling, struggling
mass, even as he struggles to think it out at a speed quick enough to
be some use. Any bullet he tries to put into Parrin is just as likely to
wind up in Ree's haunch or his shoulder. Or worse than that, in his
brain or a vital organ. These are effective silver bullets, nothing that
he can afford to take that kind of a chance with. But he can't wait,
and he can't linger and try for the perfect shot, and the perfect moment. Ree's sagging, coming back slower and slower, after every bite
and buffet from Parrin. Any minute now, he's going to fall and not
rise to fight on.

Penn's seen wolf fights. He knows how the dynamic goes, in an
unregulated dispute, and it goes nowhere that's good. Miss Lettice is
still a couple of hundred yards out in the freezing waters, easy. Easy.

She's nudging her snout underneath Sam's wet fish-bellied frozen torso, keeping him up out from the waves, from sinking beneath them and giving up the struggle to stay swimming and buoyant. It's a battle she can scarcely abandon to rush to Ree's side, and even if she was going to, it would take five minutes standing and yelling at the water's edge to get the message across. By that time Ree could have lost the last edge of vitality and strength that's keeping him fighting back against Parrin, fighting to stay on four paws when his injured thigh is trying to give out on him every second. That situation must end with the victor standing on his four paws, triumphing over the prone body of his rival. The rival he's vanquished may be living or dead at that point, but if living, it's not liable to be for ten minutes longer.

Penn can't afford to wait.

But he can hardly bear the thought of what he's going to have to do.

He doesn't think about it a lot, then. The amount of time he's already spent watching, and trying to work out the best thing, the option with the least damage all around, might yet be enough to tip the balance and doom Ree in this encounter.

He just does the thing. He rushes in, rushes straight at the pair as they roll over and over on the uneven bumps of the jetty, fighting and with jaws clashing and trying to meet canine point to canine point, through fur and flesh. They're too set and intent on each other to pay any attention or probably even to notice him. And he can't afford to hesitate, or he'd stop and lose any chance he has. He can't get a decent shot like this, with no control over movement or angles. So he doesn't stop. He just rushes straight in, and leaps between them, where they're snapping watering inch-toothed jaws and slamming at each other with hundred-pound shoulders, fifty-pound limbs.

He didn't expect it to go well, when he formulated such an idiotic plan in a split second. So it's no surprise when it doesn't. When he screams out in pain, he isn't even sure where the injury is – the pain's too sudden, and the protest too automatic. But in the next second he knows, he knows that it's his thigh, and that's Parrin's jaws set into his thigh, digging deep enough to go through muscle and almost to hit bone. What an irony, there, that after all of his careful, persistent, determined refusal of a bite offered as a privilege and an entrée into a more comfortable life, it's now that he gets it. In the middle of a fight he didn't start, of which he's not even one of the main participants, and not even deliberately. He doesn't think that Parrin went for him deliberately. At least, as far as he can guess, in the midst of scream-ing and squealing with the pain and watching the blood spurt out of a handsome set of dental indentations, the surreal visual panorama that's more intense and frighteningly vivid than normal vision, feels drug-like and hallucinatory. And although he might die – the bite is that bad, for sure – he's not worried. Not as worried as he would be if he thought it would turn him wolf, at least.

It takes a lot more than just jaws puncturing flesh, for a werewolf bite that will transform a human to a creature that runs and gallops madly under a yellow moon, that takes on fur and fangs and can run all night, heal from (almost) all wounds, and keeps a compelled and secretive assignation with the moon in a society that rules its every move and choice. Penn's seen it happen, and he knows that this isn't it. There's a lot more holding in place involved, and a stillness of both biter and bit, besides a curious dark sick-looking shadowing about the eyes that foreshadows, itself, a sudden leap and bloom of health and strength and vigour that no human could ever experience. That is, if it doesn't foreshadow a sickly failure of the body to accept the change, a sudden frenzy of death and a violent mourning. That's in accord with some of Penn's experience, too.

But he's still human – even if not whole, unmarked and breath-ing human for much longer. And so he doesn't trouble to fret over what's done and too late, and just uses it as a tool, instead. He's done what he intended – got between them, and a good shot with clear access. So even as he groans with the horrible hot sour anguish of it, the blinding weakness like a toothache all through the guts and the core of him, and he feels his leg collapsing under him, he leans back and takes aim, pulling the pretty little gun out of his pocket and putting that last bullet but one to some use.

Not in the thigh, the way that Parrin has marked and wounded him and Ree both. Nor smashing through the skull or lodging in a vital organ that would do permanent damage and remove Parrin from the lists of active service in the battle against slavery.

Penn has a little too much respect – and use – for him, for that. Parrin's an idiot, an arrogant idiot, and an idiot who can't be relied upon, if it's a choice between a slave's interests and his own, or a slave's interest put against the interests of the whole cause and body of slaves... But he battles in the service of a cause he believes in, with whatever condescension and spirit of *noblesse oblige*. Penn isn't about to grant him a capital punishment for that. After all, although he's done his best, in a spirit of fury and madness in the heat of the moment, to put an end to Ree and do him a mortal wound – he hasn't quite managed it.

Which is a good thing, because then Penn might have had to return the favour. Ree will recover from this, even if it takes a good long time longer than normal. Penn, well, perhaps not. But his life has been one long arduous labour, and disagreeable, and bothersome, even when indulgence has granted him luxurious circumstances compared to many another slave. He's damn tired of fighting against his fate.

To be frank, death would not be that unwelcome. However it would distress Ree to hear him say so.

So all of that's decided even as he struggles not to fall, as he lifts his hands and cocks the trigger. Or even before that really, because Penn's strategy and plans are perpetually fluid, and change even every second, even as any detail alters. Penn puts a bullet through Parrin's back paw, the left one, as he rears back and away from Penn. (Penn thinks, quite dreamlike and calm, that partly it's remorse, and shock at having hurt Penn so badly, when it was Ree that he was after. But it's also physical shock, and considerable pain, and fury too. He can feel remorse over Penn, and outrage at the offence of Penn shooting him, at the same time. It's no surprise that Parrin's capable of that much hypocrisy.)

And Parrin's pain and sudden debility and weakness, as well as Ree's, are both very useful, right at this moment. For both of them, it impedes their normal speed and agility, so that even with his own injury, he can stagger away, down the jetty. He can head further towards the little boat that could take him back to a life with some promise and some possibilities, to emotional ties that promise security and preferment, as well as something homelike and warm that he hasn't aspired to for so long, for years.

Well, it could have, perhaps. If he hadn't just put a bullet through a wolf, and if he wasn't bleeding heavily from a wound that might or might not be life-threatening, and isn't arterial, judging by the speed of the blood-flow. But it's sure as hell not going to do him any favours, and it could easily prove fatal given the level of medical assistance available. Even if he survives, as a piece of property his value is going to decline significantly, and that doesn't bode anything good for his future. No matter who he belongs to. (If he's damaged, if he's not pretty, if he's lamed... what value will Ree have for him? He's not sure that he's eager to find it out.)

"Parrin," he barks out – and it's as harsh as he can make it, what with his leg feeling like it's afire with blood and ripped flesh, and trying to fold under him every other minute. It's only surprising that it's holding him up at all, with a wolf-bite - not a changing wolf-bite, but still, even a regular savaging can do plenty of damage – in the muscle and meat of his leg. He must have struck lucky, to some extent, if lucky can be an accurate adjective in this situation. There has to be enough undamaged muscle tissue, out of the way with vital blood vessels and functional activity, for the basic function of muscle, mechanics and motion, to still be performed as long as his circulation allows him consciousness, whatever the damage done. The bone, too, can't be significantly affected.

Both wolves are recovering stability, getting unsteadily to their feet, though Parrin is busily howling with agony, and no doubt fury as well. Ree, though – his eyes glow, with a light that Penn's learnt to identify as a fiercely possessive glee, the kind of satisfaction that Penn has withheld this long while as far as possible. Of course they do. He's just witnessed Penn taking a massive risk – not just a risk, but incurring serious injury, perhaps life-threatening – in order to protect him. Ree is going to *love* that. Penn might as well declare eternal love and devotion, may as well get down, kneel and propose marriage. Well, they're mated already, of course. That horse has bolted over the faraway green hills, and it isn't coming back.

He lunges forward at the same moment that Parrin does the same thing – except that Penn isn't tolerating any such foolery. Even as he wobbles on his injured leg, blood oozing, dribbling out of toothmarks and the flesh contusing and rapidly turning dark, he levels his firing hand, and calmly aims the revolver – with its payload of a single bullet, not that any of them need to know that – at about a mid-point between the various wolves he's facing. And he snaps, again, at Parrin: "Parrin! Get over here, to me. And don't look at me with that dumb expression, like you think I'm going to shoot you because you just, you just savaged my *leg*. You *arsehole*."

Penn has a deep, capacious reservoir of contempt for the lupine race, built up over years and years. He very rarely has any chance to expend any of it, and if he's ever going to have a better chance than this, then–. Well, that isn't going to happen. He's never going to be at the preferable end of a gun and pointing it at three wolves, again.

Three wolves, yes. Because – for once in his life, and Penn is marking it well, noting it down and probably trying to have it made into a national holiday – Parrin is following the plan, and doing the smart thing. He's doing what Penn has told him. The gun probably has something to do with it. He moves – slowly, and keeping an eye on the business end of the revolver – towards Penn. (Penn, who is sagging a bit at the knees. Who is, actually, in some rather horrible pain, and trying to ignore it, refusing to acknowledge it.) Parrin knows what kind of bullets are in that gun. And considering their hectic chase, Penn in pursuit, through the scrubby woods of the island, Parrin probably isn't completely sure just how many bullets Penn has left in it.) He shifts back to human-form as he comes closer: and the bullet in his foot isn't any the more pretty because of it. His foot is wrecked by that bullet, unlookable at, unwitnessable: but he only winces a little as he approaches, warily. Penn's willing to bet it's more pride than invulnerability. A silver bullet hurts: it even hurts a wolf.

"Nice work, Pennorth," he says warily, his eyes on the barrel, all his focus there and none for Penn's eyes. "We should all have been keeping our eyes on the money, a lot more carefully than we actually were. Or, on the gun, to be a bit less metaphorical."

He moves up closer – limping horribly, and with body language that's on the hostile side of wary. As he gets a bit too close, Penn veers the gun barrel around to face him more exclusively, and give him a snarling face that would do credit to any wolf. "You think about it," he says, meaning any reckless grab for this nice, useful tool, "and I'll put another bullet in your leg this time – to match mine, to match his – so you have plenty of other things to think about." And he jerks a nodding head in Renally Hotstaat's direction.

Yes, three wolves, besides Parrin. He has three to consider, because Ree isn't the only one facing him on the jetty, as Parrin evens up beside him, just far enough, and crippled enough, that a grab for power and control over the situation is less of a risk. Ree's there, yes, smack in the middle of the jetty and with his stability regained, advancing slowly and carefully, with a dip and sway to his bad leg, the one that's twin to Penn's own now. But coming up is his mother the Dam, where she's thundered up, loping down from the shallow hill of the island and shaking the jetty with her approach as she runs towards them. Penn has felt her arrival, sensed it, heard it as he struggled with two wolves and put a bullet in one, to gain dominance over this disaster.

But he thinks he can be excused for not having greeted the great lady of the Hotstaat pack. Largely since he was, ahem, wrestling with a couple of enraged and fighting werewolves, at the time. The lady will no doubt forgive him. And if she doesn't, well, the blood loss that's making him a little faint and grey around the edges of his field of vision may take care of any consequences, before she can do so.

And to the other side of Ree, is the Lady Lettice. She's still in the freezing and grimly grey waters of the bay – nosing at young Sam, the slave she's finally shepherded to shore and rescued, pushing him up out of the water as he crawls, weak and cold and exhausted, onto the jetty. And she leaps up to follow him – sodden, with gouts of water streaming off her sleekly platinum grey fur – as Ree lets a low rumble emanate from his great broad wolf throat. He changes, before Penn's eyes, as Penn points the gun at him now, to keep him off.

Penn is talking to Benedict Parrin – saying, "Parrin, get back, go on. To the edge of the jetty, yes, that's what I mean. You're getting out of here, now," – even as Ree fully transforms, and speaks to Penn.

"You saved me, Penn," is what he says, as if that's any kind of a surprise, or the most relevant important aspect of this interesting kettle of fish. Penn ignores him, because it seems the only safe course of action. He's listing to one side himself, and it's hard to concentrate on anything other than the roaring fire in his thigh, the ripped tissue and damaged blood vessels that are leaking out blood and sapping his grip on consciousness every minute that passes. He'd kick out at Parrin, who's taking damn all notice of what he's being told, but instead staring at his dripping, lovely, regal sister, as she nursemaids the human fool who's almost sunk himself and perished as a result of his reckless bid for liberty. (Stares with a wild intensity, a little too passionate, and it gives Penn some pause and cause to think, has him wondering about wolf sibling bonds and if pack bonds allow for that intensity of sibling attachment.) Penn punches out with his free hand blindly instead, keeping one eye on the wolves before him, demanding Parrin's attention.

"Go on," he says, and it's for Parrin, although he's still not looking at the bastard. He jerks his head at the sail-boat bobbing between the island and the horizon, a half mile or more away, and says, "You think Canada and the liberty territories are so great, you can go and live there." He's keeping his eyes on the wolves he's nominally allied with, as he figures them more of an actual immediate danger. At least two of them, the Dam and Miss Lettice, are hale and whole. And even if both are occupied with changing to human form even as he observes them, that doesn't make them significantly less of a danger. Nor less of a potential obstacle to his hastily assembled plan. And Penn does not care for obstacles nor opposition to his plans. He's much against it, very tired of it in fact. He very fully means to have his way, and he'll take any action that that should prove to require.

That doesn't mean he isn't liable to meet with opposition, unfortunately. "You think I'm going to go running off with my tail between my legs?" Parrin asks, incredulous. His handsome face twists in disdain at the ridiculous idea, and Penn would like very much to hit him right upside the head with the barrel of the gun, in addition to the gaping hole shot through his foot, that would have a human victim laid on the ground, now, and screaming in agony. Even as a wolf, Parrin looks green and sick, much worse than he'd be with a regular bullet. He's hunched over his foot and bowed like an old man, but still the prime concern in his mind is the indignity of being required to avail himself of the same escape route as a slave seeking liberty. (And Penn could also make use of the pun that Parrin has unconsciously offered up as a weapon at his feet. Except that he has too much dignity and brisk efficiency for that. Well, given the current stress of this complex situation, at least.)

"Why not?" Penn asks drily. "It was good enough for me, and every other slave you've liberated, forcibly or otherwise, isn't it so? I'm not asking you, Parrin: I'm not giving you another option. And I'm doing you a favour. Do you imagine you're going to get a warm welcome, returning to wolf society, after this? Do you think that Alpha Hotstaat is going to protect you, even if your sister pleads for you?" It's strange how strongly old shibboleths hold on to him. It's impossible even now, to call Ree *Ree*, in front of wolf witnesses. Even though every damn one of them knows how it goes and how it's gone, between them.

It's Parrin he asks, but it's Ree who actually answers him, or at least responds to him first. He's edging forward as he does it – cautiously, wisely. Because he knows Penn, pretty damn well after these decades since they were boys together, and it's not surprising if he knows better than to think that Penn wouldn't use the tool in his hand. Hasn't Penn already demonstrated that he's quite prepared to open fire if he's provoked enough? The proof's the hole shot through Parrin's foot: and Penn relies securely on his own willingness to do whatever needs doing. Including even to Ree, if his *wolluf* pushes it far enough.

Ah, and he's proof against any weapon or assault, right now. Except perhaps one, and that's the gentleness in Ree's voice. He says, soft and seductive, "Penn. You saved me, when he was going to take me down. You proved your loyalty, you proved your love. I know you care, I know you know where you belong. What are you doing, letting him go? I know that you're not going to go running off with him, to somewhere that isn't where you belong. You belong with your mates. You belong with me." Oh, damn him. Penn really ought to shoot him, just for that wily, confident seduction, the knowledge that he has a hold over Penn that Penn can't withstand or destroy.

In fact Penn's sorely tempted. The gun wobbles in his trembling hand, or perhaps it's just pain and fatigue.

The crack of laughter from Penn's side, from Parrin's direction, rather destroys the mood set up, though. It's bitter, it's disbelieving. "You think I'm going anywhere, Hotstaat? If this crazy slave thinks he can make me go – if you think that I have any intention of it – then you're both as crazy as each other. I begin to think that maybe you're a matched pair! Lettice, are you going to let this happen? My sister won't let this happen!" He's incredulously furious, his voice lit up with it. And yes, he really does think himself too good for a fate he was happy to bless a human slave with, Penn thinks critically.

And the Dam – fully transformed, now, mud-streaked, marble-haunched, regal and incensed – surges forward. But she halts abruptly, as Penn swings his gun-hand in her direction, with a tight-mouthed look that speaks. These wolves are not fools, and they know what the gun bears. The Dam knows him, in a way, almost as well as Ree does. No doubt she remembers very well the tempers, the furies, the impulsive destruction that he was prone to as a small child. He's still fully capable of the same. She's smart enough to have detected it, a refined and brilliant woman and wolf. "Really, Parrin?" she asks, cold as ice, a lady all through and fully capable of cold homicide. It comes through in every word. "You won't deign to accept an out, an escape route? You're more of a damn fool than I imagined. You'd be wise to take it when it's offered, though. Because if you try to return to your old life, to slip right back into society as if nothing ever happened, then do you imagine we"ll allow it? That we'll protect you?" She laughs elegantly, loud but ladylike. For a delicate and bell-like sound, it's incredibly harsh. "Because your sister has married into the clan? We didn't want her contracted and brought into the pack, her or her dowry, in the first place – certainly it was done without my approval. She'd have got nowhere without the patronage of the slave you kidnapped and removed from our care without his consent or seeking it. Because he can twist my son between his pretty fingers like clay to be moulded. And now, he's offering you a deal you'll take if you have the least particle of sense in the world. Because, Benedict Parrin, you've robbed from the Hotstaats, and plotted against them, shipped an enemy into our midst like a Trojan horse, and associated us with treachery, abolitionism and criminal sedition. You've opened us up to danger and disrepute, and you didn't even do it with the free consent and choice of the slave you took. And if you don't jump into the bloody water, and swim to save your sorry neck right now, swim for that boat and the horizon and liberated slave territories, then the moment that Pennorth drops from blood loss, or sees sense and stops training a gun on those who care for his best interests, then I'm going to rip your heart out, and your throat into the bargain."

It's spoken with the warm, smooth modulation and delicate precision of any society lady. And it is utterly sincere.

But there's dissension in these motley ranks, and the Dam's son and Alpha isn't quite content with her stance. His face is uneasy – greying with the pain, and blood loss and fatigue into the bargain, but distressed more than any of those things – and he says, "Mama, it's not altogether Lettice's fault, what Parrin's been up to. He's her brother, she has a natural loyalty and it's very hard to turn your back on kin." It's more restrained and careful than Penn has ever heard Ree, except with his mother. But there's still a core of certainty at the centre of it: an assurance that Ree isn't going to give up on and abandon his hand-fasted mate, no matter what the dereliction of a wolf's duty, the betrayal. And Penn wonders if that applies to him also: and he hopes very much that it's so. Because Ree turns his attention back to Penn, and he says, with a great sincere tenderness, but also with the harshness that comes with a direct order, from the alpha of a pack, "But you, Penn, you have a choice. That bastard has offended against us, and he's offended against you. Look at your leg! Look at mine, too! He's not worth your protection and your support. He's a criminal within wolf society, and if you lend him aid, then effectively that makes you a criminal too. You can't go with him." Oh, Ree is pleading now. And theoretically, Penn should be pleased to hear it: should be happy to bring the lord and master down so low, to make him lower himself to begging the slave he's infatuated with. In fact, it hurts, hurts him just as it clearly hurts Ree's pride, and perhaps his heart too. He isn't sure why, but there's an obscure twinge at the muscle of his heart, and he feels dammed-up tears almost full enough to spill over. "Don't go with him. And don't help him, don't let him go. Look at what he's done." Ree makes a frustrated gesture: Penn's thigh, his own, Sam, Lettice. Penn isn't sure what offence Parrin's supposed to have committed against Sam, who came to liberty of his own free will, to the best of his knowledge. And to Lettice, still less, unless Ree means getting her embroiled in liberationism and sedition. But then, Ree has a very partial and biased view of those he's fond of. They can do very little wrong. Penn is pretty sure that he knows better – that Lettice Parrin is capable, of her own agency, of getting into all kinds of trouble, of her own volition.

Ree considers Benedict Parrin a bad man, and maybe a worse wolf: for stealing his property, and that of other wolves, for wounding and getting into trouble those he has an affection for. Penn wonders if Ree is actually capable of judging any issue other than by his passions and prejudices and training, on impartial and ethical grounds. It seems unlikely, at this point. Of course, Parrin has injured Ree as well: when he came to retrieve his property. And he's injured Penn, which Ree seems to take most umbrage at. But Penn thinks rather that it's his own business, whether and how much offence he chooses to take. "He doesn't deserve you," Ree glowers. "And in any case, you should have more sense. Your best interests are with us: and with helping us."

Oh, Penn does enjoy being kindly instructed about what to think. It provides him with so much entertainment, at the expense of those who think he's no mind of his own.

Not that Parrin seems to want to take the hint and be off, splashing through the Arctic waves towards freedom and escape – a good enough version for slaves, at least. "That boat of yours, and your buddy on it, I don't think they're going to wait forever," Penn points out sharply to him, over his shoulder. "You might want to get moving, if you're going. And I think you should go. The evidence points that way, very much."

"But I don't want to go," Parrin says helplessly – yes, there's definitely a helpless tone in his voice, now. "I don't want to. Letty, you aren't going to watch these bastards make me go, are you, love? You can still make Hotstaat help me, cover for me. I know you can – I know you could, if you wanted to. You're hand-fasted – not just hand-fasted, but properly mated, after all. Pennorth, you too – you could help me, if you would. You could."

Oh. Penn laughs, without even bothering to turn around. He's laughing right in Ree's direction, mostly just because that's the way he's turned. The gun shakes with it. "Perhaps I could," he says. And it says clearly enough, *but I won't.*

Chapter 9

Lettice, she's more emotional, more distressed, more manipulated. But then it's her brother, and it's hardly surprising. "I have helped, Ben. I've helped again and again, whenever you've asked – bloody hell, I sought out a bonding, an alliance because it would help you, and never mind my preferences or what I might have liked for myself. I might not have taken it as far or done as much as you'd have liked, but I've never turned you away, masked my alpha status to help you gain influence... Ben, I can't do everything, it can't go on forever. I'm mated now. I didn't know it was going to happen." Her eyes are wide, surprised, starry. She looks unfairly pretty, and very unfairly happy, suddenly. Penn can't imagine that it does her any favours, in her benighted and doomed brother's eyes. "But it has. Now, I have other responsibilities. It isn't just about you, not now."

She finishes flat, and simple, hands limp behind her back, and Parrin sighs. It's the sigh of a man who's given up. "Bloody cow," he says, but it sounds quite philosophical. There's no warning, when he takes a running jump and slides into the water without any ceremony, his pale-olive nakedness slipping into the waves as if it belongs there. Like Miss Lettice, he changes even as he begins to swim, his decision made (or made for him.)

But Penn doesn't observe much of his onward progress, towards the waiting boat steaming and bobbing in the far distance, a wolf prowling around the rails, and a manikin figure bearing binoculars leaning on the side, watching them. Perhaps it's Gus and Harry, or one of them and Parrin's freedman contact. Either way, it's further than human eyes can see, and a long way to swim. Even for a wolf, with a bullet – a treated silver bullet – in the foot.

Penn isn't watching, because it's too important, here and now, to maintain surveillance over the other wolves in his periphery, and their response to Parrin making his decision, and taking the watery option, heading for the frozen-up wastes of the northernmost Americas and Alaska.

Good thing that he does, too. Lettice hangs to the side, her arm still comfortingly around poor limp depleted Sam, maternal, supportive, comforting. She looks conflicted and troubled: and cries out into the waters, towards Benedict Parrin, "Ben! You bloody – you - I can't help it! I can't watch and cover for you forever, I can't make my whole life about your crusade! Haven't I done enough for you?" Penn doubts very strongly that Parrin's listening at all. She certainly shows no signs of jumping in after him, not like her automatic instinct to protect and retrieve Sam. Perhaps she's genuinely tired of the whole thing, of protecting and supporting a brother who has no caution or doubts. Or sense. But there's still grief and anger and sorrow etched on her pretty thin delicate face, as well as frustration and a half-ashamed kind of relief.

The Dam, she looks angry and cold, but she makes no move to go after Parrin, no attempt at physical dissuasion and retribution. Probably she's thinking *good riddance and good-bye*: certainly that's the first thing that Penn would infer from her face. And she's moving to put a hand to Ree's shoulder: to express support for her alpha and her son, to discourage him from intervening himself, to discourage him from changing to wolf, leaping into the ocean and savaging Parrin until the grey waters flow red and Parrin's offences against him, against Penn, against Lettice and who knows who else – wolves, mostly, probably – have been expunged from all records. Via a blood price, of course.

But she's too late, because Ree's too quick. Even as Lettice and the Dam are both moving, talking, Ree's taking one leap across the creaking wooden planks of the jetty – two – ready to plunge into ice-water that would freeze most human hearts after half an hour's dunking or less – and then...

Then he stops dead, very wisely. Of course he does. Because Penn isn't having that – has made his feelings on the subject a matter of perfect clarity. And, therefore, has immediately discharged his weapon, into the dusty wet wave-moulded wood of the jetty. Right at Ree's feet, of course, and by that, Penn means *right at his feet*, so close that you could count it as a precise and close manicure of Ree's toenails, or his claws after the change. And he's begun to change, even in those first strides – but now, quite abruptly, easily and quickly, the change reverts back, and hair at the temples and cheeks recedes, the beginnings of a lengthening of nails into claws reverses. Ree stops, right there, with the echo of the bullet still reverberating in all their ears. The treated silver bullet that could have been through his brain or his liver or his gut. That would have done for him, all right, farewell Ree, no more being the indulged pet and the pampered sweetheart, goodbye to being the foremost slave in unofficial status. Although not to captivity. He'd still have belonged to the Hotstaats: and been a lot less popular with them, at the same time. It would have been very awkward indeed.

But Penn is used to making hard decisions and taking drastic action. He's been doing risky things, engaging with destiny and taking it on, *changing* it, fucking with it and arguing with it, ever since he can remember. Sometimes the payoff is worth it. And if it isn't, you learn something, and if the consequences aren't fatal then it was probably worth it anyway. And anyway, a threat is no good, not if you fail to make it clear that you're extremely willing to follow through on it. They know that now, and it establishes relations on a much more cordial and advantageous level for Penn, weighted considerably more in his favour. He's willing to go to any lengths, and on that basis, they're willing to negotiate.

They don't know that that was the last bullet in the barrel – from the exact same weapon that they heard discharging as they chased off up after Penn, and Sam, and the wolves, up the hill on the island. And they don't need to know it, either. Penn gasps as the gun discharges – because that was the fourth time he's shot it, in the last hour, and his damn hand hurts, and the air smells of cordite, and he's so tired altogether. His leg hurts like fire, like his bone's made of rotting pus and the whole thing might as well be ready to drop off. It doesn't look that bad – bad, but not that bad. But still, it's certainly bad enough.

But he's done what he needed to do, to make the wolves pause and deliberate, to back off and take him very seriously. Not that Ree's going to admit it, Penn knows. He just teeters a moment, right on tip-toes where Penn's arrested his progress – and if he was human it'd be a more comic look, nude. It's a fairly comic look in any case, except that it's never a good idea to laugh at a wolf. Not openly, at any rate. Not an alpha. Perhaps least of all one you've been bedding for going on a year.

He drops back onto the heels of his feet – a magnificent creature, a perfecf raw wild male animal, smiling at Penn slyly, sweet and fond and not one bit to be trusted. "Penn. Darling. My love," he says. "Now, you know that you wouldn't hurt a hair on my head. In point of fact, there's good solid evidence of that, seeing as you put a bullet in that bastard not ten minutes ago, when he was trying to take a piece out of me. While I was practically down and out for the count, too, what with a bullet-wound in my thigh at the same time, also courtesy of that arsehole. My apologies, Letty," he adds, giving a quick glance to his other mate, standing a little bereft off to one side, a little lost and angry. "But you can understand I account myself to owe your brother very little favour at this point."

Letty shrugs, non-committal, perhaps understanding, or perhaps reserving judgement on the matter. But her mother-in-law, to the other side of Ree, has a cold quiet face, and it is trained, now, upon Penn. "Does *he* understand it, though? Your slave-mate?" she asks, pointedly. She makes no lunges, no move to take revenge, or action or sanction, to take Penn back into Hotstaat possession. Very sensible of her, considering he's the one with the business end of a firearm ready to hand. But her expression broods coldly, and promises no good things. "Considering he's just let a damned traitor and revolutionary escape, and doesn't seem one bit sorry for it, either. Not after you've hand-fasted and mated with him, even. You *moron*, Renally." Her tone is quite level, and yet Penn doesn't doubt her meaning it, not for a moment.

Ree is undisturbed, and doesn't even look his Dam's way. His attention, too, is all for Penn, which troubles Penn not one bit at this point. "Mother, Penn has his own point of view. On many things, and he always has had. You knew this already," he points out, with a very great degree of truth. "He'll come around to our way of thinking eventually. And even if he doesn't," he adds – smiling pleasantly at Penn, with a sincere warmth, that's still a little smug, that still holds an assurance of eventual triumph, "for this matter... all we have to do, is to wait. A little longer."

And well, Penn knows what he means. But he doesn't think that Ree, nor the rest of them perhaps, are ever going to really understand why it matters so much to let Benedict Parrin go free, to escape into a life that's not his former existence of covert activism and privilege and deception, perhaps... But is still free, and alive, and dignified in its way.

Especially considering the idiot has just put his teeth in Penn's thigh, and put them deep, to a depth that's frightening and life-threatening. And done it accidentally, which is almost worse – which is actually worse, for Penn, for someone who fetishises competence and efficiency – than if it was intentional. But Penn's willing to overlook it, for Parrin. Who has principles that – if really pushed to it – he's willing to sacrifice something for, to take risks and even risk his neck over. (And other peoples', too, but Penn lets that pass.) Who has a quite rigid ethical system, can see the wrong and the injustice even in a system that benefits and enriches him unjustly. And doesn't just sit around in elegant restaurants, spas, coffee-houses, and complain about it, like the fashionable young set, or the bohemian section of them. But puts himself on the line, and makes things change.

He's the utter polar opposite of Ree, in fact. And if he had a little more human feeling and passion in him, a little more sentiment and personal attachment – like Ree? If he was less ruled by chilly and inflexible moral principle, less willing to sacrifice the individual for the sake of a greater idea and a benefit to the whole community... then maybe... (Well. Or maybe, if Ree was a little less ruled by love and feeling and irrational tendernesses, less fiercely devoted where he's given his heart. If he had a little more principle and a broader, more solidly founded moral base to operate from – if he could see the great picture of human and slave suffering and injustice, instead of picking favourites and cherishing them and being so blind to all the troubles of the rest of the world... In short, if he was a little more like Parrin...)

Well. In fact, if only you could choose who you attach yourself to, Penn thinks. (It doesn't hurt that Parrin's easy on the eyes, too. That pretty maroon sheen to his hair, the hazel eyes that gleam half-silver with the wolf... Penn has noticed. He isn't blind to others, just because Ree is beautiful. It's even a point of pride.) Penn will even admit to himself that it jars a little. That he'd thought, assumed all along that surely, with all of this attention, all of this continual badgering and hinting and mysterious allusions to Penn's specialness and meaning for the Parrins... Well, he'd assumed that at least a little of it was a personal preference for Penn himself, even if not all of it. That Parrin had some measure of softness, of personal attraction to Penn.

Now? Well, now he's not sure that Parrin is even capable of a personal attraction, to anyone. He may possibly be the most impersonal, cause-obsessed individual that Penn's ever encountered.

Penn rather likes him for it, too.

Here and now, though, such musings will only get in the way of his survival and his intentions. He's a damn sight too busy for any of this. Well, too busy, and too exhausted, in too much pain. He's doing his best to stand straight, to hold the revolver level, as he stares out wolves with an insolence that he'd never have dared, days back, even hours back. (In fact, he'd have been too wise for it, not too timid. But wisdom won't get him far now. It's useful for the oppressed, and a serf's tool for one in a position of power. And he appears to have run out of it anyhow.) His arm aches – everywhere aches, in response to the red throb of pain of his thigh, screaming if torn and ruined muscle tissue can scream internally. His hand wobbles a little, but he keeps that revolver aloft, and mobile as he trains it on the three wolves before him, watching him warily with one eye on the sea, the swimmer, the boat.

"Listen, Penn," Ree begins again, more warily this time. His mother's lips are a tight thin line, his fiancée looks torn, guilty and distracted. (And little as if she's about to change her mind. Her eyes track sadly out to the grey sea, but she's still here, isn't she? Holding up a limply depressed slave, succouring who she can in the way she can, in the life she's abruptly chosen. She's been a bad naughty alpha wolf-girl. But if Ree can forgive her, then Penn supposes that he can too.) "We can just wait you out, and you know it. Look at your leg, look at what that bastard you're protecting has done to it. It's bleeding, it's not getting any better, and it's worse than for him or for me." His expression softens, is so gentle. Penn knows better than to trust that expression. It's sincere, and that's why Penn doesn't trust it. If he lets it, it could change his mind.

"You can try," Penn says, and he hates the quiet determined softness of his voice. Because of the softness, because Ree can probably – no, he's a wolf, scratch that, he can see, hear, smell, taste it – the desire to yield, that Penn can feel, down deep in himself. Is it a mate thing? Or is it just something about Ree, that's always going to do this to him? "But it depends how long I can hold out. If Parrin can swim far enough, if I hold you off long enough, then it'll be too late. That boat can out-speed even a wolf. Once he's on it, even once he's near enough, then it'll be too late."

"Bloody fool," the Dam says curtly. "Too late for who, young Pennorth?" She's chilled, and her handsome human nude form is goose-pimpled. Even a werewolf doesn't especially care to hang around in the altogether for quite this long in late autumn. There's a faint blue tang to the sway of her breasts – that would be more than impressive on a human woman – and the statuesque modelling of her hips. But she appears impervious, or perhaps only wills it to be so. "You're willing to hold us off for as long as it takes, are you?" My, but she's furious. "Until you collapse, if necessary. Which doesn't look to be that far away, from here. Bloody *fool*."

"My mother's right, Penn," Ree coaxes, gently. It's very unlike him, sits oddly on his proud masterful form, his regal head. But there are many strange things he's willing to do for Penn, after all, and have always been. Their attachment has not been one-sided, at all, beyond Penn's first infant hero-worship. "You can't keep this up. You're going to collapse, you could die, please don't do this to yourself. Don't do it to me, don't do it to Lettice. *We* care, even if you're willing to sacrifice yourself, and you are the heart in my chest and the life in my–."

Oh, and it's come to pretty words. Ree's good at that. He's not as good as he thinks at persuasion, distraction, manipulation and stealth, though. Otherwise Penn wouldn't catch immediately the first inching forward of one foot, when he tracks Penn's eyes as they linger on an intense-eyed and sad Lettice, on the Dam, and takes his chance for a move, an attempt to disarm Penn and go after Parrin.

"Try it," Penn snarls, quite wolfy himself, training the revolver more securely on Ree, right between the eyes. He's steady as granite, even if it's going to kill him. "I will blow your damned head off, by Lucifer. Damn the gods themselves, I *will*."

And if he doesn't mean it, then it's still a really excellent imitation. And if his heart's pounding, cold sweat pouring off him, from lying to Ree, from the crippling pain of the bite in his thigh, then what else can even a wolf expect from a slave threatening to murder his owners? Ree is probably pretty sure he wouldn't do it.

But not quite sure enough to take the chance, just the same. And that's how it goes, Penn holding them back, the three of them – or two and a half, because Lettice watches her brother swimming further into the distance with a look half heartbreak and half a good riddance, needing no words. And them trying it, trying it. They back off when he renews threats, and reminds them what a silver-treated bullet can do, and has already, all up and down Ree's ruined thigh.

A good thing wolves can't sense metal beyond the smell of it, for them. Penn does a damn good job, he considers, for a man with an empty gun barrel. Very convincing, in fact, or sufficiently so. And he keeps it going, keeps up the act, long enough. Long enough, he thinks, when really the muscles of his bad leg are refusing to hold him up much longer, and the pain's more than any human can be expected to bear. And he can feel the greying, soft and fuzzy at the corners, of his vision. But he thinks he'll hold out another minute to be sure, another minute, or two or five. To be certain, and he'll wave the gun around one more time and make one more threat, one more...

He's down, lopped down in his prime like a felled elm, before he knows he's going over, and that's done and a relief. The gun goes skittering over wood, and there's a splash as it flies with the force of his fall, and dimly Penn thinks that that's a bit of a shame. It would have pleased him to see Ree pick the damn thing up and open up the barrel to check it out, and to realise he'd been taken by a scam the whole time. Penn would have laughed. And now he's horizontal on the planks and no threat, no obstacle, he expects them to go run and dive after Parrin, to drag him back and make him pay the piper a pretty penny.

Except they don't, so maybe he got the job done. He held up for a good long time, after all. Well done to him, he'd pat himself on the back if he could, if he was more than barely conscious at all. Miss Lettice, she does run and go stand at the very edge of the jetty. She shades her eyes and looks out at the horizon and says, "Too late, they've picked him up, we'll never catch them now." She doesn't quite sound sorry, of course.

But Ree, and the Dam, neither of them give a moment's attention or a good goddamn to the direction of Parrin, or Parrin himself, is what it looks like. No, because the both of them are a sight too busy, diving in his direction. And Ree gets there first – of course he does. He's the Alpha, he's younger and stronger. And it matters more to him. His hands go travelling over Penn, arms and back and arse and chest, checking he's in one piece and copping a feel and poking and shaking him a bit all in one, and mostly skating, carefully, delicately as a dance, around the goring gory great bite in his leg. "You'll be all right," he's muttering, and he sounds feverish and emphatic both. He's trying to convince himself as well as Penn, perhaps. "You'll be fine. Let's get you into the little boat, and across to the mainland, and we'll have you to the nearest doctor before you can blink, it'll be fine. It will be."

He sounds a little desperate, even, and Penn thinks it but he thinks it very distantly. He supposes that perhaps he's further gone than he'd realised, and that after all perhaps he left it a little late to give in and hope for the best. But *stubborn* has always been his middle name, or perhaps *ornery like a mule*, as one of the cooks at one of his owners' houses had put it. Merely tell him that he can't have or do a thing, and there's nothing else that'll satisfy him, barring to have it, or else to do it.

In this dreamlike state, it occurs to him that Ree's courtship methods have been all arse-about-tit. It would be quite funny, now, when it might be too late altogether, to tell him that. That if only he'd played at being coldly forbidding and uninterested, had told Penn that the friendship of their youth was a cherished memory, of course, but he could never hope for anything more... Well, inevitably and of course, that would have led to Penn falling passionately in love with him, and laying siege to all of his defences and rationalizations, until he'd impregnated that impregnable castle. So you might say.

And it seems that his methods, in general, do not impress the Dam, any more than Penn. Or at least, that's the impression that Penn gets, when Ree gently pushes his arms underneath Penn's shoulders and his knees, in preparation to pick him up and to carry him. Her voice cracks out like a perfect silken whip.

"Oh, crying out to all the angels, Renally. Are you going to let him freeze and injure his leg further, before you even get him into the boat?" The Dam doesn't usually speak that way, to her eldest. He's her alpha, despite being his mother, for one thing. And since he always – almost always – accords her an immaculate and filial respect, she generally renders him the same, tempered with a little maternal asperity and fondness.

Not now, though – and the unwonted harshness appears to get the gist of her message through. Ree was wild, incoherent and frantic already, Penn thinks vaguely. But now he's only more so. "Yes," Ree says, vaguely, urgently looking about him in an uncoordinated way. But then his gaze fixes on the motorboat, still tied up, still waiting for them at the end of the jetty. "I should go and get a blanket – I should go and get a splint, something to strap his leg up with–."

"Yes, indeed you should," the Dam agrees. Penn could almost applaud the very gentle sarcasm in her voice, so gentle that only one actively seeking it out would be able to hear it. But Ree's barely aware, that's clear. He bounds off to the cabin of the boat, smooth human haunches gleaming bright and taupe-skinned in the dimmest light of day that Scotland can afford. Lovely, infuriating, uncontrollable, wrong-headed about so much. The person who cares about Penn, more than any other. Who brings him back, won't let him go, forgives him anything. Who withholds what Penn wants most.

"And now we're alone, Pennorth," the Dam says smoothly, as Ree hoves off and bounds away, setting the jetty swaying and the boat rocking as he dives into the cabin, out of sight.

"We're not," Penn says in response, dimly, softly, just because she's wrong, quite wrong. He waves a hand up, to where Miss Lettice stands off to the side, still staring out at the waters where the great sail-boat has picked up her brother, and is heading for the horizon, taking him out of her life for good. Mixed feelings show on her face, and her mind is far away from the here and now, away with the fairies. Which is no good place to be. She spares them a glance, though: and under her casual patronage, nestled under the protection of her arm, Sam watches them with uncharacteristic quietness. He's big-eyed, white-faced, his hair inhumanly orange in comparison. This experience – well, probably his whole life – has been too much for him. It shows.

The Dam laughs at Penn. Now she's kneeling over him very close, much closer than he'd realised. Her handsome bony face is unnerving. Her eyes are so bright, and so intent on Penn. Who ever looks at a slave with that degree of attention? "Well, I stand corrected," she says. "Corrected by a slave, and not for the first time, in your case. Corrected, told off, yelled at, tantrummed at... What a history you have, of telling Hotstaats their business, Pennorth. It's quite amazing that you've lived this long. And now I'm going to do for you what my son ought to do, but won't."

She says it, announces it, quite casually, a flip afterthought to her lecture on what a terrible slave he is and always has been. But Penn doesn't miss much, not even half-dead from blood-loss and fatigue and pain. That's a threat that's enough to have any slave panic and grip at the arms suddenly book-ending his head, to try to push a wolf away and shove himself up, to get free, to get safe. Ree's forgiven him, is mated with him, won't punish him. But that makes no guarantees for anything the Dam might do.

Of course it's fruitless, useless, his effort. The Dam swats him down with one hand on his chest, as if he was a mouse trying to escape the trap, tempted in by delicious cheese. The Dam, she is the household tabby, of course, the matriarch and a plump mouser who knows no mercy. "Heaven's sake, boy," she says now, irritable. "Hold still, else I'll make you do it. For you, I said, *for* you. Not *to* you." She stops, and smiles down at him. And although it's still a little detached – it's still a little as if he's a very interesting case and she's been appointed investigator by the local sheriff – the smile on her wide thin-lipped beautiful mouth is not unkind. Not unkind, no: much, vastly more complex than that.

Penn gasps up at her – it's getting a little bit hard to breathe, and it's not only the panic. He suspects it's down to so much blood lost that his body's having trouble transporting enough oxygen around, and that's bad news. But the Dam doesn't look worried. "You saved my son's life, right before my eyes, today, Pennorth," she says carefully, clearly. "Parrin was out of control, and is a ruthless little bastard besides, probably keeps a record of grudges that needs its own archive. He stands in your favour, as a Parrin, dirty liberal liberationist self-righteous bastards. And he thinks because of that, that we *don't*. He would have killed my boy and felt virtuous as an angel, doing it. But you didn't let him, even though it cost you blood and a wound that could cripple you, if it didn't kill you instead."

Well, that is true. Penn thinks, fuzzy, hazy, that it's probably not diplomatic to mention, at this point as the Dam stages his defence, that it was done with great reluctance, and an awareness that all of his affection and protection towards Ree transgresses against his own best interests in many ways. Lettice is watching them fixedly, now, along with Sam: has given up staring out at the sea, given up on wishing herself a different brother who is anything other than a trial and an irritant for her.

"And I am grateful," the Dam adds. "My son will be grateful, too. But he won't do what he should to express it. Which leaves it up to me. I know my duty, Pennorth: and I know what my clan owes you. And I pay my debts." She smiles wider, hypnotically: so hypnotically that Penn can't think through and deduce her intentions from what she's saying. Not that he could have even so, probably. Blood loss will have that effect, quite often.

It's helpful that she explains further, smiling as if his uncomprehending, blank face is amusing for her. "Freedom, young Pennorth. That's what the Hotstaats owe you: your liberty. Don't think that I don't know it. And I will give it to you, which is more than my dear well-loved son will ever do. He'll keep you hanging on forever, that's what he'll do – my dear Renally, my love, I know him well, and just what a shit he can be. Because he's too afraid to do anything else. Including his duty. I'm just going to have to do it for him."

Penn, well, Penn is injured, and he's sick, and cold, and it wouldn't take very much at all for him to pass out altogether. And yet, that's probably the one thing that anyone could say that could halfway revive him anyway. He feels almost alert, almost conscious and cognizant and sentient – in fact he jerks upwards a little way, and he can feel that his eyes are wider and more excited than anyone so half-dead should be capable of. His leg jabs a fiery poker of pain into his midriff, at the move, and he doesn't even care, he's too excited. He babbles out, "Oh, Dam Charity, oh, I am honestly so, I would, I truly–."

And then he sags, collapses back onto creaking wood and salty damp, because pain and exhaustion silence and get the better of him. And that's when he sees, when he opens his eyes properly and notices the unholy, supernatural glint in the Dam's eyes – much too familiar – and the slight, but definite, lengthening of her canine teeth.

Oh, no, no. Penn scrabbles in earnest, now, helpless but determined under her beautiful, manicured, delicately strong hands. This is not what Penn means by freedom: this is what he has refused to ever consider, what he refuses with every single rebelling atom of his being. He won't accept it, he'll never tolerate it, he'd rather die. "I'd rather die," he spits out, Adam's apple working like a piston in his throat as he swallows a flood of panic-saliva, and he thinks that that might make her understand. "I'd rather die," he repeats, but the Dam just pats his chest indulgently, her lovely dark eyes crinkling with just a flattering trace of laugh-lines. Then she shoves him down flatter on the wooden planking, hard.

This is what makes him understand that this is in earnest, there is no play-acting or make-believe going on here. And if he can't fight or beg or scheme his way out of it, then he's done for. Begging seems to be the only option he has left. His head rolls around on the plank, more weak and dizzy than by intent, and his eye meets Lettice Parrin's, where she's watching from five feet away. Her face is still, and the expression in her eyes is remoter than a million miles away. "Save me," he begs. He isn't so proud as all that. He can beg. "Save me from this. You're my mate. Save me." Perhaps his eyes are wild. He's desperate enough.

It even takes her a moment to focus her attention on him, and to answer. She might as well be high, sucking on the hookahs the young set keep discreetly out of the way of their elders. Then she looks sad,

sad and pensive. While his life veers off in a disastrous direction it was never intended to go. "Perhaps it's for the best, Penn," she says. "You want to be free. And you will be."

But not like this, Penn wants to say. I never wanted *this*. But he feels too absent of breath, too close to choking to spit the words in her direction. And anyway, the Dam is busy manhandling him into position with brisk vigour and speed, and complaining, "Such melodrama, my *stars*. For something anyone should be glad of! You'll be happy enough when it's done, my boy – you'll be well pleased then. Parrin is right about a single thing only – you weren't born to be a slave. It doesn't fit your temperament at all. You're quite unsuited. We'll fix that, easy enough. And then I shall have one son by blood, and another by making. It'll be very different, when you're changed, you'll understand."

Like my mother? Penn wants to ask. But that's his tunic, half-ripped off his shoulder, and the Dam half-changed in a matter of instants, and he's too busy screaming. Screaming for Ree, of course – the way he should have done instantly, when he understood – and screaming with the pain, too. There are teeth in his neck, jaws snapping where only his flesh and arteries should be. He's meat between a wolf's jaws for the second time today, and he can feel his eyes glow and melt and burn with the change he's seen in others. Who'd have thought it could take so quick – too quick, and he can hear Ree's feet, now, thundering out of the boat cabin and pounding down the jetty, shaking it. But it's so much too late. Serious intent must make all of the difference.

He's been through so much, and he's fought and resolved against this so long, and he's been so close to unconsciousness without giving in. Now, he gives in to it. He dives into it, a sweet drug of peace. The last thing he's aware of, before everything's black and gone and he leaves this intolerable new life behind for a little while, is Ree. Ree, running his way, running to save him. (And to keep him for himself, safely human and enslaved and bound to Ree forever, of course, yes.) Ree, screaming, "No," and, "No," and, "No!"

Much too late, really.

WHEN HE WAKES UP INTO that new life, he doesn't know how much later it is, how long he's been out of it, but it's plenty later, damn it. He knows pretty well that he's back on the Hotstaat estate, for a start. But not in any wing he's ever slept in, before. He wakes in a soft bed, a pretty room, big and light and with sun coming through big windows. This isn't a slave's bed, or a slave's room, not by a long chalk.

Everything's different. Inside his mind, he's not alone any more. He can feel a tie, a rope, a cord binding him, that spins out and travels two ways. One in Ree's direction, and one in Lettice's. The bond, he supposes. It's strong and dark and powerful, wordlessly yanking at him, telling him that he's a third of a complete whole, now, and that whole is part of something still greater. He couldn't feel it before, not when he was a slave. Not when he was... human.

Penn, he hates wolves. It's the foundation of his life, it's the fire that's kept him going, engine fully fuelled and running furiously. He has always hated wolves, and he still does.

And now, Penn, Penn's a wolf too.

THE END.

www.ingramcontent.com/pod-product-compliance
Lightning Source LLC
Chambersburg PA
CBHW051151130726
47988CB00005B/2077